e

'I can't imagine anybody not enjoying this book . . . the same winning blend of thrills, charm and local colour as Alexander McCall Smith's *The No. 1 Ladies' Detective Agency.*' *Reader's Digest*

'Keeps things heart-warmi[illegible] while tackling corruption at the highest levels and violent [illegible] *Sunday Times*

'Chopra, diligent, incorruptible and not entirely at ease with shiny new India, is a delight, as is his redoubtable wife, Poppy' *Guardian*

'Delightful' *Good Housekeeping*

'There have been many insipid imitators of the Alexander McCall Smith formula, grafting a cosy mystery into a depiction of a foreign culture dripping with local colour, but Khan has the quirkiness and hint of grit to make his portrayal of modern Mumbai memorable.' *Sunday Express*

'A quirky murder mystery . . . full of colourful characters and insightful details about human motivation.' *Irish Examiner*

'Sheer joy.' *Crime Review*

'A great warmth and wisdom infuse this and the other Baby Ganesh books.' *Booklist*

'Outstanding . . . the best entry in the series to date.' *Publishers Weekly*

'The greatest strength is the setting in the teeming city of Mumbai, from which the colour and atmosphere flows out of every page in this enjoyable, whimsical tale.' *Daily Express*

Also by Vaseem Khan

The Unexpected Inheritance of Inspector Chopra
The Perplexing Theft of the Jewel in the Crown
The Strange Disappearance of a Bollywood Star
Inspector Chopra and the Million Dollar Motor Car
(Quick Read)

MURDER AT THE GRAND RAJ PALACE

Vaseem Khan

MULHOLLAND
BOOKS
HODDER

First published in Great Britain in 2018 by Mulholland Books
An imprint of Hodder & Stoughton
An Hachette UK company

This paperback edition first published in 2019

1

A CIP catalogue record for this title is available from the British Library

Paperback ISBN 978 1 473 61240 2
eBook ISBN 978 1 473 61239 6

Typeset in Sabon MT by Hewer Text UK Ltd, Edinburgh
Printed and bound by CPI Group (UK) Ltd, Croydon, CR0 4YY

Hodder & Stoughton policy is to use ppers that are natural, renewable and recyclable products and made from wood grown in sustainable forests. The logging and manufacturing processes are expected to conform to the environmental regulations of the country of origin.

Hodder & Stoughton Ltd
Carmelite House
50 Victoria Embankment
London EC4Y 0DZ

www.hodder.co.uk

To the Indian hoteliers who welcomed me into their industry and demonstrated through word and deed their long-held maxim 'Guest is God'.

THE GRAND OLD DAME OF BOMBAY

As Inspector Ashwin Chopra (Retd) stood below the soaring arch of the Gateway to India, gazing up at the Grand Raj Palace Hotel, he couldn't help but reflect on the history of that architectural marvel that, over the decades, had graced countless covers of countless magazines around the world.

It was said that the Grand Raj Palace owed its existence to an insult.

A century earlier, India's wealthiest industrialist, the legendary Peroz Khumbatta, had been refused entry to the nearby Watson's Hotel in Khala Ghoda. Watson's – at the time the nightly scene of raucous British and American debauchery – maintained a strict whites-only policy, rigidly enforced and wholly despised by Indians such as Khumbatta, who had just begun to awaken to their own sense of national identity. Incensed, the fiery Parsee had vowed to build a hotel so opulent that even the British would be humbled, a thumb in the eye for the arch-colonialists.

And that is precisely what he had done.

For more than a hundred years the Grand Raj had served as a symbol of India's ambition, its own sense of self-worth. It had taken on the mantle of grand old dame of the city; the jewel in the crown of the Indian hospitality industry, a beacon of light and hope to which all Mumbaikers turned whenever dark clouds momentarily settled over the metropolis.

And now, somewhere within those yellow basalt walls, a terrible crime might have taken place, one that Chopra had been summoned to investigate with the utmost urgency.

His phone went off in the pocket of his grey linen trousers.

Chopra, a tall, broad-shouldered man in his late forties, with an impressive head of jet-black hair – greying only at the temples – and a thick moustache lurking below a Roman nose, was dressed conservatively, as was his wont. Below the grey trousers were sensible brogues; above, a white shirt fashioned from fine Indian cotton. This was as close to a uniform as he could now manage. Long after his forced retirement from the Mumbai Police – forced by a heart condition known as 'unstable angina' – Chopra still felt something amiss in the matter of his dress. His khaki uniform had been so much a part of his life, and for so long, that it had become more than mere clothing. In many ways, it had become a second skin.

And who could shed their skin and remain wholly the same person?

Chopra answered his phone.

It was his wife, Poppy.

'Where are you?' He heard the unusual snap in her tone. Poppy was upset, and for good reason.

'South,' said Chopra, weakly.

'South? South of what? What sort of answer is "south"? Are you in the South Atlantic? Are you at the South Pole? What, precisely, do you mean by "*south*"?'

Chopra hesitated.

The sun beat relentlessly down on him in waves of simmering heat. 'Something urgent came up, Poppy . . . I am in south Mumbai.'

He expected an explosion. Instead, after a moment of speechless silence, Poppy hung up.

In many ways, this was worse.

In the twenty-four years of their marriage, they had so rarely fought that when they did Chopra was left floundering in a sea of uncertainty. He knew that Poppy's anger was justified. He had failed to show up for a matter that was of great importance to his wife. And yet, he could not have rightly ignored the summons that had brought him to the tip of Mumbai that morning.

He would just have to explain later.

The prospect did not appeal to him.

The thought of confronting his wife when her temper was up was as attractive to him as placing his head into the mouth of a ravenous tiger.

He felt a tug on his arm.

He looked down and saw young Ganesha peering up at him with concern in his dewy eyes. The baby elephant was finely attuned to Chopra's moods. Anxiety, in particular, appeared to infect the little elephant acutely.

Chopra patted him on the top of his skull, with its little mat of short hairs. 'Can't be helped, boy,' he muttered.

Ganesha snuffled at the pulpy remains of a mango on the ground. Disinherited flies buzzed around his ears, protesting indignantly.

Chopra struck out across the crowded square that lay between the Gateway to India and the Grand Raj Palace Hotel, navigating his way through the tourist hordes that had gathered to have their picture taken beneath the Gateway's eighty-foot-high arch. A warm breeze blew in from the blue expanse of Mumbai's harbour, in which a thousand and one seagoing vessels bobbed on the chop. The tourists attracted locals of every ilk and design. Emaciated beggars, owl-eyed urchins, sombre lepers, ice-cream salesmen pedalling bicycle carts, peanut vendors brandishing twists of newspaper, eunuchs in colourful saris and designer stubble, snake-charmers, dugdugdee drum-beaters, tonga-wallahs . . . a howling menagerie of Mumbai's finest.

Chopra held grimly on to his pockets as he pushed his way through the throng.

He knew that in this crowd a man would be fortunate to reach the other side of the square with his bones intact. Better to be thrown into the path of a tide of ravenous army ants.

The front elevation of the Grand Raj Palace Hotel climbed into the sky before him, with its iconic red onion domes, arched balconies and hints of an Islamic facade.

A red carpet had been laid from the parking crescent out front into the hotel lobby. Uniformed porters pushed a convoy of gilded luggage carts loaded with suitcases through the brass doors. A beautiful Indian woman in a summer frock sashayed ahead of the porters, a golden langur monkey in a velvet waistcoat scampering along behind her. Chopra did not recognise the woman; no doubt she was another model or up-and-coming actress of the type Mumbai had always had in abundance.

The pet monkey was a particularly garish touch, he thought, darkly.

Inside the lobby, he was confronted by the unmistakable elegance that had defined the Grand Raj since it had first opened its doors. The first hotel in India to boast air conditioning, the first to open a licensed bar, the first to install a steam elevator – even now, the Grand Raj's dedication to opulence remained undimmed. The interiors, a mix of Florentine, oriental and Moorish styles, showcased vaulted alabaster ceilings, columns of tooled onyx, fretted stonework and pietra-dura floor panels. Marble was conspicuous by its sheer abundance, as were silk carpets, crystal chandeliers and an art collection that was the envy of the subcontinent.

Well-heeled visitors from all corners of the globe floated about the lobby.

Chopra approached the reception counter.

A smartly dressed young woman beamed at him. Her eyes flickered momentarily to Ganesha, then, with only the barest hint of surprise, returned to Chopra. This was the Grand Raj, after all. There was possibly no species on earth that hadn't passed through the celebrated hotel at one time or another.

'I am here to see the general manager,' said Chopra, handing her his card. 'He is expecting me.'

'Give me one moment, sir.'

While Chopra waited, his thoughts flashed back to the summons that had brought him to the hotel in such haste. The call had come from an old police colleague, Rohan Tripathi. Chopra had worked with Tripathi for a number of years, until the junior man had been posted to the southern half of the city. He remembered him as an ambitious and quick-witted policeman, one with a meticulous sense of order and getting things right.

For this reason they had worked well together.

His former colleague appeared to have a tricky situation on his hands, and had requested Chopra's help. An American businessman had died at the Grand Raj Palace, a wealthy and powerful individual. Tripathi had laid out the basic facts for Chopra, but warned him that there might be little to find. Tripathi's colleagues believed the American had committed suicide. It was simply the policeman's own uneasiness that had led him to seek Chopra's counsel. Tripathi's senior on the investigation, Assistant Commissioner of Police Gunaji, a bellicose, old-school policeman with the looks and temperament of a walrus, had taken the facts at face value. And, for ACP Gunaji, the most salient fact was that a verdict of suicide would be the least uncomfortable of the myriad possible outcomes in the matter of Hollis Burbank's death, for those who ran the city of Mumbai.

The murder of an American billionaire in India's most glamorous metropolis was a story that no one wanted to see making headlines in the world's press.

Nevertheless, Tripathi's instincts deserved consideration. For men like him, it was not enough to simply conclude an investigation, to tie up the manila folder with string and file it away to gather dust. Justice made its own demands on those who wore the khaki as a genuine calling. This desire for the truth, a notion that in his country often flickered like a candle flame, was the reason Chopra took on any new case. His investigation into the death of Hollis Burbank would be no different.

Yet he knew that he would have to tread lightly here.

Tripathi had gone out on a limb by bringing him in. Should ACP Gunaji discover him sniffing around an investigation he had personally seen fit to describe as open-and-shut, it was likely that his old friend would find himself posted to a frostbitten outpost in the foothills of the Himalayas by the end of the week.

He glanced down the hotel counter and saw the elegant Indian woman checking in further along. Her pet monkey sat on its haunches, surveying the lobby with a baleful look. Chopra wondered again who she was. If she was an actress, he didn't recognise her. This intrigued him, as he had only just completed an investigation that had taken him behind the scenes of Bollywood, the city's celebrated movie industry.

As he mused on her identity, Ganesha trotted over to the monkey and extended his trunk, an instinctive gesture of curiosity.

When the little elephant had arrived on Chopra's doorstep, sent to him by his long-vanished Uncle Bansi, he had been accompanied only by a brief letter that raised more questions than it answered. Bansi had not explained why he was sending Chopra an elephant, only that he wished him to take the helpless calf into his care. His letter had added, mysteriously: 'This is no ordinary elephant.' At first Chopra had been bemused and more than a little disconcerted by the extraordinary bequest, but over time, an unexpected bond had sprung up between himself and his ward. The little elephant had proved to possess depths that he had yet to fully fathom. He had also turned out to be an able, if somewhat unusual, companion in the detective agency Chopra had established following his retirement.

The monkey glared at Ganesha's trunk, then slapped it away, baring its teeth and shrieking maniacally.

Ganesha trotted swiftly back to Chopra and hid behind his legs, nursing his offended organ.

A young man – part of the Indian woman's entourage – dressed in absurdly tight jeans, pointy shoes, a butch T-shirt and more gold than Chopra had ever seen outside a bank vault, sauntered over to him. His square jaw jutted out belligerently. 'Here, you watch that elephant!' he said, pointing at Ganesha with the surfboard-sized mobile phone in his hand.

'What do you mean, "watch that elephant"?' growled Chopra. 'Your monkey just assaulted him.'

'Have you any idea who that is?' snapped the flunky, glaring at Chopra from above a pair of insolent sunglasses.

Chopra glanced again at the glamorous-looking woman. Before he could reply, a voice hailed him from behind. 'Sir, may I escort you to the GM's office?'

Chopra turned to find an old man in a butler's outfit hovering before him. The man had sunken cheeks, neatly oiled and perfectly parted jet-black hair, a pencil moustache and eyes that glowed with an unusual light. He stood ramrod straight, poised like a ballerina.

'Lead on,' muttered Chopra, casting a last, dark glance at the gold-encrusted young hoodlum.

'My name is Ganesham,' said the old man. 'I am the head butler here.'

'Chopra,' said Chopra.

'I understand that you are here about the Burbank affair?' said Ganesham. 'Nasty business.'

'What do you know about it?' asked Chopra.

'I think it is better you receive the details from the GM, sir. I will be available afterwards, should you need me.'

'Do you have pertinent information?'

'What is "pertinent", sir?' mused the old man. 'I have been at the Grand Raj for over fifty years. I have seen everything a man might hope to see, and all without leaving these walls. The only pertinent thing is that the hotel will endure. We have weathered everything from Partition to riots. Whatever your investigations may reveal, the Grand Raj will float serenely on.'

'They said something similar about the *Titanic*,' muttered Chopra.

A prim smile fluttered over the martinet's lips. 'The Grand Raj is unsinkable, sir.'

Tanav Dashputra, the general manager of the Grand Raj Palace Hotel, was a large, dark man, with a permanent sheen of perspiration on his brow. And this in spite of the air conditioning being turned up so high that Chopra could almost see his breath emerge in white puffs. The GM had bulbous eyes and a moustache that flowed over his bulging upper lip. An old-fashioned double-breasted suit, in blue serge, fitted snugly around his stomach.

Chopra found him in conversation with a petite middle-aged woman in a maroon sari.

The GM had his head in his hands, a glass of bitter gourd juice set on the untidy desk before him. Two tablets fizzed in the noxious bottle-green liquid. 'This hotel will be the death of me,' he said dramatically, as Chopra introduced himself. 'This is the worst possible time for something like this to happen.'

'Is there a *good* time for a guest to be murdered on the premises?' asked Chopra.

Dashputra blinked rapidly. 'Murder? What are you talking about? Burbank committed suicide.'

'Perhaps,' said Chopra.

Dashputra continued to stare at him, then dismissed his colleague. The woman left, casting inquisitive glances behind her.

'I must ask you to refrain from such speculation,' said Dashputra. 'Have you any idea how damaging such rumours would be?'

'I can guess,' said Chopra mildly.

'You cannot!' snapped Dashputra. 'Our guests have a certain expectation, founded upon a century of service. That is why the very best come to us, time and again. At this very moment, the cast of *Boom 3* are checking in to the hotel

– they are shooting on the premises. I have a royal wedding booked in – two of India's oldest noble families are practically taking over the place for the next week. And if that isn't enough, the premier of Mongolia is due here in three days' time. A state visit. He is bringing a stable of horses as gifts for the chief minister. He breeds them, wild ones direct from the steppes. I am reliably informed that one of those brutes kicked to death the manager of the last hotel he stayed at.' He shook his head ruefully, then did a double-take as he spotted Ganesha lurking behind Chopra. 'What is that elephant doing in here?'

'He's with me.'

The GM blinked. 'Animals! Truly, they will be the death of me.'

'Perhaps we should concentrate on the matter at hand?' said Chopra.

Dashputra's moustache twitched. 'Yes, of course. Let me take you to the Khumbatta suite. We'll talk on the way.'

The Khumbatta suite was the most opulent of the 500-plus rooms at the Grand Raj Palace Hotel.

A gilded elevator whisked Chopra, the GM and Ganesha up to the hotel's top floor, depositing them into a lushly carpeted corridor. Two security guards posted outside the suite snapped to attention as they approached, exchanging glances as the little elephant passed by.

The GM used an electronic keycard to open the door to the suite.

'I assume one of those keycards is the only way to get into the suite?' asked Chopra.

'Yes,' confirmed Dashputra.

'Who had access to the keycards for the Khumbatta suite on the night Burbank died?'

'Burbank had the only copy that we had issued. But that doesn't mean anything. These keycards can be reproduced by anyone on reception. It's all electronic. Guests lose them all the time.'

'I will need a list of all those who accessed the suite – or had access to it – during the twenty-four hours prior to Burbank's death.'

'It will be arranged.'

'By the way, is there CCTV on this floor?'

Dashputra shook his head. 'I am afraid not. Our guests value their privacy far too much to allow us to install security cameras.'

Chopra was silent, hovering in the doorway. 'There's always the possibility that Burbank *let* his killer in. If he *was* murdered, I mean.'

The GM shuddered. 'We have kept the details from the press so far. It is fortunate that the hotel's owners have such influence in the city. They have prevailed upon the editors of the major news outlets to confine their reporting to the scant facts that we have released, namely that Burbank passed away in his suite. We have not yet informed them of the circumstances of his death. Can you imagine the headlines when they find out that he committed suicide?'

'Can *you* imagine the headlines if it turns out he was murdered? And that someone in this hotel might be the killer?'

Dashputra blanched, but said nothing.

Chopra followed the GM into the suite, Ganesha close behind.

Although he had visited the Grand Raj before, he had never stayed there, and certainly had never been anywhere near the rarefied air of the Khumbatta suite. As he looked around, he understood why the suite – favoured by presidents and A-list actors, billionaire industrialists and spoilt scions of noble families – cost a million rupees per night. This was opulence on a scale that Chopra – living in a mid-sized apartment on the fifteenth floor of a tower block in the Mumbai suburbs – could barely comprehend.

The thought bothered him.

He was a man to whom wealth meant little. The vast inequalities in his country had always seemed to him a matter too readily accepted by his fellow countrymen, and paid lip service to by successive Indian governments. In the seventy years since India had gained her independence, the country had made steady economic progress, such that now she was being touted as a global superpower. You could not turn on the TV without being accosted by yet another self-congratulatory report of Indian advancement, the velocity of which appeared to be increasing with each passing day. Just last week, for instance, the media had foamed themselves into a fury of excitement at the news that India had launched a hundred satellites into space from a single rocket, a world first.

But the truth was that, for the vast majority of its billion-strong population, this glowing vision of a prosperous, globalised, Sputniked India was little more than a pipe dream, a billboard advert that hovered mirage-like before their swimming eyeballs – as far out of reach as those satellites – even as political slogans clanged incessantly in their ears. What did it say for a nation claiming to be a 'serious player in the burgeoning private space market' that each year thousands of farmers committed suicide at the advent of famine? In the slums of Old India, millions of men, women and children toiled beneath the back-breaking weight of their inheritance – the inheritance of caste prejudice and grinding poverty – while in the marbled halls of power, the country's leaders drove the unstoppable tank of New India into the steaming swamp of the future.

Perhaps Dashputra mistook Chopra's grim silence for a momentary awe as he began a potted description of the suite, one he had no doubt delivered many times and from which he could not keep a note of personal pride. 'You are standing in the most desired hotel room in the whole of the subcontinent,' he gushed. 'Five thousand square feet of unparalleled luxury. The floors are white Makrana marble; the upholstery and draperies cut from handwoven silk. The suite boasts a private spa area, a dining room and a master bathroom overlooking the Gateway. A dedicated valet is on call twenty-four hours a day, as well as a personal chef and a private butler.'

Ganesha stared round-eyed at Dashputra. The little elephant seemed more impressed than his guardian.

'Where was Burbank's body found?'

Dashputra led the way into the largest of the suite's bedrooms, another vast space that could have accommodated most apartments in the city. A hand-knotted carpet rippled over the marble floor, and a crystal chandelier shimmered above the four-poster bed. There was no canopy, he noted; the bedposts, fashioned from dark Burma teak, speared nakedly towards the room's mirrored ceiling.

Above the bed's carved headboard was a covered painting.

'What's that?' asked Chopra.

'That is the reason Burbank was staying at the hotel,' replied Dashputra. 'Two nights ago, the Grand Raj hosted an art auction. Burbank purchased this piece for ten million dollars. It is now the most valuable painting ever sold by an Indian artist.'

'Why is it still here?'

'The police would not allow us to move anything from the room. Everything has been logged as evidence. That is why I have a twenty-four-hour guard on the door. No one goes in or out without my express permission.'

'Can we remove the covering? I'd like to take a look.'

Dashputra frowned. 'I would rather not touch it without someone from the auction house being present.'

'Which auction house is it?'

'Gilbert and Locke,' replied Dashputra promptly. 'From London. It was quite a coup for us to convince them to host their auction here. A number of our rivals also attempted to woo them, but there is no place like the Grand Raj.' Dashputra's haughty tone folded into sorrow. 'It is terrible that Burbank has died. I don't think Gilbert and Locke will look favourably upon this at all.'

'Who is representing them here? I'll need to speak to them.'

'A woman by the name of Lisa Taylor. She is the auction director.'

Chopra wrote the name down in his notebook. 'Where can I find her?'

'She is staying at the hotel. I will give you her contact details.'

'Thank you. Where exactly was Burbank's body?'

'On the bed.' The GM gave a little shudder.

Chopra knew that the body had been taken to the morgue at the local hospital, presumably for an autopsy. He would soon have access to the report and the forensic findings, including photographs of the crime scene, if indeed that was what it was.

'I must tell you that the police believe that this *was* suicide,' said Dashputra, as if reading his mind.

'Not all of them,' muttered Chopra.

'In that case let me show you something.'

He led Chopra into the suite's master bathroom. More white marble, gleaming mirrors and a porcelain tub in which a herd of hippos might comfortably have bathed.

Dashputra pointed at the tiles on the far wall. 'This should convince you.'

On the wall, written in what looked like foot-high letters of blood, were the words:

I AM SORRY

A VERY IMPORTANT ANNIVERSARY

Poppy Chopra sat disconsolately on the veranda in the rear courtyard of the restaurant that bore her name, the restaurant her husband had established after his retirement from the police force. Her hopes that the place would provide him with a meaningful way to occupy his time – and thus keep him from the stress and excitement that his doctors had warned him might aggravate the heart ailment that had forced his retirement in the first place – had been short-lived.

Within days of leaving the service Chopra had somehow managed to embroil himself in uncovering one of the largest human trafficking rings in the country, and had then proudly announced that he was setting up his own detective agency, so that he could risk life and limb on a daily basis.

In time she had convinced herself that fighting against his perverse desire to fling himself into harm's way at every opportunity was pointless. This desire – driven by his need to pursue justice – was as ingrained in her husband as the knots in the planed boards of the veranda beneath her feet.

Besides, the restaurant practically ran itself.

Between her mother – installed in the front – and Chef Lucknowwallah – running roughshod over operations at the rear – the place had proved to be an efficient and hugely popular venture. If only her husband could understand that it was perfectly permissible for him to sit back and *enjoy* his success.

She thought about sighing, but realised that with no one to hear, the dramatic gesture would be wasted.

At the far end of the veranda, the blind tutor, Usha Umrigar, was finishing up her lesson with Irfan.

The boy, at first reluctance personified, had finally begun to make progress.

Chopra had taken him on at the restaurant, a young street urchin whose smiling, mop-headed demeanour concealed a tragic past. Irfan had been raised on the streets by his father, a cruel and exploitative man. This Fagin-like figure had bullied and beaten Irfan – and numerous other young boys – into stealing for him. The man had finally got his comeuppance, but Poppy could only imagine the scars he had left behind. Sometimes, in the dead of night, a keening ache would arise in her breast as she thought about those horrible years Irfan had endured, not knowing love or kindness, not knowing that there were people in the world who would treat him not with cruelty, but with compassion and affection.

For Poppy now regarded the boy as her own.

During the twenty-four years of her marriage to Chopra she had known only one great disappointment – that they had been unable to have children. Or, more accurately, *she* had been unable to *bear* children. Many marriages would have cracked under this burden; but Chopra and Poppy had weathered the disappointment – in many ways, their trial had brought them closer together. At times, she had mooted the idea of adoption, but for some reason, her husband had never convinced himself that he might be successful in such a venture.

And so the years had passed, childless, but not barren. Poppy had found innumerable ways of occupying her time; she believed in the mantra that if one wanted to see change in India – with its myriad ills and inequalities – then one had to get out there and do something about it.

Even now, as a woman in her early forties, her relentless dedication to the cause – whatever cause happened to have elbowed its way to the forefront of her conscience – was a source of inspiration, she felt, to those around her.

And then, miraculously, fate had chosen to turn her life upside-down.

The little elephant, Ganesha, had arrived on their doorstep, closely followed by Irfan.

Something had burst inside her then, a dam that had held her emotions in check for all those childless years.

She found herself surrendering to the torrent of maternal feelings that raged through her and there was little doubt now that both she and Chopra considered themselves guardians to the elephant calf and the ten-year-old boy who had ended up in their care.

For a parent was not defined solely by genetic inheritance. The true definition of parenthood was the ability to love, to care, to put the welfare of another before one's own.

Consider Irfan.

A sense of pride swelled inside her as she saw him develop into the fine young man she knew he would one day become. Educating him was just phase one of the masterplan . . .

The tall, thick-shouldered tutor rose to her feet, dismissing Irfan with a little pat on his head, then turned her sightless gaze to Poppy.

'What is the matter?'

'Nothing,' said Poppy, as Irfan beamed at her and skipped back inside the restaurant to begin his shift. The boy had no need to work, but refused to give up his job, or to move from the restaurant to their home. He lived here, where he had a comfortable hammock and could be close to his pachyderm partner-in-mischief, little Ganesha. Nothing that Poppy said could convince him to change his mind. And her husband was as much use as a rolling pin made of mud.

Sometimes his laissez-faire attitude was truly infuriating.

'*Something* is the matter,' said Umrigar, her large, burn-scarred hands clasped around her bamboo cane.

She was dressed in a simple navy blue sari with white trim, her iron-grey hair held back in a bun, her dark, broad face lit by mid-morning sunlight. 'You've been huffing and puffing in that chair throughout my entire lesson.'

'It's Chopra,' said Poppy. 'He was supposed to meet me here this morning so that we could plan our anniversary.'

A soft warbling sound floated over the veranda. Poppy realised that the tutor was laughing at her.

'What in the world made you think he would be interested in doing *that*?'

Poppy glared at the older woman.

Her anger stemmed partly from the fact that Umrigar had placed her finger precisely on the sore spot that Poppy had identified. Her husband didn't care, she had realised. Yes, of course, he was as committed to their marriage as he had always been, but he didn't *care*. Not about things like their twenty-fifth wedding anniversary, due to take place in precisely four days' time. He had wriggled and squirmed each time she raised the topic. He simply didn't seem to grasp that twenty-fifth wedding anniversaries didn't happen every day.

In fact, by definition, they only happened once, and after a twenty-five-year wait.

It wasn't that he was unwilling – she had expected that. It was that he was *willingly* unwilling. He said things like: 'I'm happy if *you're* happy.' And: 'Choose whatever *you* like.'

And meanwhile her friends kept going on about the big day, pressing her for news. That insufferable Jaya Sinha from the thirteenth floor, she with the tax auditor husband with a head like a watermelon, claimed that he, of all people, had booked her an all-expenses trip to Disneyland for their tenth anniversary, and had even dressed up as Mickey Mouse to serenade her in her hotel suite. The image of the brick-faced Mr Sinha wooing his wife dressed as a giant mouse made Poppy shudder, but she couldn't fault the man's commitment. Whereas her own husband . . .

Where *was* he? What was he doing in south Mumbai?

No doubt embroiling himself in another investigation just when she had asked him to set aside a few days. She wouldn't put it past the man to have another heart attack just so he could avoid their anniversary altogether.

Well, if he thought he could wriggle out of it that easily, he didn't know her very well.

Chopra *would* go to the ball.

Even if she had to drag him every step of the way.

UNDER THE HAMMER

Chopra found the auction director Lisa Taylor in the hotel's Olympic-sized swimming pool.

The blond woman was doing laps, maintaining a steady, long-limbed backstroke. Hotel guests sunned themselves on the loungers around the pool. An elderly white woman in a wide-brimmed sun hat lowered her book, and peered over her spectacles at Ganesha. 'Is that an elephant?'

Chopra felt the answer was self-evident.

It was difficult to be wrong about an elephant.

The woman continued to stare at Ganesha until he became uncomfortable and shuffled around behind his guardian. 'Hmm,' said the woman enigmatically, then went back to her book.

Chopra moved to the edge of the pool, knelt and flagged down Lisa Taylor as she swam by. She stopped, and trod water. 'I am sorry to disturb you, Miss Taylor. My name is Chopra and I am investigating Mr Burbank's death. May I talk to you?'

She stared at him, then plunged to the side and hauled herself out of the pool.

She stood in front of him, dripping, the sun glistening off her wet shoulders. Chopra couldn't help but notice that she was a very attractive woman, her luxurious figure set off by the red bathing suit she wore. She blinked blue eyes at Ganesha. 'Is he with you?'

'Yes,' said Chopra, glad of something else to focus on.

Taylor knelt down and tickled Ganesha under his ear. 'You're a handsome devil, aren't you?'

Ganesha responded with delight, waggling his ears and tapping her cheeks with his trunk.

'Until I came to India I'd never seen an elephant except in the zoo. The only pets I had at home were guinea pigs. Now I think I'd like my own elephant.' Taylor straightened up. 'Give me a moment to change. Perhaps you'd care to join me in the Banyan restaurant? I've not had breakfast yet.'

When Taylor arrived she was dressed in a white sleeveless blouse, pinstriped black trousers and glossy red shoes. Her corn-blond hair was pulled back, and red lipstick set off her fine features. If anything, she looked even better fully dressed, Chopra thought, than in her bathing suit.

The thought made him flush, and he coughed loudly to cover his discomfort.

Taylor slipped into a chair, waved at a waiter and ordered breakfast, an exotic meal of Keralan coconut rice crêpes served with pomfret molee – a fish curry from the south. She asked the waiter to bring some mangoes for Ganesha, who couldn't believe his luck when a loaded tray was placed under his trunk.

Chopra explained that he was a special investigator tasked by the police to look into the case. 'What case?' said Taylor. 'Burbank killed himself, didn't he?'

'That is what I must determine,' said Chopra. 'The circumstances of his death have raised certain doubts.'

Taylor arched an elegant eyebrow. 'I'm glad I'm not the only one who thinks so,' she said. 'To be frank, the idea that Burbank committed suicide hasn't felt right to me from the beginning. I tried to tell the man in charge of the investigation, but he seemed hell-bent on brushing the whole thing under the carpet.'

'You are talking about Assistant Commissioner of Police Gunaji.' Chopra sighed. 'I am afraid that the death of an American has set alarm bells ringing. No one wants this situation to become political. A suicide would be the most convenient explanation.'

'But not necessarily the right one?' said Taylor.

Chopra shrugged. 'It is too early to say.'

'It was that writing on the wall, wasn't it? "I am sorry". Written in blood.'

'How do you know about that?'

'Burbank's PA told me about it. He was the one who found the body. Is that why this Gunaji is so adamant it's a suicide?'

'It is one reason,' said Chopra. 'Though I am certain the statement was not written in blood. Burbank could not have stabbed himself and then got up to write those words.'

'Could he have done it beforehand? If it *was* suicide, I mean?'

Chopra shook his head. 'After I saw the bathroom I called my police colleague. I asked him if any other wounds were discovered on Burbank's body other than the fatal one to his heart. There were none.'

'Oh. I see.'

Chopra shifted in his seat. 'Please tell me about him. Burbank, I mean. How did you know him?'

'I've known Hollis – Mr Burbank – for a number of years. You see, I am the head of client relations for the India and Middle East region at Gilbert and Locke. That means it is my job to handhold the bigger collectors who want to buy art from this region. Burbank was a serious collector. He's had a special interest in Indian art for a long time; he's bought many speculative pieces in the past that are only now going up in value.'

'So he was a regular visitor to the country?'

'Actually, no. This was the first time I've been able to entice him here.'

'Yet you say he has been collecting Indian art for years?'

'Yes. But he would always buy from overseas exhibitions, or based on pictures I sent him online. He trusted my judgement.' She said this with just a trace of pride.

'I must confess I am no expert in this area,' said Chopra. 'But it was my impression that Indian art is not highly thought of on the world stage.'

'Up until a few years ago you would have been right. But

the truth is that art follows money. It's not always the other way round. India is booming. Overnight the subcontinent is crawling with freshly minted millionaires. And do you know the first thing the nouveau riche *always* want to buy?'

Chopra shrugged.

'Acceptance,' said Taylor, her blue eyes sparkling. 'Nothing screams "I've arrived, I belong" more than a very tasteful and, above all, very *expensive* painting hanging on the eggshell-washed wall of your swanky new pad. I came here a few years ago with the head of Gilbert and Locke and we were astounded at the clamour for art among Mumbai's jet set. That was when I had the idea of putting together an auction here. I was convinced I could get some of the world's biggest collectors together, if only we could put on a lavish enough production. At the same time, it would be a shot in the arm for artists from the region who I have long felt were undervalued.'

Chopra sensed that Taylor had developed a genuine affection for India. It often happened with foreigners who spent any length of time on the subcontinent.

'It's such a magical place, isn't it?' she said, as if reading his thoughts.

Chopra was tempted to nod, but stopped himself. The trouble with most Westerners was that they lived a rarefied life in India, cossetted by wealth, enthralled by the snake-charmer-and-swami 'mystique' of the subcontinent. It was the rare foreigner who got their hands dirty in the slums, the poverty, the myriad other malaises that plagued the country.

'So Burbank was only here for the auction?' he asked.

'Yes.'

'When did he arrive?'

'He flew in the day before the auction. We normally arrange a private viewing for the big collectors. The exhibition itself has been going on for a week.'

'Exhibition?'

'Yes. All the paintings have been on show to the public.'

Chopra recalled seeing something about it on the news.

'Weren't you – Gilbert and Locke, that is – worried about security?'

Taylor smiled. 'Believe me, it's the first thing we think about. We have a very experienced private security firm who deals with all of that. They know what they're doing.'

Chopra considered this. 'So you don't believe Burbank's death had anything to do with the auction? Or his purchase of what I am told is now India's most expensive painting?'

'If only that were the case.' Taylor sighed. 'It would make things very simple. But if someone did kill Burbank for the painting, then why didn't they take it?'

Chopra had no answer to this. 'Could there have been a personal motive? Assuming he *was* killed?'

She shrugged, running her fork around the edge of her plate, monogrammed with the hotel's logo. 'I know one shouldn't speak ill of the dead, but Hollis Burbank was, shall we say, an acquired taste.'

'Are you suggesting that he was not well liked?'

'That would be the understatement of the century. The man was positively loathed. Not that he cared. I suppose when you are as rich as he was why would you?'

'Please explain.'

Taylor was silent a moment. A froth of conversation rose and fell around them in the restaurant. Beside the table, they could hear Ganesha slurping on his mangoes. 'Hollis Burbank was the most driven man I have ever met. He ran an industrial conglomerate, producing everything from toothpaste to tractors. Last I checked, he was personally worth in the region of seven billion dollars.' She paused, as if to let this enormous number sink into Chopra's brain. 'By all accounts he was ruthless in his business dealings. That was my experience of him, anyway. Once he set his heart on a particular piece he would stop at nothing to acquire it. It's one of the reasons I find it hard to believe that he killed himself. He wanted this painting more than anything I've ever pitched to him. And he paid a record fee to obtain it. Why would he commit suicide, just when he'd got his hands on it? It doesn't make sense.'

Chopra rose to his feet. 'Perhaps it is time I took a look at this painting.'

As they made their way up to the Khumbatta suite, Chopra asked Lisa Taylor about the auction.

'Have you ever been to an art auction?'

'I have not had the privilege,' said Chopra dryly.

'Well, I can tell you that this one was a major production. I mean, we left no stone unturned. You see, like most things in the art world, it's all about presentation. You put a piece of cheese on a cracker and serve it at a kids' party – it's just cheese on a cracker. But you serve the same thing at an auction, and tell everyone one of the world's greatest chefs prepared it, and they'll gush over it as if you've just served them ambrosia.

'An auction like this is what you might call a high-society event. This is where the crème de la crème come out to be seen, not necessarily to buy something. We had film stars, business barons, professional socialites, even a couple of princesses. I have to admit I'd hardly heard of any of these people before I got to India, but in this business you have to do your homework. There's nothing a very wealthy art virgin likes more than to have their ego stroked. Of course, most of them wouldn't know a Monet from a Manet.' She gave Chopra a dazzling smile. 'There's no real secret to this business, Chopra. Frankly, it's all smoke and mirrors. I mean what makes Cézanne's *The Card Players* worth three hundred million dollars? No one could *really* tell you. But if enough so-called art experts say such-and-such painter is one to watch, you'll suddenly find serious collectors jumping on the bandwagon. And as soon as even one blue-chip investor makes a purchase, then the artist's price tag jumps through the roof. Rags to riches in the space of an evening.'

They had arrived at the top floor.

The security guards sprang out of their seats like a pair of jack-in-the-boxes. Chopra used the keycard that the general manager had given him and, for the second time that morning, entered the scene of Hollis Burbank's death.

'As I was saying: we had a fantastic turnout for the auction,' continued Taylor. 'The room was packed. Art whales and their reps; art assayers, dealers, critics, scholars and last – and usually least – the artists themselves. There was an incredible energy in the room. When you've been doing this for a while you get a certain feeling. As soon as the first few lots sold – all for well above the lot price – I knew this was going to be a big night.

'We moved through the sale quickly. Sculptures, bronzes, miniatures, and then on to works by lesser-known artists. Tomorrow's stars. And finally we got to the Rebello.'

They had entered the master bedroom.

Taylor stopped before the bed, a shudder passing through her as she gazed at the bedspread where Burbank's body had been found.

She shook herself, and then moved forward, climbed onto the bed and removed the cloth covering the painting above the headboard. The painting was secured behind a glass display case, a numerical keypad set below it. A red light winked on the keypad, indicating that it was alarmed.

Taylor returned to the foot of the bed and stood beside Chopra – and Ganesha – as all three regarded the painting.

'Behold!' said Taylor. 'Zozé Rebello's masterwork: *The Scourge of Goa*.'

Chopra stared at the enormous canvas.

It was painted in a distinct visual style, reminiscent of the miniatures favoured by the Mughal emperors, depicting hundreds of tiny but highly detailed human figures. The background of the canvas was a deep yellow with reds and umbers running through it, giving the impression that the protagonists were wading through a lake of fire. As he focused on different sections of the canvas he realised that the figures all appeared to be engaged in violent or aggressive behaviour.

'Disturbing, isn't it?' said Taylor. 'It gets everyone that way the first time. You start off by thinking it's harmless, and then you actually focus on what all those little people are doing to each other. I confess I gasped the first time I understood.'

'Understood what?'

'That this is Rebello's depiction of hell. Or, more accurately, hell on earth. Art experts think this is an indictment of the tumultuous past of Goa, his home state, the fact that it was ruthlessly plundered by various factions throughout history, both Indian and foreign. Hindus, Muslims and, most notably, the Portuguese, who turned Goa into a governing seat for their "Empire in the East". They converted the locals to Christianity – at the point of a sword, naturally – and transformed Goa into a major seaport for the spice trade. Spice was the gold of that era, and whoever controlled the spice routes became enormously powerful. No one asked the Goans whether they wanted any of this. Whether they wanted to speak Portuguese, or worship at one of the three hundred churches they were forced to build. Whether they wanted to be tried, tortured and executed by the Goa Inquisition on the flimsiest of pretexts.'

Chopra mused on how history had a way of smoothing over even the worst of humanity's excesses.

Goa was now recognised as a tourist paradise for those seeking sun, sand and sea. For decades, it had been popular with the hippy trail; now it had become a retirement Mecca for many Mumbaikers, a place for the wealthy to keep a second home that they could jet down to in an hour on the many domestic airlines that now clogged the subcontinent's airways.

He wondered just how many knew of the region's turbulent past.

Chopra focused again on the canvas. Each figure was precisely drawn, he noted, down to the expression on each face. In all there must have been a thousand individuals depicted on the canvas: Hindus, Muslims and Christians; Portuguese and native Goans.

Death was the common motif that drew them together.

There were a great many bodies, strewn over the canvas like corpses over a battlefield. Rebello had found every conceivable manner of death to inflict upon his cast: shot, strangled, clubbed, stabbed, impaled, beheaded or simply hacked to pieces. Some were already dead, sightless eyes turned to a roiling sky, others caught in the act of dying. He saw one figure kneeling on the ground, grasping at his intestines as they spilled from his torso. What made this particular scene so horrific was that the man's apparent killer was a nun, a grey-clothed woman in a white wimple whose face shone with beatific light.

An involuntary shudder passed through him.

Ganesha's trunk slipped into his hand, and he gave the elephant a reassuring squeeze. No doubt his ward was experiencing a similar feeling of disquiet. He wondered briefly why anyone would want to buy a painting like this. Who in their right mind would want this hanging anywhere in their home?

'Did Burbank have any trouble in acquiring the painting?' he asked eventually.

Taylor smiled as if he had said something foolish. 'The Rebello was the highlight of the auction, Chopra. Every collector worth his salt wanted this. We had a real bidding war. The lot price was set at two million dollars. Burbank had to pay ten to get his hands on it.'

'*Had* to pay?'

'Yes. The bidding went on for nearly an hour. We had collectors calling in from all over the world. But, in the end, it came down to a battle between Burbank and an Indian businessman, Agnihotri. He's been quite vocal about not letting the Rebello go out of India. Vowed to buy it, but in the end Burbank simply outbid him. To be frank, Burbank paid a ridiculous sum for the painting. The previous record for an Indian artwork was for an abstract by Gaitonde, which sold for over three million.'

'How did Agnihotri react, after Burbank outbid him?'

'Badly. In fact, I saw his face when the hammer came down. The man was livid. He tore up his auction catalogue, and stormed out of the room. There was an ugly rumour circulating that he confronted Burbank, but I don't know if there's any truth to that.'

Chopra made a note to check this out. Agnihotri's name sounded familiar. He recalled that it was on a list that Tripathi had given him of individuals he had briefly questioned or had intended to question before ACP Gunaji had started interfering with his investigation. 'And what happened next? After the auction, I mean?'

'Well, there was a champagne reception, of course. A

chance for the big bidders to preen a little. We also find it's a good way to prevent buyer's remorse from setting in. There's nothing that helps calm an art virgin's insecurity after he's just blown a few million pounds on what looks like a child's doodle than a roomful of sycophants telling him what a cultural maven he is. You could say my livelihood depends on it. I earn a commission on each artwork I sell. And the Rebello estate is one of my most prestigious clients.'

'Has the sale gone through? In spite of Burbank's death?'

Taylor looked glum. 'I'm afraid not. It's in what we'd call art auction limbo. You see, once the hammer came down, Burbank was technically the owner of the piece. He certainly thought so – that's why he insisted that the Rebello was moved up here, into his suite, right after the auction. He was planning to be in Mumbai a few days, and he didn't want the painting out of his sight.'

'Was he not worried about security? Weren't you?'

'I am *always* worried about security. But as you can see, we had the painting installed by our security team. It's fully alarmed. No, the real problem is that Burbank purchased the painting through one of his company accounts. An offshore shell company to be precise. It's a common way for richer collectors to minimise their tax liability when they buy major works. And that means the payment hasn't yet been processed. It requires a second director from this particular company – which is registered in the Cayman Islands – to sign off on the transfer of funds. And given that Burbank is now dead – and the painting is being held as evidence – this other director has decided to put things on hold until he understands exactly what happened to Burbank. Which is bad news for me, because it means that my commission on the deal is now stuck.' She gave a grim smile. 'We – and by that I mean Gilbert and Locke – need to know exactly what transpired here.'

Chopra led Taylor to the bathroom.

He wanted to take another look at the writing on the wall.

Taylor raised a sceptical eyebrow. 'I've known Burbank for years. And I can tell you that in all that time I never once heard him apologise.'

'You do not believe that he wrote this?'

'All I can say is that if he did, then it must have been something truly earth-shattering he was sorry about.'

Chopra allowed a moment's silence to pass. 'You mentioned that the body had been discovered by Burbank's personal assistant. Do you know where I can find him?'

'I have a pretty good idea,' said Taylor, archly.

THE GREEN FANDANGO

Chopra found Ronald Loomis in the Grand Raj's world-famous bar, the Green Fandango.

The Fandango was steeped in history. As the first bar in Mumbai to hold a liquor licence, it had, for the better part of the last century, served as the smoky haunt of movie stars, gangsters, shady businessmen and the city's subterranean movers and shakers. Recently redecorated in a bold art deco style, it harkened back to an earlier, simpler time at the Grand Raj, a time when the bar represented a shadowy oasis outside society's normal rules.

Loomis, a rakishly handsome young man with a sandy widow's peak, round-rimmed tortoiseshell spectacles and a red bow tie, was slumped at the bar, staring out into the harbour.

Saddlebags of sweat were prominent under his arms, in spite of the air conditioning.

In response to Chopra's query, he merely stared glassy-eyed at Ganesha, then looked back down into his drink, a

Green Fandango Special, made to a recipe that had been around since the end of the Prohibition era and was an institution in its own right.

'I've been with Mr Burbank for a decade,' said Loomis woodenly, in a nasal American accent. 'He plucked me right out of Princeton. Gave me a career, a purpose. He was a brilliant businessman. I got to see him in action, up close. Yes, he could be ruthless, but you show me a successful businessman who isn't. He was a tough boss. Demanding. Expected the highest standards, and didn't tolerate stupidity. I learned a lot from him. Everything, in fact.'

Chopra allowed Loomis's rambling monologue to wind down. He could see that the young man was upset by his boss's death, and possibly a little worse for the time he'd spent in the Fandango. 'I am told that you discovered the body,' he finally said.

'I did.'

'What time was this?'

'About six-thirty a.m.'

'What were you doing in Burbank's room at six-thirty in the morning?'

'Mr Burbank is – was – an early riser. He liked to go over the day's schedule at precisely six-thirty every morning.'

'So you knocked on his door. Presumably, he didn't open it. What happened next?'

'I dialled Mr Burbank's phone, but he didn't answer. In fact, I heard it ringing from inside the room. He has a very loud and distinctive ringtone. "The Ride of the Valkyries". Wagner. I became worried and so I called the front desk. They sent someone to open the room. When we got inside I saw that his phone was on the table. And then we went to the master bedroom.' Loomis halted, then continued. 'It was horrible. He was just lying there, staring up at the ceiling with glassy eyes, that . . . that knife sticking out of his chest.'

'Is there anything else you recall about that moment? Immediate impressions? Anything you felt was out of place?'

Loomis looked at Chopra as if he had gone mad. 'You mean other than the dead body of my boss?'

Chopra waited. Finally, Loomis said, 'No. Nothing.'

'What did you do next?'

'I called the hotel's general manager. *He* called in the authorities.'

'And it was the police who decided that Burbank had taken his own life?'

Loomis looked up sharply. 'What's that supposed to mean?'

'Exactly what I said, Mr Loomis. The police concluded that Hollis Burbank had committed suicide . . . That is correct, yes?'

'Well, what else could it have been? Haven't you seen the writing in the bathroom?'

'I have. What do you think that means?'

Loomis gave Chopra another long look. 'Are you sure you're an investigator? When a man scrawls "I am sorry" on a wall, then stabs himself in the chest, it's pretty much obvious what he means.'

'So you believe Burbank killed himself?'

Loomis hesitated. Something strange passed over his face. 'The truth? I find it difficult to reconcile the idea of suicide with the man that I knew. It's just that that policeman, Gunaji, was so adamant. He practically put the words in my mouth.'

'Did Mr Burbank have enemies?'

Loomis snorted. 'Of course he did. Plenty of them. He's a man who doesn't take prisoners. But it's hard to believe someone killed him out here. We're in a five-star hotel in the middle of India, not some back alley in Queens. He certainly wasn't mugged by some lowlife looking for his wallet.'

'What if I told you that you are not the only one who thinks Burbank wasn't the type of man to commit suicide.'

Loomis picked up his glass, took a long gulp of his drink, then set it down again carefully on a coaster. 'Look, I've worked with Mr Burbank every day for ten years. And I tell you, even I never knew what he was thinking. He was inscrutable. Never revealed what was going on inside him. Never talked about himself, his past. The only emotion I ever saw him express was anger. He always let people know when they irritated him.' He flashed a grim smile.

'Can you think of any reason why Burbank *would* commit suicide?'

'I've been asking myself the same thing, and the answer is no.'

'Nothing at all?'

Loomis grimaced. 'He'd been stressed lately, but that was just business. He'd started taking Valium. Not that he had a prescription for them. I have no idea where he got hold of them. He didn't want anyone to know he needed them, I suppose. Not even me.'

'Any personal problems? Family matters that had upset him recently?'

'Mr Burbank is divorced. Has been for years. His ex-wife lives out in Colorado somewhere; she got custody of their only child, a daughter. Turns out *she's* all grown up, and recently got married. I think he felt bad about that, about being estranged from her. But nothing to suggest he was thinking of killing himself.'

Chopra considered this.

As Loomis suggested, it seemed a tenuous reason upon which to hang a man's suicide. Then again, he'd seen men die for lesser reasons – both by their own hand and at the hands of others. In his younger days, he had believed in the concept of certainty. It had been a chastening experience to feel the sand being sucked from under the shoes of that belief. The human condition was truly inscrutable, he now knew, the sewage wallowing at the bottom of a man's soul dark and turgid.

Another thought occurred to him. 'There is also the question of why he would kill himself after buying a painting he had apparently been chasing for a very long time.'

'Exactly,' agreed Loomis. 'Though for Mr Burbank it was never the attainment of a goal that was the key. It was the hunt. He loved the battle; he loved crushing his rivals.' The PA's face darkened. 'Look, if you're really serious about looking at something other than suicide, then the person you should be talking to is Agnihotri.'

Chopra mentally flicked through his notes. 'The man Burbank outbid for *The Scourge of Goa*?'

Loomis nodded. 'The pair of them were at each other's throats the whole evening. Agnihotri's been in the press sounding off about how he'd make sure that painting never leaves India. And then Mr Burbank came along and just blew him out of the water.'

'Did they exchange words?'

Loomis snorted. 'They exchanged more than words. A little while after the auction I was in a private toilet with Mr Burbank—'

'I'm sorry,' interrupted Chopra, 'but did you just say that you were in the toilet *with* Burbank?'

'He wanted me to take some notes. Dictated them while he sat on the bowl. Look, do you want to hear this or not?' Loomis's eyes flashed with irritation.

'Please, continue,' muttered Chopra. Perhaps it was true, he thought, privately. The rich did do things differently.

'So, while we're in the middle of this, I got a call from our head office. I stepped outside to take it. When I walk back in I see Agnihotri in there. He's got Mr Burbank by the lapels, shoved up against a wall. Agnihotri's a big guy. He's red with anger, shouting at the top of his voice, calling Mr Burbank a cheat, a rogue, all sorts of things. The man was out of his mind, totally out of control.' Loomis drained his drink, then banged the counter for another.

Chopra considered what the PA had told him.

He felt sure that Loomis was not lying, yet it was still hard to picture. Two of the world's wealthiest men fighting like street kids inside a toilet at India's most prestigious hotel. What a story that would make!

'What happens to Burbank's estate?' he finally asked. 'Who will inherit his enormous wealth?'

'Good question,' said Loomis. 'I've been in touch with his lawyers, and they're reviewing his will. Short answer: I don't know. It was never something Mr Burbank discussed with me.'

'And the company? Who runs –' Chopra checked his notes '– Westland Industries now?'

'I suppose control will pass to Donnie,' said Loomis, as if he had only just thought of this. 'That's Donald Cassidy. He's the company's Chief Operating Officer. Sits over in our California HQ. Wears black turtlenecks and Gucci loafers. Eats that protein mush all day, spouting Foucault.'

Chopra got the impression that Loomis did not approve of Donnie Cassidy.

'Once the circumstances of Mr Burbank's death are settled, the board will meet and elect a new chairman,' continued the PA. 'And I guess that's when I'll decide whether I want to work for my new boss, or throw a drink in his face and quit.' He gave a high-pitched, slightly hysterical laugh.

'I understand Burbank has business interests here,' said Chopra.

'Yes. A few years ago, he decided there was a fortune to be made in India.'

'So Westland Industries have a base here?'

'A subsidiary company,' affirmed Loomis. 'But it's not called Westland Industries. Mr Burbank wanted an Indian name. He finally plumped for Shakti Holdings Ltd. I suppose you know Shakti means "power", the primordial energy of the cosmos?' Loomis smiled ironically.

'Where is it based?'

'Right here, in Mumbai. They have offices in midtown. Area called Powai, by the lake.'

'Who runs it?'

'Indian chap by the name of Gavaskar.'

'Did Burbank visit the offices while he was here?'

'No. But Gavaskar was scheduled to see him tomorrow. Here at the hotel.'

'I'd like to talk to him. Can you arrange that?'

Loomis grunted. 'Why not? What does it matter now, anyway?'

The barman placed another tumbler under his nose. Loomis picked it up, waved it at Ganesha – who was staring at him owl-eyed – and said: 'Here's mud in your eye, Dumbo.' He took a long pull, wiped his mouth with his sleeve, then slipped off his stool. 'I should have done more. I should have seen this coming.' He glared blearily at Chopra. 'I'll be in my room if you need me. Getting drunk.'

Chopra watched him stagger away.

A RECKONING AT THE RESTAURANT

As he drove back north through the city, Chopra's thoughts lingered on the day's events.

Following his meeting with Ronald Loomis he had interviewed a number of the hotel staff, all those with access to the Khumbatta suite prior to Burbank's death. The interviews had revealed little of use. He now knew that Burbank had entered his suite for the final time at 11:53 p.m. on the night of his death. That was when the businessman's own keycard had been logged in. The data was all stored on a computer, and had been simple enough to check. Five minutes later Burbank had placed a call to room service. The order had been delivered thirty minutes after that.

And that was the last time anyone had seen Burbank alive.

Chopra had next attempted to interview the Indian businessman Avinash Agnihotri, but had found himself confronted by a brick wall. A visit to Agnihotri's suite had proved fruitless. Undaunted, Chopra had obtained the mogul's phone number from the hotel's general manager.

Calling it, he had found himself redirected to Agnihotri's personal assistant, a stern, older woman whose iron-cast admonishments reminded Chopra of Mrs Subramanium, the tyrannical president of the managing committee at the building complex in which he and Poppy lived.

Having weathered the fiery gatekeeper's wrath, he had finally extracted a grudging admission that Agnihotri would be in the hotel tomorrow around lunchtime. Chopra could try his luck then.

And herein lay the essential problem.

Although he had been brought onto the case by Tripathi, the fact was that Chopra had little official authority to compel anyone to cooperate.

And yet his initial impressions had left him more than intrigued.

Hollis Burbank had clearly been a man few would miss. His enormous wealth had isolated him from a world that he appeared to hold in some measure of contempt. He was, by all accounts, a ruthless individual with little in the way of charm or warmth. And yet he had inspired the loyalty of Ronald Loomis and the admiration of Lisa Taylor. He had built a global business empire, and had managed to do so while keeping his private life exactly that.

Private.

All of which meant that Chopra's search for the truth was going to be . . . complicated.

From the rear of the specially converted van Ganesha looked out at the snarling Mumbai traffic.

The little elephant could sense that his guardian was preoccupied, so focused instead on the streams of people moving along the side of the road in the early evening. Many were barefoot, either because they owned no shoes or because they were making the weekly pilgrimage from all corners of the city to the gold-roofed Siddhivinayak temple in midtown Mumbai. A Jain holy man swept the street before him, unwilling to crush even insects in his zeal to protect life. A fruit-seller juggled an enormous pyramid of watermelons on a handcart.

Chopra suddenly thumped the horn and cursed loudly, startling the elephant. Ganesha's ears flapped rapidly, like a hummingbird's wings, as he stared out of the windscreen.

A rickshaw had stopped in the middle of the road, beside a white Tata Nano. The car – billed as the world's cheapest – had, in line with the company's promises, transformed the average Mumbaiker's life. In fact, by adding immeasurably to the chaos on the city's over-congested roads, it had transformed the average Mumbaiker's life into a living hell.

Chopra ground his teeth as he watched the rick driver and the owner of the Tata Nano arguing bitterly, in that particular fashion that only Indians were capable of, gesticulating wildly at the sky, the ground, the very air, shouting at the top of their lungs, without – and this was the key to all such altercations – anyone actually advancing the matter towards resolution. The argument could go on indefinitely. It mattered not that half the city was piling up in the traffic jam behind them. It mattered not that both protagonists had other, more pressing business to attend to. The argument was all that mattered; it was a living, breathing thing in and of itself. The argument was India, its very essence;

gloriously infuriating, perpetually maddening, *argumentum ad ridiculum*, essential in a way that only gods and madmen could truly comprehend.

By the time he reached the restaurant it was almost nine.

Chopra parked the van on the congested Guru Rabindranath Tagore Road, let his ward out, then followed the little elephant as he trotted down the alley that ran by the side of the restaurant to the courtyard at the rear.

Inside the courtyard Ganesha found Irfan waiting for him with his evening meal, a mass of pulped fruit and green shoots, followed by a bucket of milk laced with the Dairy Milk chocolate to which he was addicted.

Chopra watched the pair of them happily at play beneath the mango tree.

He left them there and walked into the restaurant through the back.

In the kitchen he paused, watching for a moment, as the sous chef Romesh Goel and the assistant chef Rosie Pinto whirled about the narrow space like a pair of dervishes. Though it was late in the evening the restaurant was packed, and would remain so until close to midnight. The fact that it was crammed largely with policemen was something that filled Chopra with a quiet sense of satisfaction.

He recalled his devastation following the heart attack that had forced him into retirement. He had heard of the expression 'having the rug pulled out from under you'.

After thirty years in the service he had felt that not only had the rug been pulled from under him, but he had then been wrapped up in it and dropped off a cliff. The restaurant had been a means for him to keep himself occupied, to stay in touch with his old colleagues on the force.

Its success was merely a bonus.

Yet it was that very success that had afforded him the time to devote to the second venture he had embarked upon, one that he had not planned, but that now provided him with a much-needed sense of mission – the detective agency that had sprung up after Ganesha's arrival, following Chopra's investigation into the murder of a local boy.

Since then Chopra's fledging agency had found itself approached by a steady stream of clients, his reputation growing by the day. Lately, he had been invited to work with the same police force that had summarily ejected him from its ranks.

If he derived a quiet pleasure from this, he kept it to himself.

Gloating had never been one of Chopra's traits.

He suddenly realised that there was a booming absence in the kitchen.

'Where's the chef?' he asked.

Romesh froze, a half-sliced aubergine in his hand. Chopra was suddenly aware of the mouth-watering smells wafting about the kitchen, a melange of spice and nose-tingling warmth.

His stomach gave an eager rumble.

'Chef is in Lucknow, sir,' said Romesh.

Chopra remembered that the chef had told him about his

trip last week. He was visiting his home state to pay his final respects to a dying aunt. He could hardly have begrudged the man his leave. Azeem Lucknowwallah – once a renowned chef – had come out of retirement to work at Poppy's, simply because it was run by a former policeman. Lucknowwallah's own father had worn the khaki, before being killed in a tragic accident involving a bullock. The man was temperamental, and a prima donna about his food, but Chopra considered him a friend. The chef was responsible for the restaurant's success and, what's more, had recently gone above and beyond the call of duty when Chopra had found himself in serious trouble during an investigation.

He would miss the chef's straightforward opinions, not to mention his incredible butter chicken special.

He walked out of the kitchen and into his office, where he found his associate private investigator – and former sub-Inspector at the local police station where they had both worked – Abbas Rangwalla, face-down in a fragrant mutton biriyani.

Rangwalla leapt to his feet as Chopra entered, his dark, pitted cheeks flushing, grains of rice lodged in his short beard.

'I'm sorry. I wasn't sure what time you were getting back, and I missed my lunch—'

Chopra waved Rangwalla's concerns away. 'Sit. Finish your meal.'

He watched as the junior man folded uneasily back into the seat on the far side of his desk and resumed eating, somewhat mechanically now that his boss was seated before him.

After almost twenty years of working together Rangwalla was still something of a mystery to him. The man was plugged into the streets of Mumbai in a way that Chopra never had been – this was what had made him such an invaluable deputy at the Sahar station, and now made him such an able associate at the agency. And yet the man himself remained stubbornly inscrutable. He had two children, and a terrible smoking habit. Beyond that he had never revealed much about what went on in his life, or inside his bearded head.

'How are you getting on with the Persimmon case?' asked Chopra.

Rangwalla shrugged. 'The man is mentally unstable.'

Harish Persimmon, a seventy-year-old local resident, had approached the agency with what he had described as 'a case of the highest importance'. This highly important case had been to follow Persimmon's cat around, a cat that the old fool was convinced was the reincarnation of his father. Chopra had politely declined the work, but the man had kicked up such a fuss that finally he had tasked Rangwalla to handle the matter.

'He's convinced that the cat – or Papa as he insists on calling him – will lead him to a hidden treasure trove. Undeclared wealth that his father accumulated before his untimely death.'

'And did it?' said Chopra, with the ghost of a smile.

'Did it what?'

'Lead you to a hidden treasure trove?'

Rangwalla gave him a sour look. 'No. It wandered around aimlessly, went up a tree, rooted around in a garbage heap, soiled the streets, then attacked me when I got too close.'

Chopra stifled his laughter. Rangwalla pushed back his plate. 'So, while I was wasting my time on a wild cat chase, what were you doing?'

Quickly, Chopra filled his deputy in on the day's events at the Grand Raj Palace Hotel.

Rangwalla scratched his beard. 'Sounds like you are going to have your hands full. Is there anything I can do to help?'

'Yes. I want to know more about Hollis Burbank. I want you to see what you can find out.'

Rangwalla looked mystified. 'How?'

'Talk to Kishore Dubey at the *Mid Day*. This sort of thing is precisely what he excels at.'

Dubey was an old newspaper contact of Chopra's. He excelled in writing profiles of the many celebrities who lived in or passed through Mumbai.

Rangwalla nodded unhappily. 'Okay. Anything to get away from that damned cat.'

Chopra ignored him. 'The trouble is that for almost everyone concerned it would be much better if I find nothing. A verdict of suicide would spare a great deal of embarrassment all round.'

'Well, you cannot make an omelette without breaking eggs,' said Rangwalla, philosophically.

'What?' Chopra frowned. 'Who's talking about making an omelette? What's an omelette got to do with anything? I didn't ask you to make an omelette, I asked you to do some investigating.'

'It's just a saying,' said Rangwalla hastily. 'My daughter said it to me the other day. To be frank, it confused me too.'

The pair of them stared at each other, on opposite banks of a river of misunderstanding, and then the door swung open.

Chopra blanched.

Poppy was standing in the doorway, her slender figure rigidly erect, hands planted firmly on hips.

She did not look happy.

Over the long years of their marriage Chopra had developed a deep appreciation for his wife's generous nature, her eternal optimism, her willingness to believe the best of the world, even in the face of irrefutable evidence to the contrary. These qualities balanced out her sometimes volatile temperament, which would erupt in lightning bursts of anger whenever something got under her skin.

Such as now.

'So,' said Poppy, acidly. 'The big hero returns.'

'I was just on my way home, Poppy,' said Chopra. He felt a sudden tightening around his chest, and wondered if it was his traitorous heart fleeing for the hills.

'Were you?' said Poppy. 'Because it seems to me that what you were actually doing was sitting in *your* little office in *your* restaurant with *your* associate detective discussing *your* oh-so-important investigation.'

Rangwalla looked from Poppy to his boss, and back again. He made as if to stand. 'Perhaps I should be getting along—'

'SIT!' thundered Poppy.

Rangwalla's knees buckled and he fell back into his chair. He hunkered down into it like a man in a foxhole.

'Perhaps this isn't the time or place—' Chopra began before being unceremoniously cut off.

'But it is *never* the time or place!' growled Poppy. 'Not when it comes to discussing something that is important to *me*.'

'I can explain—' began Chopra again.

'Oh, can you?' said his wife, advancing into the room.

He saw that red spots of anger floated on her cheeks; the black bun of her hair quivered atop her head and her gold bangles jangled on her wrists.

She turned to Rangwalla. 'Tell me, Abbas, do you think he can explain why I am having to chase him all over town for the occasion of *our* twenty-fifth wedding anniversary? Can he explain why, having agreed to visit the temple with me this morning so that we might discuss arrangements for our anniversary with the priest, and having reminded him every single day for the past week not to forget, he failed to show up? Can he explain why there is always some case that is more important, some appointment that is more pressing, some work that is more essential than his own marriage?'

The sudden silence quivered in the room, balanced precariously on the edge of the cliff to which Poppy's rage had ascended.

'Um, no?' ventured Rangwalla. He felt beads of sweat popping out on his forehead. Poppy had always managed to discomfit him. For one, she was the only person in the world who insisted on calling him by his first name.

Chopra flashed his deputy a grim look. Rangwalla subsided, deciding that it was in his best interests to keep any further input to himself.

The door suddenly opened again and Irfan tracked in, closely followed by Ganesha.

The boy, still in his shocking pink waiter's uniform, waved a small gift-wrapped parcel around. 'I'm so glad you're both here,' he said. 'Ganesha and I have got you a present. For your anninanniversary.' In spite of the situation, Chopra found himself suppressing a smile. Irfan's command of English was coming along in leaps and bounds. But 'anniversary' was a word he found easy to begin, yet exceedingly difficult to end.

Poppy turned to the boy and the elephant.

As she looked down at them, standing side by side, their big round eyes overflowing with affection, she found her anger evaporating.

She knelt down and wrapped an arm around each one. Ganesha's trunk curled around her shoulders. 'My boys,' she sighed, burying her face between them. Silently she began to weep.

'Why are you crying?' asked Irfan. 'You haven't even seen it yet. You might like it.'

'I am sure I will love it,' snuffled Poppy. 'I am crying because I am happy. I love you both very much.'

'We love you too,' said Irfan, brightening. Ganesha gave a soft bugle, and patted away the tears on her cheek.

Chopra rose from his desk and made his way to the trio.

Poppy got to her feet and examined his face gloomily as he approached.

Chopra felt terrible.

He realised that there was some truth to Poppy's accusations. Throughout their marriage he had rarely felt that he had neglected her needs – nor would he ever wish to. He had married his wife for love, and had never regretted his choice. They had weathered all that life had thrown at them. She remained his closest companion, his fiercest and most loyal friend.

And yet, looking at the present situation through her eyes, he realised that perhaps, on this occasion, he *had* been unfair to her.

'I will find the time,' he said softly.

Poppy waved him away. 'Don't make promises you cannot keep. I would rather you just did what you had to.'

'This case . . . it could have political repercussions, Poppy. I must devote time to it. But I promise you I will clear it up as soon as I can, and then you and I shall go on a holiday.'

'A holiday?' Poppy's ears perked up. 'You mean an actual trip? Out of the city?'

'Yes. Anywhere you wish.'

She eyed him doubtfully, then her attractive face flowered into a smile. 'I will hold you to that. I have witnesses.'

'It's a promise,' said Chopra.

A FIRST LOOK AT THE EVIDENCE

The next morning Chopra drove south again, this time to the Colaba Police Station, just minutes from the Grand Raj Palace Hotel.

He parked his van on Shahid Bhagat Singh Road, let Ganesha out of the back, then walked past the Wesley Church with its pointed arches and uplifting white signboard proclaiming: Peace Be Unto You! He passed through the police station's blue and yellow gates, and into the building proper.

He paused in the doorway, early-morning sunlight backlighting his tall frame, as he took in the scene. The hustle and bustle of a police station at work brought a gladness to his heart, one that was tinged with a sense of loss, like a violin note sounding from deep within the undergrowth of his emotions.

After all, this had been *his* life for almost thirty years.

In his own station, back in Sahar – over which he had presided as the officer-in-charge – he had found the peace that only comes to a man when he discovers his allotted role in the grand scheme of things. His days had been filled with routine, order, purpose.

And then: the heart attack that had derailed the dependable train of his existence, hurling him into the mangrove swamp of the unknown.

Yet, with Poppy's help, he had weathered the storm, and emerged on the other side, stronger and, possibly, wiser. A man in his position had few reasons to complain. In comparison to so many of his fellow citizens – those who eked out a living on the margins of society, not knowing where their next meal was coming from – he was a man blessed by good fortune. He loved and was loved in return. His life had stability, and now, thanks to the detective agency, he had a renewed sense of purpose, one that fitted him like an old glove.

Chopra made his way through the chaotic tumult to the office of Inspector Rohan Tripathi.

He knocked on the door, waited for Tripathi's familiar voice to bellow 'Come!', then entered, leaving Ganesha behind in the main station area.

It had been years since Chopra had last seen his old colleague, but Tripathi had changed little. A thin man with a streamlined head like a bullet, the dark hair swept back as if he had been exposed to a fierce wind. A rakish moustache, the moustache of an aristocratic polo player or a freedom fighter, the type of historical hero that Tripathi had always professed admiration for.

'Chopra,' said Tripathi, by way of greeting, holding his hand over the receiver of the phone plugged to his ear. He waved at a chair on the far side of his neatly ordered desk.

Chopra chose to stand, waiting until the call had ended.

When Tripathi finally put it down, his shoulders sagged with relief. 'That was Gunaji,' he said. 'Wants to know why I'm holding up the press release. He's desperate to tell the world how he has "solved" Burbank's suicide.' Tripathi shook his head, picked up a file from the top of a teetering tower of manila folders and threw it at Chopra. 'Here's everything I have so far. Forensics, interviews, autopsy report, the lot.'

Chopra recalled that Tripathi was a man who wasted little time on trivialities. Small talk was alien territory for the intense policeman.

'How are you, Rohan?' he asked anyway.

'How am I? I am a man hanging from the edge of a cliff by his fingernails. At the bottom, splattered on the rocks, I can see the corpse of my career. That's how I am.'

'You could just go along with Gunaji,' said Chopra mildly.

Tripathi snorted. 'Gunaji is a CBI goon. He loves to throw his weight around. Luckily for him he has plenty of it to throw. The word is he wants to run for the chief ministership when he retires.'

Chopra had come across officers from the Central Bureau of Investigation before.

The CBI was tasked to investigate corruption in the police force and other branches of the civil service. The only problem was that, in Chopra's personal experience, CBI officers sometimes succumbed to the very same rotten habits they were attempting to eradicate.

The CBI was also responsible for investigating cases of a political or sensitive nature. Hence Gunaji's involvement in the Burbank affair.

'The man would sell his own mother to get in front of a TV camera,' continued Tripathi sourly. 'Luckily, I still have some say in this investigation. Just not enough to deploy the full strength of resources that I would like to. Hence my call to you. It's a grim day, Chopra, when politics ties the hands of the police service.'

Chopra sat down, opened the file and began to read.

Hollis Burbank's body had been discovered in the master bedroom of his suite, a knife embedded in his chest. Burbank's fingerprints had been found on the handle of the knife – and no one else's.

A half-empty glass of vintage Glencoyne single malt whisky had been discovered on the bedside table – the price of the bottle, which Burbank had ordered the same evening from the hotel's bar, was four thousand dollars. A small brown tablet bottle of Valium was found beside the glass. A toxicology report showed that Burbank had taken a large dose, dissolved in the whisky.

Burbank's fingerprints were on the glass, and the Valium bottle.

Chopra looked up. 'Why would Burbank take Valium? I mean, if he was about to kill himself with a knife anyway?'

'I wondered that myself,' said Tripathi. 'Gunaji thinks he was calming his nerves. That he was anxious about stabbing himself.'

'Then why not just take an overdose? And why *stab* himself anyway? Why not sit in the bathtub and slit his wrists?'

'Like those old Roman senators, eh?' said Tripathi. 'The answer is: we don't know. Maybe he was making a statement. I mean, you saw what he wrote in the bathroom, right?'

Chopra nodded.

I am sorry.

'Is there a last known movements timeline in here?' he asked.

'Of course. He was at the auction, then an after-party till late in the evening. He went from that straight back to his room – alone as far as we can tell. He entered his suite at 11:53 p.m. Ordered room service, and after that . . . nothing.'

'I understand he ordered caviar and champagne. An extravagant meal for someone planning to kill himself.'

Tripathi grimaced. 'Gunaji says that if *he* was planning to end it all, he'd order a lavish last meal too. A shame he isn't,' he added. 'Planning to end it all, I mean.'

Another thought occurred to Chopra. 'Where did Burbank *get* the knife?'

Tripathi waved at the folder. 'There's a report about it in there somewhere. The knife was taken from the suite's kitchen area. It's Japanese, the best that money can buy, hand-forged from Damascus steel, with a nine-inch blade and an edge so sharp it could shave off your moustache from a yard away. By the way, it wasn't blood.'

Chopra frowned. 'What wasn't blood?'

'The statement on the bathroom wall. "I am sorry". It wasn't written in blood. But I expect you gathered that already. That was why you called to ask me about any other wounds on the body, wasn't it?'

Chopra's moustache lifted in a smile, but he said nothing. There was no need. 'So if it wasn't blood, what was it?'

'Paint. Red paint. We found a small pot of it in the bathroom. Together with a flat-headed artist's paintbrush. His fingerprints were on them both. And before you ask what they were doing there, we found an easel in the suite. Turns out Burbank was a closet artist himself. Liked to dabble. He'd been painting. A picture of sunflowers. Between you and me, it was pretty terrible.'

Chopra considered how this revelation cast a different light on the victim, a man so far described only as a ruthless businessman. The fact that Burbank painted revealed something more about him, he felt, something hidden, and intimate.

'Was there anything missing from the room? Valuables?'

'Nothing,' said Tripathi, emphatically. 'The suite has a wall safe. Burbank hadn't bothered to lock it. It was stuffed with cash, designer watches, diamond cufflinks. Nothing to a man of Burbank's wealth, but a tidy haul by anyone else's standards. Yet none of it was touched. If this was murder, then it wasn't about robbery. It was personal.'

Chopra turned his attention to the autopsy report, which had been prepared by his old friend Homi Contractor.

'How did you get Homi to do the autopsy?'

'Not easily,' admitted Tripathi.

Chopra could sympathise. Homi was notoriously busy and even more notoriously difficult.

'But he's the best pathologist in the city. I didn't want anything left to chance, not for this.'

Chopra skimmed the report.

Burbank had died from a stab wound directly to the heart. The knife had pierced the left atrium, one of the two upper chambers of the heart. Homi's report explained how the penetration had caused massive and profuse bleeding, resulting in acute tamponade – compression of the heart by an accumulation of blood in the pericardial sac surrounding the heart. The result had been a very rapid death.

A number of photographs accompanied the report, including one of Burbank stretched out on the bed, the knife handle jutting out from his chest. He was dressed in one of the suite's luxurious bathrobes, monogrammed with the hotel's logo. A flower of red soaked the thick white cotton over his heart. Chopra paused for a moment, staring at the glassy eyes, the grey, lifeless face. He had seen numerous bodies during his long career. So rarely had the faces of those corpses been imbued with the peace that was said to come from man's final release.

Hollis Burbank certainly did not look like a man who had gone to meet his maker with a clear conscience.

He took out his phone and dialled Homi Contractor. The need to speak to the pathologist had become acute.

Homi was his usual caustic self. 'So they've pulled you into that steaming pile of horse manure too, eh? Well, I suppose it's my fault. Rohan told me about his doubts and I made the mistake of mentioning your agency to him. Told him you were still as sharp as you'd been on the force. Perhaps what I should have said is that you're just as keen to chase your tail around the city looking for murderers and rapists and whatnot. Can't keep a good fool down, eh?'

Homi had often said that he couldn't understand why, after retiring, Chopra hadn't gone to live the high life somewhere. And yet, he secretly suspected that his friend would be exactly the same once he was forced to hang up his surgeon's gloves. The man was a dynamo.

'The angle of the knife,' said Chopra. 'Was it consistent with a man stabbing himself?'

'Consistent, yes,' said Homi. 'Practical? Usual? No.'

'What do you mean?'

'I mean, it was all very clumsy, wasn't it? A man wants to kill himself with a knife – why not slice open his wrists? Instead, he chooses to stab himself in the chest. I mean, cardiac penetrations are hardly the most fatal of traumas. You have a far better chance of surviving a stab wound to the heart than, say, a wound to a major artery in the neck or thigh.' Homi sighed. 'If you're asking me whether this was staged, whether Burbank was helped along on his journey to the next world, then the short answer is: I don't know. On the face of it there's no evidence to support that conclusion. His prints were on the knife handle – in exactly the right configuration to indicate a two-handed grip, with a strike downwards into the heart. My guess is he was lying on his back when he did it. That way he wouldn't have to fall down afterwards. All very inelegant. And besides, lividity was fixed. The body wasn't moved after the heart stopped. He definitely died on that bed.'

'What about time of death?' Chopra asked next.

'Based on the liver temperature taken by the on-scene pathologist, I'd say he died somewhere between one a.m. and two a.m.'

Chopra thanked Homi, and ended the call. He tapped the phone thoughtfully against his thigh.

Homi's opinion was something he had relied upon for many years while running the Sahar station. And yet, balanced against this were his own instincts, honed over decades of sifting through crime scenes and often murky preliminary investigations. Like Tripathi he could sense that something was out of kilter with Hollis Burbank's death. It was not, of course, beyond the bounds of possibility that such a man might contemplate taking his own life, but there was a world of difference between impossible and improbable.

He finished looking through the file.

There was very little forensic evidence collected from the scene.

Fingerprints – but none from anyone who couldn't or shouldn't have been in Burbank's room; some trace fibres and, in one corner of the bedroom, by the mirror, some shards of coloured broken glass that might have come from a bangle or other piece of decorative jewellery. Dried blood had been discovered on the shards, but it had been unidentifiable. The report supposed that the shards had been left there by the prior tenant of the suite, a glamorous actress, and that they had somehow escaped the cleaning crew.

He was intrigued by a note saying that staples had been discovered on the bed Burbank had died upon. They had been found in the gap between the headboard and the top of the mattress.

He raised an eyebrow. 'Staples?'

Tripathi shrugged. 'There was a lot of paperwork in Burbank's room. Thick sheaves of it. Apparently, he liked to take his work with him when he travelled, probably read it in bed, the same way I read investigative reports. Hence the staples. Before you get excited, we've been through it.

It's all reports and legal documents relating to his various operations around the world. Instant cure for insomnia.'

Towards the end of the file was an inventory of all the personal belongings discovered in Burbank's room. Aside from a number of very expensive suits, Burbank appeared to travel lightly.

Something at the bottom of the list caught Chopra's eye.

#Photographs 1–4 [found inside inner lining of deceased's briefcase]

'What does this entry about photographs refer to?' he asked.

'Oh, just a bunch of old pictures we found inside his briefcase. Why?'

'I'd like to see them.'

'They're meaningless.'

'I'd like to see them anyway.'

Tripathi shrugged, then picked up the phone and asked one of his junior officers to fetch the photographs.

A constable in blue shorts arrived at a breathless rush, handed an evidence bag reverentially to Chopra, then glanced nervously at Tripathi. Chopra guessed that his old friend was keeping his men – and women – on their toes. The preservation of evidence from crime scenes had often been a haphazard endeavour in the Indian police service. But now, conscientious, forward-thinking officers like Tripathi were putting paid to such lackadaisical attitudes.

'What do you want? A medal?' barked Tripathi, glaring at the constable.

The man fled from the room.

Chopra took out the photographs and laid them out on Tripathi's desk.

There were four, all black-and-white prints, all eight inches by six, with deckled edging.

They showed a group of people, the same group, lined up in various configurations in and around what seemed like an industrial building. It wasn't clear from the photos what sort of plant it was, and there were no landmarks to determine where the site might be.

The figures in the pictures, four of them, were equally ambiguous. Three men, one woman.

They wore hats – sun hats, rather than protective hard hats – and white lab coats. Three of the figures were Indian. The fourth was a tall, handsome white man, clean-shaven, wearing a blue button-down shirt and aviator sunglasses.

Chopra paused on this figure. He didn't recognise the man. He half-expected it to be Burbank, a younger version, but the face was too different.

He held up one of the pictures, tapped it with a finger. 'Who is that?'

Tripathi shrugged. 'Your guess is as good as mine. I asked Burbank's PA. He didn't know either. Didn't know anyone in those pictures. Burbank had them hidden inside the lining of his briefcase. They must have been very personal.'

Chopra turned the photo over.

On the back, written in faded black ink, were the words: 'Faulkner, Murthi, Sen, Shastri. Chimboli, Feb. 1985.'

He checked the other pictures, but there was nothing on the back of any of them.

'There are names here,' he said.

'Only surnames,' said Tripathi. 'From thirty years ago, if that date is accurate.'

'Where is Chimboli?'

'Out near Pune. It's a backwater. Mostly just villages and dust. And if you're thinking of tracking down whatever that facility is, forget it. Even if it still exists, *I* don't have the manpower to chase ghosts. Gunaji would have a fit just knowing I'd asked you to poke around.'

'Do you mind if I hang on to this?' Chopra asked.

'Why? Those pictures haven't got a thing to do with Burbank's death.'

'You're probably right. But I'd like to hang on to it just the same.'

'I can give you a photocopy,' said Tripathi. 'Chain of evidence, and all that. You'll probably want to take a look at this too,' he added, opening the drawer of his desk and handing Chopra another evidence bag.

Inside he found a charcoal sketch on butcher paper. The sketch was of a half-naked figure in a loincloth, slumped against a wall in a dark alley, the face a grotesque parody of a man laughing at something only he could see. There was no signature on the sketch, only initials in the corner: K.K.

'We found this in the same place, in the lining of his suitcase.'

'Did he buy it at the auction?'

'No.'

'Then he may have brought it to India with him.'

'Possibly. It's not something we've spent much time looking into. More pressing leads to pursue and all that,' said

Tripathi dryly. 'It's probably just a piece he really likes. I'm an absolute philistine when it comes to all this art guff, but it's got a certain something, I'll admit.'

'I'll need a copy of this too.'

Tripathi shrugged. 'Okay. Who am I to second-guess my old mentor? Just remember: Gunaji has his boot on my throat. Time is of the essence. Unless you can come up with a convincing reason to declare Burbank's death as something other than suicide, he is going to shut the door on this investigation.'

Chopra stood, turned to leave.

'By the way,' said Tripathi. 'Is it true you're wandering around the city with an elephant?'

'Yes,' said Chopra, his expression stiffening. He knew where this was headed. Many of his old colleagues thought he must be addled when they discovered he had taken in an elephant. 'Why?'

Tripathi looked embarrassed. 'Well, it's just, er, you know I grew up in the south? There was this elephant orphanage outside our village . . .'

Chopra smiled with relief. 'His name is Ganesha. Would you like to meet him?'

'He's here?' Delight spread across Tripathi's features.

Once again Chopra reflected that the mere thought of encountering an elephant could knock ten years off a man's age.

'Come on,' he said. 'He's probably got half your station trying to feed him chocolate by now.'

POPPY CHECKS IN

A few hundred yards away, in the lobby of the Grand Raj Palace Hotel, the general manager Tanav Dashputra was staring in disbelief at Poppy Chopra and Irfan. A semicircle of porters and room-boys lounged beside the luggage carts they had just pushed into the hotel, looking on, goggle-eyed, failing to disguise their delight at the GM's discomfort.

'But, madam, I cannot just *give* you a room!'

'I did not ask for a room,' said Poppy. 'I asked for a *suite*.' She waved at the train of luggage carts. 'I have a few essentials with me, as you can see.'

The GM gaped. A vein throbbed at his temple. The collar of his shirt seemed about to burst from his throat. 'This is-is—' he began, but Poppy cut him off with a flattened palm, as if she were conducting traffic.

'My dear Mr Dashputra,' she said primly, 'three days from now it is my twenty-fifth wedding anniversary. I had high hopes that this would be an occasion that my husband and I might enjoy together. That we might spend some time in each other's company. Instead, I now discover that he will be otherwise engaged, in *your* hotel, investigating the death of one of *your* guests. Now, another woman in my shoes might well have accepted the situation. But I, Mr Dashputra, am not "another woman". I do *not* accept. I do not turn the other cheek. Turning the other cheek was yesterday. Today it is: kindly give me my suite or I will bring the ceiling down on your head.'

Dashputra stared queasily at the woman.

During his twenty-five or so years in the hotel industry he had encountered every type of guest imaginable: the smugly irksome, the routinely obnoxious, the inexplicably hostile, the drooling lunatics. And yet, in all that time, he had never deviated from the guiding principle that underpinned the hospitality business on the subcontinent, an ethos inscribed on wooden plaques in the offices of innkeepers and hotel managers up and down the land: Guest is God.

Well, if the guest standing before him now was a god, then she was Kali, black-tongued and vengeful, goddess of death and destruction.

Woe betide any man foolish enough to tangle with the dark mother.

And there was also the small matter of discretion.

He wouldn't put it past this insane woman to begin shouting about her husband's investigation into Burbank's death in the middle of the lobby. Already he could see that the porters' ears had perked up. The wretches lived on gossip, even though he had warned them a thousand times about indulging in idle talk about the guests.

All things considered, a complimentary room seemed a small price to pay to nip a possibly calamitous situation in the bud.

'Very well, madam, I will see what I can do.'

'Thank you,' said Poppy. 'And I would prefer a sea view, if you don't mind.'

An hour later, Poppy and Irfan had settled into the Rani of Jhansi suite on the ninth floor.

Being in the Jhansi suite filled Poppy with a quiet delight.

The Rani of Jhansi was a particular heroine of hers; a Maratha queen who had fought – and died – against the British in the Indian Rebellion of 1857. Now there was a woman who had rarely suffered from self-doubt, even when charging into the guns of the 8th Hussars, 'raining a fire of hell', as the old poem went!

The suite itself was magnificent, so plushly decorated that Poppy had the feeling that she had stepped inside a wedding cake. The concierge proudly informed her that film stars and politicians had stayed there, that it was the preferred choice of one of the country's top cricketers. He gave Poppy the grand tour, then stood by the door coughing ostentatiously.

Poppy, misunderstanding the gesture, took out a bottle of cough syrup from her handbag and insisted he take three spoonfuls.

As the hapless concierge reeled away, Irfan made himself

at home on the enormous sofa, which had the sturdy look of a seventeenth-century naval vessel about it. He switched on the TV, and instantly became glued to a cartoon show called *Mighty Mohan* about a small boy with superpowers who raced around the city fighting evil, oblivious to his own safety.

In many ways this Mighty Mohan resembled her husband, Poppy thought, with a shake of her head.

Chopra was, in some respects, still a boy at heart. He thought in childlike terms, in black and white, with nothing in between. In truth, it was one of the things she had always admired about him. He remained the most honest man she knew. In a country seemingly ravaged by corruption this was not something to be taken lightly . . . If only he would learn that it wasn't up to him to solve *every* problem, to right *every* wrong, to cure *every* ill. Why couldn't he let others take the reins now and again?

'Would you like to take a look around the hotel?' she asked Irfan.

'After the show,' mumbled Irfan.

Poppy gave a semi-exasperated smile. Like many of the boys in her class at the St Xavier Catholic School for Boys – where she taught classical dance – once he was installed in front of a screen he became as lifeless as a zombie.

Well, if anyone deserved a little leeway it was Irfan.

He worked as hard as anyone at the restaurant, and the trauma he had suffered early in life had failed to subdue his spirited demeanour or basic good nature.

'In that case, don't leave the room. I'll be back soon.'

A BAD BUSINESS ALL ROUND

Chopra returned to the Grand Raj Palace at eleven, and headed straight for the business centre. Here he asked the way to the VIP members-only club.

At the door to the lounge a tuxedoed concierge barred his entrance, looking Chopra up and down with ill-disguised disbelief.

'I am here to see Avinash Agnihotri,' said Chopra.

'Is Mr Agnihotri expecting you?' said the concierge archly. 'Is he expecting your, ah, elephant?' The stooge behind him gave a soft snigger.

Chopra's brow furrowed.

He took out his identity card, which identified him as a 'Special Advisor to the Mumbai Police,' duly signed and stamped by the commissioner of police himself, a concession Chopra had won following an earlier case. 'I am investigating Hollis Burbank's death. If you don't let me in to see Agnihotri right away I will be forced to drag him out by the collar. I will be sure to let him know *you* were responsible for his humiliation.'

The concierge blanched. 'Come with me, sir. And please, feel free to bring your, ah, associate.' He bobbed his head at Ganesha. '*Sir.*'

Ganesha twirled his trunk, and swaggered through the doors behind Chopra.

Chopra met Avinash Agnihotri in a private room, with carpet so thick it reminded him of the northern Indian grasslands where the grass was so tall elephants became lost inside it. His own elephant, Ganesha, appeared delighted with the squishy flooring, and moved around in happy circles while Chopra sank down into a faux empire armchair opposite Agnihotri.

The Indian businessman was aggressively sipping a martini. 'My own brand,' he said, pompously. 'Indian-made.'

Chopra recalled that Agnihotri – who was based in Bangalore, down in the southern half of the country – had made his fortune in software. He was one of the crop of Indian IT czars who had grown rich seemingly overnight in the outsourcing bonanza that had convulsed the developing world during the past two decades. Chopra had recently read that the wheels were beginning to come off that particular cart, as the backlash from local customers and workers' unions in Western markets made itself felt. Agnihotri, for his part, had successfully diversified and was now involved in a range of manufacturing enterprises around the country. He was known for being fiercely patriotic. His mantra of 'Make Indian, Buy Indian', a philosophy that hearkened back to the days of the Independence movement, had given him a popular, man-of-the-people appeal.

Of course, the ordinary Indian didn't stay in five-star suites at the Grand Raj Palace, or fly around on a private jet run by his own airline, Agni Air.

Agnihotri had a head of dark, close-set curls peppered with grey; aggressive eyebrows; and a nose like a vulture, below which lurked a grey-black moustache.

'What's this all about, Chopra? I was about to deliver a seminar to some of the city's top chief executives.'

Chopra explained quickly.

Agnihotri put down his martini. He took a silver cigar case from his pocket, and lit up a thin cigarillo. He didn't offer one to Chopra. 'So you think there was more to Burbank's death than meets the eye?'

'That is what I am attempting to determine.'

'Hah. Trust Burbank to make a production out of his own suicide.'

'I take it you and Burbank didn't see eye-to-eye.'

'The man was a crook,' said Agnihotri angrily.

'You have had previous dealings with him?'

Agnihotri hesitated. 'No. I simply meant that in business circles he is known as a ruthless predator. Doesn't really care how he makes his money, or who gets chewed up along the way. Like an elephant on the rampage.' He glanced at Ganesha, who was running his trunk over a marble statue of a Nandi bull, guardian of Kailasa, the home of Lord Shiva.

Chopra dwelt for a moment on Agnihotri's words.

There seemed to be a depth of hostility there that hinted at something more than a spat over a valuable painting. 'It is my understanding that at the auction the battle between yourself and Burbank to acquire *The Scourge of Goa* became quite heated.'

'Define heated,' said Agnihotri.

'You were disappointed losing out to Burbank.'

'I did not *lose out* to Burbank,' snapped Agnihotri. 'I simply chose to stop bidding. I could easily have carried on. It's not like I don't have the money.'

'Then why did you stop? By all accounts you were vociferous before the auction about acquiring that particular painting. About ensuring that it stayed in India.'

'Is being a patriot a crime?' said Agnihotri, his eyes flashing angrily. 'You see, that's the problem with our country. We're so carried away with where we're going, we seem to have forgotten where we've come from. It's true that I've made a fortune through globalisation. But where does it say that if you grasp the opportunities of the future you have to cast aside everything from your past?'

'Nowhere,' murmured Chopra. It surprised him to learn that in some ways Agnihotri was a man after his own heart. Certainly, he was expressing the very views that Chopra routinely espoused, views that, in these heady days of Shining India, few wished to hear.

'Yes, I made a lot of noise about *The Scourge of Goa*,' continued the businessman. 'I'm not a big collector, but that wasn't what this was about. I just couldn't stand by and watch another piece of our national heritage sold off, particularly to a man like Burbank, a marauder with no respect for the thousands of years of Indian history that have brought us to where we are today. That painting is another stitch in the great tapestry of our national identity. Stitch by stitch I see that identity unravelling. We have become so thoroughly seduced and brainwashed by the West that we are becoming unrecognisable to ourselves.' Agnihotri shook his head. 'So, yes, I did the best I could to stop Burbank from getting his hands on it. But I'm no fool. Once I realised that he *wouldn't* stop, that it didn't matter to him how much money he spent to get that painting, that it had become just another contest of wills for him, I pulled out.'

Chopra paused as behind him Ganesha bumped into a coffee table and almost knocked over a very expensive-looking vase.

Agnihotri pointed his cigarillo at the little elephant. Ganesha froze guiltily and looked down at his square-shaped toes, his trunk hanging down in embarrassment. 'I travel all over the world and never have I seen an elephant inside a hotel. But that is precisely what makes India *India*. Because there *is* nowhere else in the world where you could walk into a five-star hotel and see an elephant and it would do no more than raise a curious eyebrow.'

Ganesha appeared to realise that he was not about to be castigated, and slunk away from the vase, hiding from Chopra's admonishing gaze behind an antique rosewood writing desk set in the centre of the room.

Chopra resumed his questioning. 'All that is very well, Mr Agnihotri,' he said, 'but the fact is that you accosted Burbank immediately after the auction.'

'Accosted?' echoed the businessman.

'It is my understanding that there was an altercation. In one of the VIP toilets.'

For the first time Agnihotri's arrogant demeanour slipped. He poked his cigarillo into his martini glass, extinguishing it. Then he picked up the glass, and moved it towards his mouth absent-mindedly before realising what he was doing. He set it down again.

'I wouldn't call it an altercation.'

'Then what would you call it?'

'A . . . straightening-out. A clearing of the air.'

'Do you usually clear the air by grabbing your rivals by the throat?'

'I barely touched the man!' protested Agnihotri.

'You threatened to kill him.'

'I'd had a lot to drink,' spluttered the businessman. 'Look, I admit, I got a bit carried away after the auction. My emotions got the better of me. If I did threaten him, it was simply in the heat of the moment.'

'What did you hope to achieve? By confronting him?'

Agnihotri waved a hand around. 'I don't know. I just . . . He was so smug. After he won. Made a point of coming over and shaking my hand in front of the cameras, just so he could rub my nose in it. I confess, I saw red.'

Chopra had known men to kill for less. 'Can you tell me where you were on the night of Burbank's death from roughly one a.m. to two a.m.?'

Agnihotri shot him a venomous look. 'I don't have to answer that question. You're not even a real policeman.'

'Technically, you are correct,' said Chopra, stifling his

urge to grab the man by the collar. *Not a real policeman?* After thirty years on the force?

He held the businessman's gaze until finally Agnihotri buckled. 'Very well. If you must know, I was in my room. Sound asleep. Like I said, I had had a lot to drink and it had been a draining evening.'

'Is there anyone who can confirm this?'

'Who would that be? The president of India? A team from the UN?' said Agnihotri belligerently. 'I was alone. My family is back in Bangalore.' He glared at Chopra. 'Instead of wasting your time harassing upstanding citizens, perhaps you should be talking to those who genuinely wished Burbank harm.'

'And who would that be?'

'Why don't you start with Padamsee? The art critic,' said Agnihotri. 'The man took a swing at Burbank right after the auction.'

'Why?'

'Why don't you ask him?' said Agnihotri, heaving himself upright. 'I think I've had just about enough questioning for one day.'

Chopra rose to his feet. 'Very well. May I ask if you will be staying here for a few days?'

'I'm here for another week,' said Agnihotri irritably. 'I have some business matters to attend to.'

'Thank you for your time.'

A LOVE STORY FOR THE AGES

Poppy was lost.

The maze-like corridors of the hotel – all painted and carpeted in the same luxurious shades of umber and maroon – quickly disoriented her. She turned a corner and stepped into a bowl-shaped nook in which a young woman wearing breezy slacks and a plain white kurta was looking at a magnificent portrait set above a red leather sofa.

The portrait drew the eye, and was clearly intended to be the focus of the space.

The painting was of a regal couple, a beautiful woman in a green-and-gold sari seated on a wooden bench, a handsome man in a peacock-feather turban standing just behind her. The man's right hand rested lightly on the woman's shoulder. *Her* left hand was raised to gently touch the tips of his fingers, an oddly intimate gesture for what at first seemed a formal portrait.

The dusky young woman facing the painting seemed lost

in thought. A cloud of distinctive perfume wafted from her, twitching Poppy's nostrils.

Not knowing what else to do, she joined her; together they gazed at the painting.

She saw that a plaque accompanied the portrait. It said, in block capitals: *THE RAJA OF KAMALPUR AND HIS BELOVED SECOND WIFE, THE RANI OF KAMALPUR. A LOVE STORY FOR THE AGES.*

'Do you think they were happy?' said the woman suddenly.

'I am sorry?' said Poppy.

'These two. The lovebirds. Were they happy?'

'Well,' said Poppy, somewhat flustered by the odd question, 'I am sure they must have been. They were married, yes?'

'That's the point, isn't it?' said the woman. 'Where does it say that marrying someone guarantees happiness?'

Poppy smiled. 'There are no guarantees in life. Like everything else, marriage is something one must work at.'

The woman eyed her warily. 'Why do people say that? True romance is supposed to be . . . the opposite of hard work.'

Poppy's smile faded.

Well.

The girl clearly had strong opinions, and didn't appear to mind sharing them. Perhaps a dose of common sense was in order here . . . And then, just as she was about to speak, a flash of insight came to her. 'You're getting married, aren't you?'

'Is it that obvious?' said the girl, glumly.

'It is meant to be a happy occasion,' said Poppy. 'Not the cause of misery.'

'Really? Then how come everyone I know had a nervous breakdown before the "big day"? Not to mention all those marriages where it never worked out? For whatever reason.'

Poppy could not argue against this.

India might well be a superpower now, but the social stigma that came with divorce or a broken home – particularly for women – would take far longer to dispel. The truth was that many Indians stayed together, happy or not. Sometimes it worked out – after all, time and maturity often brought accommodations to offset initial years of frustration – but Poppy herself knew of many examples of sham marriages, couples trapped in lifeless relationships but unable or unwilling to break free.

The shackles of societal expectation were cast in iron, she had often felt.

'Are *you* married?' said the girl.

Poppy nodded. 'Yes.'

'Happily?'

'For twenty-four years.'

'He must be a good man.'

'The very best.'

'But did you know you would be happy together on the day you married him? On the day you moved to his home?'

Poppy hesitated. Had she known that? Had she known that Chopra would be the man he had proven to be? Honest, ethical, hard-working and, yes, in his own way, a romantic – in spite of current evidence to the contrary – though he would rather be boiled in hot lead than hear himself described in that fashion. 'What is your name, dear?' she asked.

'Anjali.'

Poppy gestured for the girl to sit with her on the claw-footed sofa beneath the portrait of the Raja and Rani of Kamalpur. She took her hand and patted it. 'My husband and I grew up in the same village. Then he went away to become a policeman. He returned one day, and saw me passing by the river. We exchanged a greeting, nothing more. A few days later his father came to see my father, and asked for my hand in marriage for his son. My father gave me the option of saying no, but it wasn't really an option. I loved my father, and wanted to make him happy. It was, after all, tradition for a daughter to marry the husband her father chose for her. And the man he had chosen seemed a good match. He was educated; he had a good career in the big city; he was the son of a man my father admired, his oldest friend. And yes, I found him handsome.' Poppy's eyes became moist with nostalgia. 'But did I know he was going to treat me well? Did I know that he would stick with me through the darkest days of my life? For instance, the day I was told I could never have children? Did I know that he was honest in a way few would understand, that this honesty would never waver, never bend, never break, even if it cost him his life? Did I know he would turn out to be generous, and kind, and warm?' She smiled. 'Did I know he would be allergic to ginger, adore cricket and Gandhi, and some English detective called Sherlock Holmes? No. I knew none of those things.'

'You sound as if you adore him,' said Anjali, wistfully.

'I do. But there are still times when I would like to put hot chillies in his tea.' She said this with such feeling that Anjali stared at her until she looked away. 'How well do you know this boy you are due to marry?'

'Like you, our parents brokered the marriage. I didn't get much of a say in it.'

Poppy was surprised at this admission.

One of the things that *had* changed in modern, urban India was the freedom of the younger generation to choose their own partners; though perhaps it wasn't freedom in the way that people in the West thought of it. Nowadays, many parents arranged for children to meet through family networks, at supervised social gatherings. Once potential candidates had been identified in this way, parents could involve themselves in making the formal arrangements. It was still rare for Indians to marry outside of their caste, religion or class, and these sorts of 'flexible arranged marriages' were an effective compromise.

For a modern, clearly educated, woman such as Anjali, Poppy would have expected such an informed choice.

'You realise that no one can make you marry a man you do not wish to?' she said sternly.

'No one made me,' said Anjali, her eyes flashing. 'It's just . . . I can't explain.'

'Try,' said Poppy, but the girl shook her head, her beautiful features suddenly shadowed by misery.

'Is it because there is someone else?' asked Poppy delicately.

'No,' said Anjali. 'It's nothing like that.'

Poppy gave her hand a squeeze. 'Well, in that case, I advise you to go with your heart. If you don't want to get married, then don't.'

The girl gave a watery smile. 'As I said, it's complicated.'

Poppy reflected again on how beautiful she was. Dusky skin, a graceful neck, black hair like liquorice. The air of tragedy about her only served to bring her beauty into sharp relief.

'What I really want to do is focus on my career.'

Poppy gave a small clap of delight.

Having recently joined the 'rat race' after twenty-four years of not having a regular job, she now considered herself a world expert on the trials and tribulations of the working woman. 'And what is it that you do?'

'I, uh, run a hotel. Of sorts.'

'How splendid,' said Poppy. 'Is it as grand as this one?'

'Oh, it's just a small place, out in the countryside. You could say it's a new venture.'

'Well, I am sure that with someone as sensible as you in charge it will surely prosper.'

'You're a real optimist, aren't you?' said Anjali. 'Sadly, I've always been a realist. As hard-headed as a donkey, my father says.' She got to her feet. 'Thank you for the advice. Perhaps you could give some to my family too? About marriages and weddings not always being the answer. They're staying at the hotel. You can't miss them.'

'You're welcome,' said Poppy. 'And perhaps I can ask something of you in return . . . Could you possibly tell me how to get off this floor?'

HELL HATH NO FURY LIKE A CRITIC SCORNED

Following the meeting with Agnihotri, Chopra made a call to the auction director Lisa Taylor.

'Padamsee? Yes, of course I know who he is.' She suddenly burst into a fusillade of panting noises, which, for some reason, ignited a lurid warmth under Chopra's collar. 'I'm on a bicycle in the gym,' she explained. 'Padamsee . . . huff . . . Not exactly . . . puff . . . my favourite person.'

'Why is that?'

He heard Taylor swinging herself off her bicycle, catching her breath. 'Well, he's an art critic, and a particularly vicious one at that. His speciality is attempting to derail the careers of young artists by penning the most scathing reviews you could imagine. I, on the other hand, make my living by *promoting* artists. I make the most money when a young artist suddenly becomes hot, and the value of his or her work skyrockets. That process is helped along immeasurably by critics offering positive reviews. But for that to happen one needs critics who are open-minded, willing to give fledgling artists a chance. Padamsee is not that type of man. He is a cynical, bitter, hateful snob. He was an artist in his youth, but not a very good one. His work was brutally dismissed by the critics of his day, and I suppose that has stayed with him.'

'Hitler was a failed artist too,' observed Chopra.

There was a momentary silence, and then Taylor's tinkling laugh came down the phone. A surge of well-being ballooned inside him. This made him strangely uncomfortable.

'Where can I find him?'

'At this time? He's usually in the Banyan restaurant for lunch.'

Chopra noticed an incoming call on his phone. It was Tripathi.

'Could you hold for a second.' He answered the call.

'I'm afraid I've got bad news, Chopra,' began Tripathi. 'Gunaji somehow got wind of your investigation. He crashed into my office ten minutes ago and ordered me to take you off the case.'

'What did you say?'

'I told him to go to hell. I've had just about enough of that stuffed baboon.' Tripathi sighed. 'That's when he got the commissioner on the line. I've got no choice. I hate to do it, but I can't risk my career for this.'

'But I've just begun to make progress,' protested Chopra. 'Your instincts were right. I think there may be more to Burbank's death than suicide.'

'Believe me, if I had my way, we'd see this through to the

bitter end. But I really don't have a choice. I'm sorry for wasting your time.' Tripathi hung up.

Chopra stared at the phone, his jaw grinding with anger and disappointment. 'Hello?' It was Lisa Taylor. 'Are you still there?'

'Yes,' said Chopra.

'Not many men put me on hold,' said Taylor. But she sounded more curious than angry. 'Must have been important.'

'It was.'

'You were asking about Padamsee.'

'It doesn't matter now,' said Chopra. 'I'm afraid my investigation has come to an end.'

'What? What do you mean?'

Chopra quickly explained.

'But that's ridiculous!' protested Taylor. 'You're the only one who's really taken this seriously.'

'It's out of my hands. My client has terminated my services.'

Taylor was silent. When she spoke it was with a curious excitement. 'Don't give up just yet. Meet me in the restaurant in twenty minutes. I may have a solution.'

Precisely twenty minutes later, Chopra entered the Banyan restaurant. Immediately, he heard Ganesha's bugle, and then the little elephant shot past him in a grey blur.

'Poppy!' he said, staring in astonishment at his wife

seated at a table with Irfan, with what looked like half the restaurant's menu spread out before them. A sweating waiter hovered at Poppy's elbow, nervously awaiting a verdict. 'What are you doing here?'

Poppy rose to greet her husband. 'I have found a solution,' she announced.

'A solution?' Chopra was nonplussed. 'What was the problem?'

'The fact that you don't know what the problem is, is itself the problem,' said Poppy, her tone stiffening.

Chopra's mouth flapped open, but any words therein appeared to decide that rushing out into the line of fire was not worth the risk, and stayed right where they were.

'Look,' said Poppy, her expression softening, 'I understand that your job is important to you. I understand that you feel responsible for everyone who asks for your help. But you need to understand that, right now, *this* is important to me. Our anniversary is not just another day. And since you cannot be at home to participate in it with me, I have decided to come to you instead. If the camel will not go to Mecca, then Mecca must come to the camel, yes?' Poppy smiled.

Chopra's eyes crinkled.

He had always understood that his wife was an emotional person, and that was fine. It balanced out their relationship. But this, this was . . .

'Don't worry about the expense,' said Poppy hurriedly, the words floating from her mouth in a nervous rush. 'We have been given a complimentary suite.' She hesitated, perhaps sensing her husband's real consternation. 'And don't worry about us getting under your feet. Irfan and I will enjoy our stay here until you are ready to join us. Perhaps we can have dinner together? You can stay in the suite with us, of course.' She looked hopefully at her husband, as did the waiter, and a number of other diners who had stopped eating to listen in on the developing melodrama.

'Poppy, we cannot accept this suite,' said Chopra gently.

'But the general manager said it was not a problem.'

'It does not matter what he says. It is a matter of principle.'

'But—' Poppy began, but was cut off by Lisa Taylor materialising at her husband's elbow.

'Hello, Chopra. Have you spoken to Padamsee yet?'

The young Englishwoman was wearing a short red satin dress with spaghetti straps, and designer heels. She had showered and changed after her workout, and was now dressed to the nines. Or, at least, *partially* dressed, whispered a hot little voice in Chopra's ear.

'No,' said Chopra. 'As I said on the phone, I am no longer charged with this investigation.'

'That's where you're wrong,' said Taylor brightly. 'I've just got off the phone with the managing director of Gilbert and Locke. We would like to retain your services. To investigate Burbank's death.'

Chopra's jaw slackened. 'Why? How?'

'Burbank was one of our biggest clients. We want to get to the truth about his death.' She lowered her voice so that only Chopra could hear. 'We need to know exactly what we are dealing with, Chopra. If it *was* suicide, fair enough. But if it was murder, then we need to be armed with the facts.

The good name of Gilbert and Locke must be protected at all costs. Somehow I don't believe that that is foremost on the agenda of ACP Gunaji.'

'This . . . this is—' began Chopra.

'No need to thank me,' said Taylor. 'I should warn you that there is a clock ticking here. My boss wants this all tied up in the next few days. Before the police can make a statement.'

Chopra nodded. 'I understand.'

'So you accept?'

'Yes. I accept.'

'Splendid! Now, since you haven't yet spoken to Padamsee, why don't we go together? I'd like to see what that oaf has to say for himself.'

Chopra suddenly sensed the pressure of Poppy's stunned gaze, as well as the goggle-eyed scrutiny of the lookers-on. He flushed in the sudden silence.

'Yes, Chopra,' said Poppy icily. 'Why don't you carry on? In the company of – I'm sorry, madam, I did not catch your name . . .'

'Lisa. Lisa Taylor.' Taylor gave a photogenic smile. 'I'm helping him with his investigation.'

'Is that so?' said Poppy. 'He did not mention that he was working with a *partner*.'

'She's not my partner,' said Chopra hurriedly. 'Lisa is an auction director. She, ah . . .' He glanced around at the impromptu audience. 'Perhaps this isn't the place to discuss this.'

'There is nothing to discuss,' said Poppy flatly. 'As you told me last night, this is a *very* important case. I can see that you have much to keep you engaged. Why don't you run along? I shall go back to my suite.'

'But Poppy, I thought we had discussed the matter of the suite—'

'*You* had discussed it,' interrupted Poppy, curtly. 'That is not the same thing as *we*.'

'Perhaps I can help?' said Taylor. 'Gilbert and Locke will be happy to pick up the tab. For your suite, I mean.'

Chopra stared at the woman. 'That is very generous, but—'

'Then it's settled. Now, I don't see Padamsee around.' She smiled breezily at a waiter. 'Hello, Shiva. Do you know where Adam Padamsee is? He usually drinks his lunch here.'

'Yes, madam, he was here.'

'Do you know where he's gone?'

'Yes, madam.'

They waited.

'Well, are you going to keep us in suspense?'

'Oh! Sorry, madam. I believe he has gone to the Nehru Room.'

Taylor turned to Chopra. 'That's where we're exhibiting some of the artwork that wasn't sold at the auction. I'm due to show a collector around now, actually. A millionaire dung baron from Kerala. I've always been fascinated by how you can make so much money out of dung. Fertiliser, apparently.' She turned and patted Ganesha on the head. 'I still can't get over the fact you've got your own little elephant. No one would believe me back home in Oswestry. Right, let's go, Chopra.'

She walked off briskly towards the exit.

Chopra hesitated, vacillating between leaving and staying to smooth things over with Poppy. He could sense that his wife was unhappy, though she had no cause to be.

'Go on, *Chopra*,' said Poppy archly. 'She does not seem like a woman who likes to be kept waiting.'

'Poppy—' he began, but his wife raised a hand.

'There is no need to explain. You have work to do. Clearly it is much more important than standing here wasting time talking to me.'

She turned, sat down and went back to her meal.

Not knowing what else to say, Chopra nodded, then followed Taylor out of the restaurant, slipping out his phone so that he could apprise Tripathi of developments. It was important, Chopra felt, that his friend knew he hadn't yet abandoned his quest for the truth.

The Nehru Room was a sumptuous space with monstrous crystal chandeliers, shimmering maroon wallpaper and a brilliant white marble floor. Artwork had been set up around the walls, with various pieces of sculpture and pottery displayed on stands in the main space. A number of well-dressed people were being shown around the gallery.

They found Adam Padamsee standing before a painting consisting of a large white canvas with a single black dot in the very centre. He clutched a notebook, and was scribbling in it furiously.

Padamsee was a squat man with a protruding gut, a widow's peak, a pointed goatee and bloodshot eyes. He wore beige chinos above tasselled loafers, and a breezy sports jacket that hung awkwardly across his rounded shoulders.

'And whose career are you destroying today?' said Lisa Taylor, by way of greeting.

Chopra sensed the hostility and instantly regretted allowing Taylor to join him.

Padamsee gave Taylor a sour look, his eyes lingering for a moment on her bare legs, then said: 'Who's this? Another fool you've found to palm some worthless piece of rubbish off on?'

Chopra realised that Taylor had not been exaggerating when she had described Padamsee as rude and obnoxious.

'You wouldn't know a real work of art if it came and bit you on the backside,' responded Taylor hotly.

'Really?' Padamsee waved his notebook at the white canvas with the black dot. 'Do you know how the so-called artist of this "masterpiece" describes his work? I quote: "A reflection of infinity in the eye of the Creator; a journey into the soul of oneness; a mote of dust adrift in the cosmos." ' Padamsee looked unimpressed. 'It is a dot.'

'Context is everything,' said Taylor, defensively. 'I happen to know that the artist meditated for three years on a mountaintop in the Himalayan foothills eating only boiled grass and fermented yak's milk before the inspiration for this work came to him.'

'Next time tell him to stay there.'

Chopra interrupted before Taylor could reply. 'Mr

Padamsee, my name is Chopra and I am investigating Hollis Burbank's death. I'd like to talk to you about the evening of the auction.'

Instantly, Padamsee's face underwent a change. He became uneasy, blinking his reddened eyes rapidly. 'What for?'

'My understanding is that there was an altercation between yourself and Burbank. You tried to assault him.'

'Assault!' Padamsee's eyes widened in alarm. 'I never touched the man.'

'That's a lie!' said Taylor. 'You took a swing at him. We all saw you.'

Chopra had had enough. He turned and faced the auction director, fixing her with a stern look. 'Lisa, I must ask you to allow me to handle this. Please.'

She continued to glare at Padamsee. 'Fine,' she said eventually. 'I have to see to my buyer anyway. But don't say I didn't warn you – he's a habitual liar.'

She turned and stalked away.

Chopra focused on the art critic. 'What was your fight with Burbank about?'

'Why do you care? The man killed himself.'

'That is what I am trying to determine.'

Padamsee looked uneasy again. 'Look, unlike most of the people who knew him, I won't pretend that I've been shedding tears for Burbank. I'm not glad he's dead, but neither am I sorry about it. He was a terrible human being, and believe me I know something about that. I have never pretended to be a saint, but there are lines even I would not cross.'

'What line did Burbank cross?'

Padamsee hesitated, then said, 'Fine. You will probably find out anyway . . . After the auction we both attended the after-party. One of those post-coital soirees where the Lisa Taylors of this world fawn over the likes of Burbank, stroking his ego, telling him what a discerning eye he has for buying the latest piece of garbage she's managed to foist onto him.'

'You believe *The Scourge of Goa* to be garbage?' said Chopra, with a raised eyebrow.

'Of course not,' snapped Padamsee. 'For once Taylor managed to get her hands on something worth selling. It was just a shame that Burbank prevailed in the bidding. I am no weeping nationalist like that Agnihotri, but to see such a work in the hands of a boor like Burbank made my blood boil.'

'And yet you went to this post-auction party with him?'

'It's part of my job, Chopra. We humble art critics don't get paid much for our opinions,' he said bitterly. 'We have to play the game to earn our crust. We labour for years to become experts, and then spend the rest of our lives being treated like lapdogs. When we deliver an honest review we are accused of being vicious, bitter. If we offer flowery praise for worthless rubbish we are fools. Well, I've spent my life calling it exactly as I see it. It has made me many enemies. And yet no major art event would be complete without my presence, hovering about the edges like a leper.'

Chopra realised that Padamsee's resentment ran deep. He wondered what would possess a man to continue to work with a community of people who despised him.

He must have the hide of a rhinoceros.

'What did you and Burbank argue about?'

Padamsee sighed. 'If you must know, Burbank insulted my wife.'

'Your wife?'

'Yes. Her name is Layla. Layla Padamsee.' He looked expectantly at Chopra.

Chopra hesitated. 'I am sorry. Should I be familiar with her?'

'She is a renowned sculptor,' said Padamsee testily.

'How exactly did Burbank insult her?'

'You have to understand that my wife is not like me. She is a warm and gregarious person. And she is very attractive. Well, Burbank had been flirting with her all evening. I say flirting, but what I really mean is letching. The man had a reputation for that sort of thing. I warned Layla, but she just laughed it off. Said she could handle herself. Towards the end of the evening he managed to trap her in a corner. He was drunk, leaning in to her, *breathing* all over her. When I came over, instead of backing off, he grinned at me, told me what a "talented" wife I had. I told him that if he thought she was so talented why didn't he buy one of her sculptures. That's when he leaned over, and said: "Why don't I just buy *her*?"' Padamsee's face flushed with anger at the memory. 'I stood there for a second, not sure if I'd heard him correctly, and then he said: "I'll pay you a hundred thousand dollars. For one night with your wife." I can't tell you how terrible I felt right then. It was like that movie, the one with Robert Redford, I can't remember the name now. This man, with all his money, felt he could buy my decency. Well, when it comes to Layla, my blood runs hot. And so, yes, I took a swing at him. But the truth was I was as drunk as everyone else there that night. I missed him by a mile. But he got the message. He left – without a mark on him. You can check that with whoever you wish.'

'I shall,' said Chopra. 'And I would like to start by speaking with your wife. Do you know where I can find her?'

'She's running a sculpting workshop in one of the gardens.'

Chopra paused. 'Can you tell me what happened *after* Burbank left?'

'Nothing happened. I stayed at the party for a while longer, then went to my room.'

'You never left your room again?'

'No. Like I said, I'd had a lot to drink, and needed to sleep it off.'

'Was your wife with you?'

'Of course. Where else would she be?' But his eyes drifted away, unable to meet the detective's searching gaze.

'Thank you for your time,' said Chopra.

THE WEDDING OF THE SEASON

While Chopra headed off to find Layla Padamsee, Poppy found herself drifting into the Mughal Ballroom on the ground floor, the largest space in the hotel. Irfan and Ganesha followed behind her, engrossed in their own play.

An odd feeling of listlessness and despondency had fallen over Poppy.

The encounter with her husband had not gone as she had hoped.

She had, of course, anticipated that he would be less than overjoyed to discover that she had followed him to the Grand Raj Palace – she had not really stopped to question the wisdom of her strategy, fearing that if she did she would simply surrender to the inevitable and remain at home.

But that was often the way with her.

She acted first, and thought later.

Nevertheless, she had hoped that, once he got past the initial shock, he might appreciate the fact that his wife – who had graciously stepped aside while he charged off on yet another of his never-ending investigations – was close by on the occasion of their twenty-fifth wedding anniversary.

But the encounter in the restaurant had proved discomfiting, and had left her feeling inexplicably upset. It wasn't even the presence of the very beautiful Englishwoman that her husband appeared to be gallivanting around with. She knew him well enough to trust him implicitly, though the woman's carefree familiarity with him had almost caused her to give the underdressed strumpet a piece of her mind.

No. What really bothered Poppy was the tiny sliver of suspicion that perhaps her husband was *embarrassed* at having her around.

During the years that he had run the Sahar station, he had been a stickler for the rulebook, a dedicated and incorruptible policeman. These traits had set him apart – his solemn nature, his moral rectitude – and she had grown to love him as a personification of these same ideological idiosyncrasies. Yet now, she found herself wishing that, for once, he would bend his mighty principles and simply embrace the fact that the woman he had been married to for a quarter of a century wished to be near him.

'Hey, look where you are going, madam!'

Poppy stopped short, having almost walked into a giant cardboard cut-out of Sachin Tendulkar, India's legendary cricketer. The sight only served to remind her of her husband – Chopra was a big fan of the game and had avidly followed Tendulkar's batting exploits for years. Glancing around her, she realised that Tendulkar was just one of a gallery of colossal cut-outs stationed around the ballroom.

A man in a blue safari suit was peering down at her from the top of a ladder as he fiddled with a light fixture beside Sachin's ear. 'And mind that elephant, too,' he said, belligerently.

'Why don't you mind yourself?' said Poppy, glad of something else to focus on. 'Why are you cluttering up the place with these ridiculous things, anyway?'

'They are for a wedding,' said the man, unfazed. 'The hosts have invited many celebrities and want to greet them with twenty-foot-high cut-outs of themselves. Only in Mumbai.' He gave a wolfish grin.

'Who is getting married?' asked Poppy, glumly. She couldn't seem to get away from the subject, apparently. Marriages and anniversaries!

'Some real big-shots. The heirs of two royal families, apparently.' He scratched the side of his nose with a screwdriver. 'It is the most lavish wedding I have ever seen at the Grand Raj. Half the city is coming. Anyone who is anyone. There's a cut-out of the royal couple out in the garden,' he added, pointing with the screwdriver to a door at the far end of the ballroom. 'Some people have more money than sense, if you ask me. When I got married, we had a rice menu. Rice dumpling to start, plain rice for mains and rice pudding for dessert. God, I hate rice.'

In the garden, Poppy found a number of people milling about, and what looked like a film crew winding up a shoot.

She saw a beautiful young Indian woman with oversized sunglasses sitting on a chair beneath a parasol. A pet monkey in a ridiculous yellow waistcoat lurked on a chair beside her. Attendants fawned around them.

Poppy caught hold of a passing waiter bearing a tray of drinks. 'What is going on here?'

'They are shooting a movie, madam,' said the waiter excitedly. '*Boom 3*.'

Poppy, who prided herself on being a lifelong devotee of Bollywood, had not heard of the production.

'They are from the south,' said the waiter.

Ah. That explained it.

India was so vast that one movie industry was simply not enough to cater for the multiplicity of languages and cultures that divided the subcontinent. Bollywood, based in Mumbai, was just the largest and most influential of India's movie machines. Others centred in regions around the country inspired equally fanatical devotion.

This production must be from the Telugu film industry based in the state of Andhra Pradesh. She knew that recently there had been a trend for crossover movies between Bollywood and Tollywood – as it was known – with actors and producers looking to expand their reach to new audiences.

She re-examined the beautiful starlet, wondering if she could place her.

Unable to do so, she instead resumed looking for the cut-out of the wedding couple.

She found it at the far end of the garden, stationed beside a garlanded wedding podium set up in the lee of a banyan tree. A saffron-robed priest impatiently paced up and down beside the podium, glancing at his watch every few seconds.

The twenty-foot-tall cardboard apparition of a young couple in traditional dress smiled breezily down on him.

They made a very handsome pair, Poppy thought wistfully, once again taken back to her own wedding day.

And, then, as she looked at the female figure, she realised that there was something familiar about her. It was the girl she had met on the ninth floor . . . Anjali!

The girl who had had doubts about getting married at all.

This realisation set off a shrill alarm in her stomach.

Suddenly, the gaiety of the planned occasion seemed to sour. Anjali had been decidedly unsure about her upcoming nuptials. And now that Poppy knew what a grandiose occasion it was going to be, she could almost sympathise. Though she herself loved this sort of over-the-top spectacle she knew it was not for everyone, particularly not for a young woman – a young princess, in actual fact, if Ladder Man was to be believed – who seemed unsure of the direction in which her life was headed.

She looked around the garden, wondering if Anjali was present.

Perhaps another heart-to-heart might be in order . . .

At that moment, a party of voluble Indians burst into the garden, propelling themselves across the lawn towards the podium. They were all ostentatiously dressed, in shimmering silk saris, embroidered churidar trousers, loose-fitting, ankle-length lehenga skirts and brocaded jodhpuri suits. A gaggle of overstuffed peacocks. As they approached, Poppy realised that they were split into two factions, with an older couple at the head of each group.

It was these two senior couples whose voices rang the loudest.

'For God's sake, all you had to do was keep an eye on her,' griped the tall, thin man at the head of one group, flailing at the air with a mahogany walking cane as he made long strides across the lawn. The man had grey hair, a pinched, clean-shaven face and pitted cheeks.

'What do you mean?' retaliated the rounder specimen leading the second mob, a heavy-browed man with a shaggy moustache, wearing a shimmering jacket, the buttons of which appeared in imminent danger of popping off like champagne corks. 'She is a grown woman. She does not need anyone to keep an eye on her.'

'Well, where is she then?' replied the first. 'We are already two hours late for the rehearsal.'

The two parties seemed to run out of steam as they reached the wedding dais. They milled around in aimless confusion, like chickens pecking at grains of rice, as the two irate leaders continued to squabble.

Poppy singled out a young woman who was standing apart from both groups, scrolling on her mobile phone. 'Excuse me,' she said, 'Can you tell me what is going on?'

The young woman – who was cudding gum, Poppy couldn't help but notice, a habit she loathed – gave her the evil eye. 'You must be from the other side.'

'The other side?'

'The groom's mob,' clarified the girl.

'No,' said Poppy. 'I am . . . a friend of Anjali's.'

The girl lowered her phone. 'Is that so?' she said, in a tone that suggested she would struggle to believe this if someone painted it on her forehead in neon yellow. 'Well, I have known Anjali since we were both in school, and I have never seen you before, Mrs . . .?'

'My name is Poppy,' said Poppy. 'And I am not that sort of friend.'

'What sort of friend are you then?'

'I met Anjali upstairs earlier today. She seemed anxious about her upcoming marriage. I offered her a few words of advice.'

'Really?' said the girl, her interest suddenly quickening. 'What did you say to her exactly?'

'I merely suggested to her that she must follow her instincts. Sometimes, when one is uncertain about a particular course of action, it is best to trust one's own feelings.' Poppy felt pleased with herself for phrasing her thoughts so elegantly.

The girl stared at her. 'Well, good for you Mother Teresa,' she said flatly. 'But maybe that explains why Anjali has now vanished.'

'What?' Poppy's alarm rang sharply through the garden. 'What do you mean "vanished"?'

'Is it such a difficult word?' said the girl sarcastically. 'Vanished. Disappeared. No longer around.'

'But she is due to be married!'

'Really? And here's me thinking we were all here for a pyjama party.'

Poppy felt flustered. 'I assure you I said nothing to her that would make her just . . . leave.'

The girl continued to eye her sourly, then her face compressed into worry. 'I knew she had doubts, but I never expected anything like this. And the worst thing is: we can't work out what happened.'

'What do you mean?'

'I mean that she simply *couldn't* have vanished from her room. Not unless she's a magician.'

Poppy began a reply, but was forestalled by raised voices behind her.

She turned to find that the two men who had been arguing had now squared up to each other.

'Have you any idea how much money I have spent?' bellowed the tall, thin one.

'I have spent no less,' countered the plumper man, his voice shaking with indignation.

'She is *your* responsibility,' said the first, waggling his cane.

'Give him a good belt,' piped up a voice from the back of the crowd. 'Who do they think they are, blackening our faces like this?'

'Yes,' came another voice from the rear. 'Show him we won't be trifled with.'

This set off another round of belligerent grumbling.

'I missed an appointment for my bunions for this.'

'I knew this was going to happen. My astrologer told me – don't go, he said, it'll all end in tears.'

'Best bunion doctor in the state. Took me four months to get an appointment.'

'They should have locked her up. This is what happens when a girl gets modern ideas in her head.'

'It's not easy living with bunions. Everyone thinks if you just buy the right shoes, but—'

'Will you shut up about your bloody bunions!'

With each complaint the two men – presumably the fathers of the bride and groom – were pushed closer together, a circle of baying, not-so-well-wishers closing in around them like the jaws of a steel trap. A light of panic entered the patriarchs' eyes as they suddenly realised that their bloodthirsty guests expected them to somehow settle the matter there and then, in the time-honoured tradition. After all, just that week there had been chaos in the Lok Sabha – the Lower House of Parliament – when one member had thrown a shoe at another over a new bill demanding a state pension for cows, resulting in an unseemly brawl that had lit up the media for days.

A shriek scythed through the din.

Poppy turned.

The priest was hopping around, holding his hands over his private parts. His lungi – the cloth that wound around his lower limbs – had disappeared.

The remarkable spectacle finally stuttered the mob into an awed silence.

'That elephant!' spluttered the priest, his bulbous eyes contorted with rage.

Poppy swung her gaze to Ganesha.

The little elephant was under the banyan tree, sensibly avoiding the sun, investigating a hole in the gnarled trunk. An incriminating orange splash behind his rump indicated the presence of the missing lungi.

Oh dear.

Poppy knew that Ganesha possessed a mischievous streak, a trait encouraged by little Irfan. Although she was learning to accept this as part of the young calf's burgeoning personality, sometimes, inevitably, this put her and Chopra into embarrassing positions.

Such as now.

Denuding a holy man was more than a prank – it was a sacrilege. She couldn't imagine that the frayed tempers of the two wedding parties would be improved by the situation.

She strode over to the elephant.

'Ganesha!' she scolded, scooping up the priest's lungi and holding it out in front of her. 'Bad boy!'

'But he didn't do it!' yelled Irfan, from somewhere above her head.

She looked up to see the boy perched in the upper branches of the tree, all but concealed by the banyan's leafy canopy.

'What are you doing up there!' cried Poppy. 'Come down before you fall and hurt yourself!'

'Ganesha didn't take the priest's lungi,' protested the boy. 'I saw everything. It was that stupid monkey. He pulled it off the priest and planted it behind Ganesha.'

Poppy turned.

Behind the priest, perched malevolently on the edge of the wedding dais, was the langur in the yellow waistcoat they had seen earlier, the movie star's pet. The monkey was shelling and eating peanuts, plucking them from a pocket sewn onto its jacket.

Poppy hesitated. Could Irfan be telling the truth?

'What nonsense!' came a voice from behind her. 'That elephant should be locked up! Humiliating a man of God!'

'And see how the boy shamelessly lies for his friend,' echoed another. 'They should both be given a sound thrashing. Children these days are a menace to society.'

Poppy's eyes narrowed, scanning the mob.

'Who said that?' She shook the lungi at the crowd. 'If my boy says it wasn't Ganesha, then it wasn't him. And if anyone dares lay a finger on either of them they'll answer to me.'

There was an uncomfortable silence as the mob considered the wisdom of a confrontation with this clearly insane woman.

The silence was broken by the priest's voice. 'Madam, may I have my lungi back?'

Poppy handed the lungi back to him, averting her eyes as she did so.

The priest snatched the cloth, wound it around himself, then stalked away with the tattered remnants of his dignity. 'Find yourself another priest,' he muttered as he passed the prospective fathers-in-law.

'What? Wait! You can't leave!' cried the taller of the two in alarm.

'We've paid you a fortune!' spluttered the other.

Poppy watched as the wedding crowd trailed off after the indignant holy man, leaving her alone with the girl she had first spoken to.

'Well done,' said the girl sourly. 'Just when I thought things couldn't get worse. That was the top priest in the city. All the big movie stars use him. Do you know how difficult it was to convince him to officiate at this wedding? And now he's gone too.'

'But we didn't do anything!' protested Poppy.

The girl shook her head and wandered away.

Irfan clambered down from the tree, and took Poppy's hand. Ganesha plodded over and slipped his trunk into her other hand.

She bent down and looked them both in the eye. 'You know that I would never be cross with you – as long as you tell me the truth.'

'But I *am* telling the truth,' said Irfan. 'It was the monkey.'

Poppy hesitated. 'I believe you,' she said eventually, and gave them a hug. 'Come on, let's go and find out more about this runaway bride.'

THE SCULPTOR

The Bhagat Singh garden was named after the Indian freedom fighter and folk hero who, in 1929, had thrown a bomb into the Central Legislative Assembly in Delhi. To the bemusement of the British soldiers guarding the assembly, he had subsequently hung around waiting to be captured, chanting revolutionary slogans and scattering badly printed leaflets into the smoking chaos. Shortly thereafter, at the tender age of twenty-three, he had been hanged, marking another seminal moment in the Independence struggle.

The garden was an enclosed space in the Grand Raj Palace's west wing, surrounded on all sides by the hotel's looming walls. The green oasis consisted of a tiled courtyard, a short lawn hemmed in by willow trees and a water fountain from the centre of which rose an imposing stone statue of Bhagat Singh himself, complete with his trademark felt hat and insouciant moustache.

A group of a dozen people – mainly foreigners – were stationed around the lawn, working lumps of glistening clay on top of pedestals. Chopra thought that the provisional sculptures were intended to be busts of Bhagat Singh, but, if this were the case, he was glad that the man himself was not around to judge the results.

An attractive, middle-aged Indian woman in a bohemian skirt and halter top circulated among the amateur sculptors, offering advice and words of encouragement.

As Chopra looked on she paused behind a small, mousy woman with ginger hair wearing a broad-brimmed summer hat. 'That's very good,' said the Indian woman. 'But he doesn't really look like Bhagat Singh, does he?'

'No,' agreed the white woman, in an English accent. 'That's because this isn't Bhagat Singh. It's my ex-husband.'

The Indian woman gave an encouraging smile. 'Well, bravo to you. It's a rare woman who would make a bust of her ex-husband. You must be on good terms.'

'Oh, we aren't on good terms,' said the woman brightly. 'I'm making this bust so that I can keep it by my bedside and stab it in the eyes with a fork every night before I go to sleep.'

'Mrs Padamsee?' said Chopra, as the Indian woman noticed him hovering on the edge of the lawn and turned towards him.

'That depends on who is asking.'

Chopra quickly explained his mission. A cloud passed over Layla Padamsee's face.

Her curly hair – highlighted by a single blond zigzag down the middle – was scrunched back behind her head into a messy ponytail, and she flicked at it now, nervously, as she considered her response. 'I must apologise for my husband,' she said. 'He suffers insanely from jealousy. And he isn't very good with liquor.'

'Not many people are in my experience,' said Chopra dryly. 'Your husband tells me that Hollis Burbank was, shall we say, *indiscreet* with you on the evening of the auction.'

'My husband tends to exaggerate,' said Layla. 'Yes, Burbank was a boor, but have you any idea how many men behave in that way at these sorts of things? An art exhibition is like a watering hole in the desert. It attracts all sorts of predators because they know easy prey will be around. There's a reason the big art houses employ lots of beautiful young women. It's part of the allure for rich older men like Burbank. They somehow think everyone is fair game, that if you're involved in the art world – particularly if you happen to be a female artist – you must be up for anything.'

'But you were not so . . . amenable?'

'No,' said Layla, coldly. 'I most certainly was not. I love my husband. And I know how to fend off men like Burbank without alienating them. There was no need for Adam to get involved.'

'Did your husband seek out Burbank later, to finish the argument?'

'No. He went back to his room and slept off his evening of free Scotch.'

'And you?'

'I went with him,' she said promptly. 'Neither of us left our room again that night.'

Chopra paused.

This last statement by Layla Padamsee had been unusual. She had answered a question that he had not yet asked. In his time as a policeman, such a response would have set alarm bells ringing. He made a mental note to examine the alibis of both Padamsees. Effectively, they were alibi-ing each other. Given that they were husband and wife, this deserved closer scrutiny.

He examined her anew, his eyes travelling the length of her, the unease in her face, the nervous body language. His gaze fell on a large plaster wrapped around her right wrist. 'What happened?' he asked.

She followed his gaze. Her left hand involuntarily attempted to cover her right wrist. Then she seemed to realise what she was doing, and smiled uncertainly. 'Oh, just a little accident.'

'What sort of accident?'

'I, uh, had an accident with my pottery wheel.'

'Are you certain about that, Mrs Padamsee?' Chopra asked softly.

She hesitated, looking at him with troubled eyes. Chopra felt the truth bulging at her lips, but in the end, she said, 'Yes. I am.'

'In that case is there anything else you can tell me about that evening? Anyone else that Burbank might have argued with?'

She began to shake her head, but then stopped. 'I don't know about any arguments, but I did see Burbank talking in a corner with Swarup. It seemed to be a very intense conversation. Swarup didn't look very happy about it, whatever it was.'

'By Swarup do you mean the artist? Shiva Swarup?'

'Who else would I mean?' said Layla scathingly. 'I take it you've heard of him?'

Of course Chopra had heard of Swarup.

Shiva Swarup was, according to the national media, India's most famous living artist. A painter whose work had risen to prominence three decades earlier, and continued to headline major art exhibitions around the country. He was often called 'India's Matisse', renowned for his bold use of colour and heavy-handed brushstrokes, and his work routinely sold for extravagant sums. Indeed, a number of his contemporary paintings had sold well at the Grand Raj Palace auction.

'Did Burbank buy one of Swarup's paintings?' asked Chopra.

'No.'

'Do you know what they were talking about?'

'I have no idea.'

Chopra examined the woman's handsome face, the trace of belligerence that swelled her beautiful jawline. 'Do you know where I can find Swarup?'

'He has a studio on Marine Drive. Spends most of his time holed up there. Frankly, he is known for being reclusive. It took a great deal of pleading by Gilbert and Locke to get him to participate in this auction at all.'

Chopra thanked the woman, then turned to leave, before turning back. 'May I ask how long you are staying at the hotel?'

'I am here for another week, running classes.'

Chopra nodded. 'I may return to ask further questions.'

Layla blinked uneasily. 'Will that be necessary?'

'Let us just say that I am not quite inclined to take everything that you and your husband have told me at face value.'

The wedding parties, Poppy discovered, had taken up a large proportion of the hotel. By trailing the guests, and eavesdropping on their animated chatter, she discovered that Anjali had been staying in a bridal suite on the same floor as her own room.

Arriving at the suite, Irfan and Ganesha padding along behind her, she discovered Anjali's gum-chewing friend slouched against the wall outside the door.

'You again,' said the girl.

'Me again,' said Poppy brightly. 'I want to help.'

'Don't you think you've done enough?'

Poppy decided that she had had just about as much sassiness from this slip of a girl as she could tolerate. 'Stand up straight!' she said, in her most no-nonsense voice.

Reluctantly, the girl straightened.

'Tell me this,' Poppy continued. 'Do you consider yourself to be Anjali's friend?'

'Of course.'

'Then start acting like it. From what I can see the people who *should* be sitting down calmly and trying to work out what has happened are too busy running around like headless chickens. Which means that someone with a sensible head on their shoulders must take charge of the situation.'

'Possibly,' conceded the girl grudgingly.

'Well, that is what I do,' said Poppy. 'You might even say that solving problems is my middle name.'

'Funny middle name,' muttered the girl under her breath.

Poppy ignored her. 'Now, what is *your* name?'

'Huma. Huma Dixit.'

'Tell me about Anjali, Huma.'

'What do you want to know?'

'Everything.'

'Well—'

'Wait,' said Poppy. She rummaged in her bag, and took out a tissue. 'Your gum, please.'

'Are you serious?'

'Very. We cannot give this matter its due attention if you are chewing gum all the time.'

The girl stared at Poppy in disbelief, then seemed to surrender. 'Fine.' She plucked out the gum and put it into the tissue, which Poppy wrapped up and put back into her bag. 'By the way, why do you have an elephant following you around?' She glared at Ganesha, who was looking on with some interest.

'He is not following me around. I am his guardian.'

'Well, I don't like the way he's staring at me.'

'He is just being friendly.'

'Tell him to be friendly somewhere else,' said Huma belligerently.

Ganesha continued to stare at her, perhaps hoping for some chewing gum.

'You were telling me about Anjali.'

Huma focused again on Poppy. 'Anjali's always been a high achiever. Top marks in school, the first girl in her family to go to university, a real pioneer.'

'Is it true that she is from a royal dynasty?'

'Yes. Her family can trace their ancestry back to the Peshwa rulers of the Maratha empire. Her full title is Rajkumari Anjali Tejwa Patwardhan, and her father is the Raja of Tejwa.'

Poppy's eyes sparkled. How incredible that the seemingly simple girl she had met earlier had turned out to be a princess! 'Anjali told me that she wished to focus on her career. She said that she ran a hotel.'

Huma Dixit released a bark of laughter. 'Hah! Trust Anjali to call it that. The "hotel" she is talking about is the Rajwada, the Royal Palace of Tejwa.'

Poppy considered this, uncertain whether the girl was joking. Another question occurred to her. 'Who exactly is she getting married to? I mean, when I spoke to Anjali she seemed unsure of the match. Is he, perhaps, much older? Or, ah, lacking in certain departments?'

'What departments would those be?'

'Well, Anjali is beautiful, educated, ambitious. I am sure she would not wish to be chained to some sort of gargoyle with the brains of a lumbering ox. There are plenty of men in this country who don't appreciate a woman with a mind of her own, you know.'

'No, I suppose not,' said Huma. Her eyes suddenly gleamed with a mischievous light. 'And gargoyle is about right.'

'What does this groom-to-be think of Anjali's desire to focus on her career?' continued Poppy.

Huma smiled wickedly. 'Why don't you ask him? The lumbering ox is standing behind you.'

Poppy turned to find a tall, handsome young man lurking nervously in the corridor behind her. 'I am sorry, Aunty,' he began. 'Do you know Anjali?'

Poppy turned to look behind her.

But the only ones present were Irfan and Ganesha, staring up with interest at the newcomer.

And then it dawned on her that the young man was referring to her.

Her face coloured.

Aunty? The cheek.

'My name is Poppy,' she said stiffly. 'And I am not your aunty. I am a friend of Anjali's, and I am helping to locate her.'

The young man, who was dressed in a dashing charcoal grey Nehru suit, and twisting a silk turban around in his large hands, looked downcast. 'I can't understand it,' he said. 'They say she just vanished. Into thin air.'

'No one vanishes into thin air,' said Poppy firmly. 'My husband is a detective, and one of the things I have learned from him is that there is *always* an explanation.'

'I hope you are right, Aunt— er, Poppy Madam,' said the boy.

'What is your name?' asked Poppy. She could see that the boy seemed quite put out.

'Gautam. Gautam Deshmukh.'

'He means *Yuvraj* Gautam Deshmukh Patwardhan,' said Huma. 'Or Prince Gautam the Great, as we like to call him.' Her voice had a sarcastic sneer to it that did not escape Poppy.

'It is true,' said the boy sadly. 'I am the sole heir to the Deshmukh branch of the Patwardhan royal dynasty. We are the neighbouring princely realm to the Tejwa family landholdings.'

'What you mean is that you are the neighbouring *enemies*,' snapped Huma.

'Enemies no more,' protested Gautam. 'That is the point of this marriage, isn't it? So that finally, after centuries of enmity, the Deshmukh and Tejwa clans may be united as one?'

'Hah!' said Huma. 'Why don't you tell that to your father?'

'My father agreed to the marriage.'

'Well, now he seems to think we have deliberately spirited Anjali away.'

'I am sorry,' mumbled Gautam. 'He is just worried. We all are.'

Poppy patted the boy on the arm. 'I am sure there is a simple explanation for all this. Many brides become nervous just before their wedding. It is, after all, a daunting prospect. To leave everything and everyone you have ever known and enter a new household, a new life. Particularly if, as in this case, there is bad blood between the two families.'

'It isn't that,' said Huma. 'Anjali isn't afraid of anyone, let alone *his* mob.' She jerked a thumb at Gautam. 'I'm afraid that if you're looking for a simple explanation here, there isn't one.'

Something in her tone jarred. 'What do you mean?' asked Poppy.

The girl hesitated. 'Okay. If you're serious about helping, then come with me. I had better show you what happened. The fact is that Anjali *has* vanished – and none of us can work out how, let alone why.'

WHEN A COW IS NOT A COW

Chopra drove the short distance from the Grand Raj Palace to Marine Drive, taking the scenic route past the Oval Maidan. It always gladdened him to see young cricketers playing on the palm-lined field, with its patchy grass and kutcha wickets. No matter the season or the weather, they were out there, hollering and shouting, running and jumping, not a care in the world. They may not have known where their next meal was coming from, but he was certain that even if the field had been under two feet of water they would still have been happy to play.

The Tata van puttered past the Bombay High Court, and Bombay University with its iconic Rajabhai Clock Tower, modelled on Big Ben in faraway England. The tower was one of many Raj-era buildings dotted around the city. It had originally been commissioned by a prosperous Indian stockbroker, Premchand Roychand, as a means of alerting his blind mother to mealtimes.

Once, Chopra knew, it had played 'Rule Britannia' and

'God Save the King', but those days were now well in the past.

Shiva Swarup's studio was located halfway along Marine Drive, not far from the Wankhede cricket stadium, taking up five floors of one of the ubiquitous white towers that graced the Drive.

Even beneath the full heat of the afternoon sun, pedestrians thronged the curving Back Bay promenade, offering a brisk trade to the dozens of cart vendors selling coconut water, lime juice, jasmine flowers, peacock-feather fans and pani puri snacks. A yogi sat atop one of the giant tetrapods lining the promenade, gazing mysteriously out to sea, a mirror-flat expanse of deep blue, blazing with prisms of light. The air quivered in the heat, giving the impression that both yogi and tetrapod were levitating above the water.

The ground floor of the studio comprised a gallery of Swarup's work – and the work of other young artists that the maestro had deigned to nurture – and was a bold white space that gave the eye little else to focus on.

Chopra supposed that was the point.

With no distractions, the only thing to hold the gaze was the artwork . . . If indeed that was what one could call it.

It hung from the ceiling, jutted from the floor and adorned the walls. Art of all manner and description. Paintings, sculptures, installation pieces that, frankly, left him puzzled as to whether they were exhibits or part of the building's superstructure.

A group of men in business suits were gathered around what looked like a stuffed cow standing on a podium. A reedy-looking man in a white kurta, blue jeans, Kashmiri sandals and a thick moustache that seemed to weigh down his head described the piece to them in a nasal drawl. 'We are now gazing upon the secrets of infinity,' he said, haughtily.

Chopra was as mystified as the visitors. The cow suddenly moved its head and he realised, with a start, that it was alive.

One of the businessmen raised a tentative hand. 'Excuse me, but isn't that a cow?'

The man reared back. 'This is *not* a cow, sir.'

'Umm. It looks like a cow to me. I mean it has horns and everything.'

'Those are not horns. Those are physical manifestations of the essential duality of conflict and harmony evident in the cosmos.'

'Ah. Because I could have sworn they were horns.'

'Really?' sneered the artist. 'And I suppose these are just udders, hmm? And not the intrinsic symbols of the succour that each soul craves from the teat of the ultimate being?'

A second businessman raised a hand. 'But what if the cow wanders off?'

'It is not a bloody cow!'

'Sorry. I mean what if the manifest symbol of the cosmos wanders off?'

'It is the nature of art to be fluid,' said the artist archly. 'One cannot cage art. Art must be free to express itself.'

At that precise moment, the manifest symbol of the cosmos chose to express itself by raising its tail and defecating onto the podium.

The first businessman spoke confidently. 'I get it now.

That's a searing indictment of the capacity of mankind to pollute everything it touches.'

'That, sir,' said the artist, his eyes bulging with fury, 'is a pile of excrement.'

Chopra had had enough. 'I'm looking for Swarup,' he said, brandishing his identity card. 'Police business.'

The artist stared at him, his eyes growing cautious. 'He is in his studio.'

'Thank you,' said Chopra, moving towards the grand spiral staircase at the rear of the space.

'But, sir! Maestro is not to be disturbed when he is painting!'

'It seems to me everyone around here is pretty disturbed already,' muttered Chopra.

Shiva Swarup's personal studio was on the fifth floor.

Chopra entered the studio and found himself in a large, high-ceilinged space, lit by a swathe of light that fell in from a bank of high windows running across the far wall of the room. The room itself was whitewashed, and littered with a jumble of large easels, some covered in tarpaulin sheets and some holding half-finished paintings.

Beside the door, a workman in white gloves carefully unpinned a canvas from its wooden frame with a pair of pliers. He watched for a moment, then made his way to the far end of the room where a naked dwarf was standing on a plinth holding what looked like a cuddly snake toy. The dwarf, Chopra realised, was quite old, his small, hairless body wiry, the ribs prominent across his malformed chest.

The dwarf watched him approach, then said: 'If you're looking for Shiva he's just gone out onto the balcony for a smoke.'

'Thank you,' said Chopra.

'Have a quick look at the painting and tell me what you think,' said the dwarf. 'He won't let me see it until it's finished. He's very particular about that.'

Chopra hesitated, then walked to the easel set up opposite the dwarf.

Once again he found himself mystified.

On the canvas was an Olympian, godlike figure, standing atop a cloud, wrestling a mighty, seven-headed cobra. If he squinted his eyes he could just about make out the face of the dwarf on this Herculean being.

'Well?' said the dwarf.

'Ah, it's, er, very good.'

The dwarf's face fell. 'You hate it, don't you?'

'No. Not at all,' said Chopra, hurriedly. 'It is very, ah, potent.'

The dwarf sighed. 'I suppose I should have expected it. Something's been off the past couple of weeks. He's not been his usual self.'

Chopra's interest was suddenly piqued. 'What do you mean?'

'Ever since this auction rolled into town, he's been as tense as an elephant on a hot tin roof. He should never have agreed to do it, if you ask me.'

'Why *did* he agree to do it?'

'I have no idea. I suppose he just felt he had to be there. You know, with it being the "biggest auction of Indian art ever". How would it have looked if India's number-one artist wasn't there?

'He's a good man, you know,' continued the dwarf conversationally. 'I've posed for all sorts. There was this one chap, from the Absurdist school, very emotional fellow. Used to get into terrible rages. Burned his own studio down three times, twice with me in it. I never minded. I was his muse, you see. Though, sometimes, I wondered why I was bothering to pose for him. He'd ask me to stand on a stool, holding a clay pot; or do a handstand; or pose as if diving from a high board. Then he'd paint an ass in a sombrero. He once told me that the real world was duplicitous. That it takes a true artist to look beyond the falseness of reality, to the truth within.

'He was a big one for Truth,' said the dwarf with a sigh. 'In the end, I think it was Truth that killed him. One day he asked me to hold a rose in my teeth while I posed. When he was done, he took one look and then shot himself with a revolver. Before I called the police I snuck a peek. He'd painted me as a baby, my thumb in my mouth, an expression of beatific innocence on my face. I still don't know what made him shoot himself, what he saw in that painting. I like to think he'd reached the pinnacle, that he'd realised he just couldn't paint any better than that.' He sighed again. 'There's not many careers around when you're a dwarf. It's all: you're a dwarf? Welcome to the circus, and a lifetime of being shot out of a cannon or having custard poured down your pants. I mean, what sort of demented mind even finds that funny?' His eyes glinted briefly. 'I always wanted to be a miner, but they told me dwarfs don't know the first thing about mining. We don't have the hands for it, apparently.'

Chopra found Shiva Swarup on the balcony, staring out over the Marine Drive promenade, smoking an acrid roll-up.

He was a small, grey-haired man, with an untidy white beard, square-framed black spectacles and a hooked nose. He wore a plain white kurta above jeans, the kurta spotted with paint stains. Spots of paint also marked the artist's beard.

Chopra introduced himself, and explained his mission.

Swarup's face darkened. 'It is terrible that Burbank is dead,' he said woodenly. 'But I was told that he committed suicide.'

'Did you know him well?'

'I did not know him at all,' said Swarup.

'Ah. I would have thought that, with Burbank being a collector of Indian art, your paths may have crossed.'

'He didn't collect *my* art,' said Swarup.

There was something in his tone that pulled Chopra up. 'I am informed that he spoke at length to you on the evening of the auction. The conversation appeared to be very intense.'

Swarup blinked rapidly. 'I do not recall that.'

'Are you saying you didn't speak to him?'

The artist hesitated. 'I spoke to a great many people that evening. I am, as you may have realised, considered something of a celebrity, though I personally detest the limelight.'

'I am certain you would have remembered speaking to Mr Burbank,' said Chopra softly.

Something about his tone communicated itself to Swarup, who blinked again, then said: 'Now that I think about it, perhaps you are right. We *did* have a conversation, a very short one. He asked me about *The Scourge of Goa*, about Rebello.'

'You knew the artist?'

'Briefly. Many years ago. I had just "arrived" on the art scene; he was already an established master. I spent a short period in his studio in Goa.'

'And that is all you spoke with Burbank about?'

'That is all,' said Swarup, his voice becoming firmer.

Chopra reached into his pocket. 'I'd like you to take a look at something,' he said, holding out the copy of the sketch discovered inside Hollis Burbank's suitcase. 'Can you tell me anything about this?'

Swarup's eyes widened as he took in the image of the slumped, half-naked man with the death's head grin. He coughed, to cover what appeared to be surprise, then said, gruffly, 'No.'

Chopra stared at the man. 'Are you sure? It seems as if you recognise this work.'

'No,' snapped Swarup. 'I do not.'

'Then do you have any idea who might have drawn this? There is no signature. Just the initials. K.K.'

'No idea at all.' Swarup crushed his roll-up on the sill of the balcony. 'I am sorry to rush you, but I really must return to my work.'

'Yes, of course,' said Chopra, though he was reluctant to

let go of the matter. His antennae were up. He was certain that Swarup was holding something back. 'Just one last question: was there anything else that you saw or heard that evening that seemed out of the ordinary to you?'

Swarup shook his head. 'No. I have no idea why Burbank took his life. Whatever it was, it must have been terrible.'

AN IMPOSSIBLE DISAPPEARING ACT

'We'd just finished lunch together,' said Huma Dixit, as she led Poppy, Irfan and Ganesha into the bridal suite, Gautum following them. 'Then we came back up here. Anjali was supposed to get ready for the dress rehearsal in the garden. She wanted to have a bath first and so I ran the tub for her. She got in for a soak while I sat out in the living area, watching TV. After an hour, I realised we were getting late for the rehearsal so I knocked on the bathroom door. When she didn't answer I tried to get in, but it was locked. That's when I called the hotel reception. They had to break the lock. When we got inside there was no sign of her. The water in the tub was cold. The windows were all latched from the inside.' Huma frowned. 'She just . . . vanished.'

Poppy walked into the bathroom.

The theme was Egyptian, with beige marble tiles adorned with hieroglyphs, a Cleopatra bathtub sitting in the centre of the room and a pyramid-shaped structure in the corner, which, she discovered, was a towel bin.

As large as the bathroom was, there was simply no place for Anjali to have hidden.

'Are you certain all the windows were locked?' she asked.

'Yes. And even if they weren't, we're on the ninth floor. Last I checked Anjali didn't have wings.'

'Have you noticed anything strange about the bathroom?'

'The only thing strange about it was that Anjali asked housekeeping to stay away.'

'Why?'

'She didn't want them in here. Said she wanted one completely private place, an oasis of calm in the madness surrounding this wedding.'

'Didn't that strike you as odd? Not having the bathroom cleaned?'

Huma shrugged. 'It's her wedding, not mine.'

Poppy considered this. Why would Anjali not have wanted the bathroom cleaned? Privacy didn't seem a good enough reason. It's not as if housekeeping would have barged in to clean while she was in the tub. The only logical explanation was that there was something in the bathroom that Anjali didn't want anyone to see. But Poppy had gone over every inch of the room. There was nothing out of place.

A furore erupted in the living room.

She stepped back outside to find a gaggle of wedding guests and family members crowding into the suite. They were still arguing.

The two patriarchs stepped forward to confront Huma.

'Has she called you?' asked the round one, anxiously.

'No,' said Huma.

'But this is ridiculous!' exclaimed the taller man. 'I have guests arriving every hour. If Anjali does not return soon, we will have to call off the wedding. The scandal is unthinkable!'

'We'll find her,' said Huma.

'I presume you have asked the hotel staff to search the premises?' said Poppy, stepping forward.

The two men focused on her. 'Who are you?' asked the taller of the two, looking at her along the impressive length of his nose.

Poppy glanced at Huma. Reluctantly, the girl introduced her. 'This is Poppy, a friend of Anjali's.' She managed to keep the contempt from her voice. 'And this is His Highness Raja Shaktisinghrao Deshmukh Patwardhan. Father of the gargoyle. I mean, the groom,' she corrected herself hurriedly. 'And *this* is His Highness Raja Prakashrao Tejwa Patwardhan, Anjali's father.'

The round man looked at Poppy with sad eyes. 'The hotel's general manager is organising a discreet search of the public areas. But the real question is *why* would Anjali be hiding? She agreed to this marriage. I did not force her into this.' His voice took on a defensive edge. 'She told me she was happy to go through with it.'

'Hah!' muttered Shaktisinghrao. 'She is a Tejwa. Her word means nothing.'

'What did you say?' said Prakashrao, wheeling round to the taller man.

'I merely pointed out that it is nothing new for a Tejwa to betray a Deshmukh. No one here has forgotten the Battle of Badwalkar Plain, I am sure.'

'That's a damn lie that your family has been spreading around for two centuries!' Prakashrao's round cheeks quivered with fury.

'It's all there in the history books,' said Shaktisinghrao airily. 'You are fortunate indeed that I am so enlightened, accepting your daughter into my family.'

'Accepting!' For a second Poppy thought Prakashrao's eyes would pop from his face. His thick moustache danced beneath his round nose. 'Why, you ungrateful snob! It is I who am doing you the favour. Your son is famous in ten states for his stupidity. He can barely remember to breathe and speak at the same time. You should be kissing my feet that I have deigned to allow my daughter to marry such a clod.'

'I'm going to beat you to a pulp!' roared Shaktisinghrao.

'You and what army, Deshmukh?'

The two men flailed ineffectually at each other, without actually coming to blows.

'Father!' said Gautum, looking on anxiously.

Poppy regarded the pair with astonishment.

She had attended innumerable weddings, and had borne witness to all manner of bad behaviour – rudeness, backbiting, familial intrigue – which was almost par for the course at an Indian wedding.

But this was beyond the pale.

She was about to wade in and give the two men a piece of her mind when a deafening klaxon sounded from the doorway.

The crowd hurriedly parted as an enormous wheelchair trundled into the room. It was motorised, a large, black-framed contraption that had the general look and unstoppability of a tank. It was the sort of vehicle that one might see moving through war zones, having obliterated a small city.

And seated in this steel leviathan was a tiny woman in a white widow's sari.

With her hawkish face, thin frame and claw-like hands deftly operating the wheelchair's control pad, she resembled a baby bird, albeit a predatory one. Something about her beady, ill-favoured expression reminded Poppy instantly of her own mother.

The room had fallen silent. The old woman glared at the two patriarchs. 'If I catch you two fighting again I'll take a cane to both of you.'

'Madam—' began Shaktisinghrao.

'Mother—' said Prakashrao nervously.

'Don't you "mother" me, you big oaf. My granddaughter – the only one of the entire lot of you that is worth a mung bean – is missing, and the only thing you two preening peacocks can think about is yourselves. Scratching at each other like a pair of washerwomen. I am ashamed to call you my son.'

'But *he* started it!' mumbled Prakashrao, a note of pleading in his voice.

'It's not *my* daughter that has gone missing,' protested Shaktisinghrao.

'That is where you are wrong,' said the old woman. 'I've known you since you were a boy, Shaktisinghrao. You were an oily little squirt then, and so you are now. You open those big ears of yours and listen to me carefully. On the day that you accepted my granddaughter into your family *you* became her father. *You* are responsible for her. And if a single hair on her head comes to harm you shall answer to me.'

She glared at both men, then ran her narrowed gaze over the crowd. 'Now get out of my sight, the lot of you.'

The guests stampeded for the doorway, eager to place as much distance as possible between themselves and the cantankerous old woman. Gautum escorted his father out.

With the room empty, the woman's eyes suddenly alighted on Ganesha, who also looked as if he wished to flee. 'Why is there an elephant in here?' she said, in mild astonishment.

'He is with me,' said Poppy.

'They let you keep an elephant in the hotel?'

'Why not?' said Poppy defensively. 'There are guests with dogs, cats, parrots. I know for a fact there is a woman with a monkey staying here.'

The woman trundled her wheelchair over to Ganesha hovering nervously beside Irfan. She bent forward to peer at him closely. Then her face broke into a broad, gummy smile. 'I used to have an elephant when I was young. He was my best friend. My only friend,' she added wistfully. 'What's your name, little one?'

'His name is Ganesha,' supplied Irfan helpfully. 'And my name is Irfan. He is *my* best friend.'

'Let me tell you a secret about elephants,' the woman said. 'They are the most loyal creatures on earth. Once they decide to love you they will love you their whole lives. They will never forget. You must never betray an elephant's trust. Do you understand?'

Irfan nodded solemnly. 'Yes.'

'Good. Now, who is this,' she said, turning her chair to face Poppy. 'Your mother?'

'Yes,' said Poppy, firmly. 'My name is Poppy.'

'And my name is Big Mother. At least that's what everyone calls me. I am the head of the Tejwa clan. Well, technically, my idiot of a son is, but we all know where the real power behind any throne lies, do we not?'

Poppy's face split into a smile. 'Yes, we do.'

'You know my granddaughter?'

'We met briefly. She struck me as a woman after your own heart. I, ah, spoke to her this morning. She seemed troubled by her upcoming marriage. I may have offered her some advice. It may have led to her vanishing.' Poppy gave the old woman a guilty look. 'I want to help, Big Mother. I feel . . . responsible.'

Big Mother sighed. 'The accommodations we women have to make. I never wanted this for Anjali. I have watched her grow from a child into a fiercely intelligent and independent young woman. I wanted her to spread her wings and fly out into the world.'

'Then why is she being forced to marry against her wishes?'

'She is not being *forced* to marry,' snapped the old woman. 'Anjali agreed to the match. She understood that it was necessary.'

'Why was it necessary?' said Poppy. 'If you truly valued her freedom to choose why put her in a position where she must choose *this*?'

Big Mother looked ready to snap again . . . and then the anger seemed to fizzle out of her. 'The truth is a tiger,' she sighed. 'You can hold on to it by the tail as tightly as you like, but there is always the danger it will slip loose and devour you. Some years ago Anjali discovered a difficult truth. It is that truth which, in the end, persuaded her to agree to this match.'

'What truth?'

'That the Tejwa household is all but bankrupt.'

Poppy's face slackened in shock. 'But-but you are a royal family! How can you be bankrupt?'

'Very easily. The princely houses of India have been in a long, ruinous decline since the end of the Raj. After Independence, when India became a democracy, our land was seized, our power stripped from us. And then, the ultimate betrayal: the Indian government took away our federal grants, forcing us to feed ourselves. I still remember the day the government official came to tell us. An oily-headed Collector. Do you know what he said? "It is not me doing this to you, madam. It is the People." Hah! Long live the republic.

'For decades we have lived off past wealth, pride forcing us to put on a pretence of grandeur, while behind the velvet drapes we have sold off the family silver, the fleets of Rolls-Royces, the land that we formerly taxed to those who shouted our names in the street, who bowed and called us "Huzzoor!". Once there were more than five hundred royal households in this country – one by one I have watched them grow silent.' Big Mother's eyes had taken on the smoky haze of memory. 'Five years ago, I visited an old friend, the last remaining princess of Oudh. She was as old as me, but had never married. Her ancestors had ruled over a princely state that took days to ride from edge to edge. Now she sits alone and forgotten, a lonely old woman in an eight-hundred-year-old stone building falling down around her ears, black mould creeping over the walls, darkness encroaching as the electricity flickers on and off. There is a sign outside the gates: *Intruders shall be gunned down*. But there are no intruders. There is nothing left to steal, except her vanity.' She sighed. 'A handful of royal households have survived, by adapting to the new world. Two generations ago, the Deshmukh clan went into business. Now they own diamond mines and an exceptionally profitable jewellery chain. My own son, good-hearted fool that he is, realised too late that the clouds on the horizon would engulf us. His father was the same, a man who buried his head in the sand, deafening his ears to the trumpeting of his own doom.

'Anjali was my last hope. When she discovered the truth about our finances – shortly after she graduated from university – she became determined to rescue us from our fate. While her father sat around playing tabla and singing songs with his wastrel friends, she decided that our only option was to turn our royal palace into a hotel. Other princely states have made a success of such a venture, she told me. Apparently, ordinary people will pay fortunes to experience the "lifestyle of the Indian maharajahs and maharanis". Hah! If only they could experience the life we live now.' She paused. 'But the hotel will not save us, not before we slip into ruin. At some point Anjali realised this. I offered her an alternative, though I was loath to do it. But the gods had chosen to send salvation to me – who was I to ignore it? Shaktisinghrao, the Raja of Deshmukh, sent word that his son wished for Anjali's hand in marriage. The boy was quite adamant, apparently.

'I was not surprised. Marriage offers have been flooding in for Anjali since she turned sixteen. She is beautiful and intelligent – though in some circles this latter trait is still considered a liability,' she added acidly. 'I have shielded her from them all. I wanted her to fulfil her desire to study, to follow her dreams. But my granddaughter has a practical head on her shoulders. She understood that by marrying into the Deshmukh family our financial woes would be solved. Deshmukh cannot afford to allow us to go bankrupt – how would it look if his daughter-in-law's household were ruined, forced to stand outside their palace and watch their possessions being sold off to scavengers?'

'But why did he agree to the match in the first place?' Poppy asked. 'I mean, if the two households have been enemies for so long?'

'Because he has a weakness for his son. Gautam is his only child. He has never denied him anything. Perhaps if he had applied his cane to his son's backside a little more we might not be here today.'

'You believe Gautam is the reason Anjali has run away?'

'What else could it be? The boy is no match for her. He has the wit of a stunned donkey. Though I do wonder why Anjali chose to leave now. I mean, she has had months to think about this.'

Poppy said nothing, feeling guilt descend on her once

more. Could her advice to Anjali have triggered the young bride's decision to flee?

'There *was* something,' said Huma. 'A few weeks ago, she witnessed an almighty row between her father and Gautam's father. They were fighting about money again. I think Gautam's father made some comment about buying the newly-weds a Rolls-Royce, so Anjali could visit her old home in the style befitting a Deshmukh daughter-in-law. And then Anjali's father said, if that was the case, *he'd* be the one to pay, and it went on from there. She was very upset.'

'Those dolts!' fumed Big Mother.

A silence descended, broken by Poppy. 'From what Huma tells me it is still not clear how Anjali actually got out of the bathroom.'

'Does it matter? She is gone, and she must be found. If she wishes to call off the wedding, then I must know. I must prepare. You see, Deshmukh insisted on the grandest wedding imaginable for his only son. He made the mistake of telling *my* son that he would foot the entire bill, given our financial situation. Well, that was a red rag to a bull. My son did something foolish, without consulting me. He mortgaged the palace, took out a loan that he has no hope of repaying, not without Deshmukh's help. I am afraid, Poppy, that if Anjali does not go through with this wedding, then we really shall be out on the streets. All of us, including me.'

THE PLOT THICKENS

On his return to the hotel Chopra tracked Lisa Taylor down to her room.

He knocked on the door. It swung back to reveal the Englishwoman wrapped in a short towel, another twisted around her hair. She had just stepped out of the shower. 'I-I am sorry,' stammered Chopra. 'I shall return later.'

'Oh, nonsense!' Lisa waved him in. 'I'm sure you've seen a half-naked woman before, Chopra.'

She turned, her towel snagging on the door handle. She caught it as it half swung away, revealing more than Chopra would have wished. His face turned scarlet and he felt, acutely, the unbearable lightness of seeing.

'Whoops!' said Taylor, juggling her assets back into the towel. 'Sorry.'

She disappeared into the bathroom, much to Chopra's relief.

When she returned, she wore a bathrobe and was towelling her long blond hair. 'So, how is our investigation going?

I'm afraid I am going to need regular progress reports to feed to my boss back in London.'

Chopra nodded, then took out the sketch. 'Did the police show you this? It was found in Burbank's possessions.'

'No,' she said, frowning. 'They did not. And I don't recognise it, though it does look oddly familiar. Who's the artist?'

'That is what I was hoping you could tell me.'

'Is it important?'

'I'm not sure.'

'But you suspect.' Taylor grinned brightly. 'It's those famous police instincts at work, isn't it? A little feeling in your gut.'

Chopra's guts were doing something, and he distinctly did not like the feeling. 'Can you help?'

'Leave it with me.' She took a picture of the sketch using her phone. 'By the way, where's that adorable elephant of yours?'

'Ah, he is with my wife.' Chopra felt the word 'wife' sticking in his throat like a fishbone. This made him flush once more.

'She didn't like me much, did she?'

Chopra frowned. 'On the contrary, my wife is very much in favour of independent-minded, successful women.'

'Then we would probably get on famously. At any rate, I'll contact a couple of colleagues who might know something about this sketch. Perhaps we can meet later? Let's say eight? In the Banyan restaurant? It's practically our special place now.'

She gave a breezy grin.

As Chopra staggered from the room, he had to remind himself that Lisa Taylor's only interest in helping him lay in the fee she – and Gilbert and Locke – were still owed on Burbank's purchase of *The Scourge of Goa*. As Padamsee had said, Burbank had been a golden goose to her, nothing more.

Someone had killed the goose, and she would not rest until she knew who and why.

Chopra spent the next two hours interviewing more employees of the hotel, meticulously working his way through the staff roster on the evening of the auction, and the night of Burbank's death. He knew from Rohan Tripathi that the initial police interviews, hampered by Gunaji's interference, had been cursory at best. He was also keen to follow up on some of the alibis he had been given by the likes of Agnihotri and the Padamsees.

It was while he was thus engaged that he was interrupted by the sudden, unexpected arrival of Tripathi, accompanied by the hotel's general manager, Tanav Dashputra and the large, bullish form of Assistant Commissioner of Police Gunaji.

Gunaji introduced himself with a blast, then thundered: 'What the hell do you think you are doing? This is a police investigation. You have no right to go charging around making a mess of our enquiries.'

'What enquiries?' said Chopra, his hackles instantly

raised by the man's overbearing attitude. 'As far as I can make out you did nothing except try to force through a verdict of suicide.'

Gunaji snorted steam. 'I heard about you, Chopra. Rao told me you weren't a team player.'

Chopra bristled. ACP Rao was an old nemesis of his, also in the Central Bureau of Investigation.

Gunaji leaned over Chopra. 'I order you to stop your investigation and vacate the hotel.'

Chopra glared at the man. 'You have no authority over me.'

This only incensed the senior policeman further. 'I'll have you arrested, dragged out of here by the heels!'

'Arrested? On what charge?'

'Obstructing an official investigation.'

'Try it,' said Chopra. 'I have been employed by Gilbert and Locke to investigate the death of one of their most prominent clients. If you attempt to stop me from completing my mission, I am sure they will want to know why. I don't think it will have escaped your notice that they have access to the most powerful people in this city.'

Gunaji's face quivered with fury. His lips squirmed as he struggled for his next words. 'This isn't over,' he finally choked out, then turned on his heel and stormed out, Dashputra fussing after him like a tugboat behind a runaway tanker.

'I'm sorry about that,' said Tripathi. 'I have a feeling someone at the hotel tipped him off. Possibly even the general manager. I don't think he's too happy with you wandering around accosting his guests.'

Chopra waved his friend's apology aside. 'Just try and keep Gunaji off my back.'

Tripathi shrugged. Easier said than done. 'Have you made any more progress?'

'Give me another day. There's definitely something here. Too many questions left unanswered.'

'If anyone is going to find those answers, it is you, old friend.'

After Tripathi had left Chopra resumed his interviews.

It was while speaking to the front desk manager that he finally made a breakthrough.

He had asked the man to report anything unusual, anything at all, even if it seemed unrelated to Burbank. The manager had considered this, then said, 'Well, there *was* one thing . . .'

Chopra found Adam Padamsee by the pool, enjoying afternoon tea with his wife.

'You lied to me,' he said. The sounds of splashing drifted over his shoulder.

Padamsee's eyes swivelled, lizard fashion, towards his wife. He stood up, puffing out his chest. 'What are you talking about?'

'You told me that after your altercation with Burbank you went back to your room, and spent the rest of the night asleep. I have just spoken with the hotel's front desk manager. At 1:05 a.m. a call came through to the front desk. It came from room 224, the room next to yours. A complaint was made. Raised voices in your room. So loud that your neighbour was forced from his sleep. Following the complaint, the hotel reception sent someone to your room. By the time the porter arrived the noise had subsided. He knocked repeatedly, but there was no answer. He assumed you had both left.

'I spoke with the guest in 224, a businessman from Orissa. He said that, shortly after he made the complaint, he heard your wife leaving the room. He couldn't make out the details of what you were arguing about, but one thing he clearly recalled under questioning – the name Hollis Burbank.'

Padamsee swayed on the soles of his feet, as if Chopra had punched him in the gut. His round face had turned scarlet, and he seemed suddenly short of breath. 'We had nothing to do with Burbank's death.'

Chopra turned to Layla Padamsee. 'Soon after you left your hotel room Hollis Burbank was dead. I must ask you: where did you go?'

'You don't have to answer that, Layla,' snapped Padamsee. 'He has no authority to question us.'

Layla chewed her lip.

She was wearing another halter top. Chopra's gaze drifted down to the thick plaster around her right wrist. Once he had realised that the Padamsees' alibis were no longer credible, he had gone over his initial interviews with the pair. His thoughts had flashed to the plaster, the way Layla Padamsee had unconsciously fingered the injury as she had talked.

And, just like that, it had come to him.

He reached into his pocket and took out his phone. He flicked through to a photograph, held it up for them to see. 'These are the remains of a broken bangle. They were found in Burbank's room, after his death. He had no other bangles in his possessions, and they do not belong to any of the hotel staff. The housekeeper swears that the room was personally inspected by her before Burbank's arrival. There was no bangle.' He pointed at Layla's wrist. 'How did you get that injury, Mrs Padamsee?'

Layla blinked, looked at her husband, but said nothing.

'It is my belief that this bangle belongs to you,' continued Chopra. 'It is my belief that you sustained that injury when this bangle was broken. And that means you were in Burbank's room on the night that he was killed.'

'This is preposterous!' exclaimed Padamsee, causing a white man on a nearby sunlounger to lift the newspaper from his face and crane his sunburned neck in their direction. 'That bangle could belong to anyone.'

'I am certain that if we examine your wife's possessions, we will find other bangles to match it.' Chopra waited. He sensed the woman's inner turmoil. 'There is blood present on the shards. If necessary, I can have it tested.'

Finally, the sculptor spoke. 'You are right—' she began, but was cut off by her husband. 'Layla!'

She reached out, took Padamsee by the hand, gave him a watery smile. 'I want to speak, Adam. I want to tell him the truth. It's been eating away at me. I need to confess.'

If there was one thing Poppy had learned it was that if you really wanted to know what was going on, you had to go the people at the bottom, the people no one thought to ask because they considered their opinions to be of little value. The silent witnesses to the foolishness of the world.

She found the Grand Raj Palace's head butler, Aryan Ganesham, in the staff meeting room, down in the basement of the Grand Raj Palace, a place of echoing whitewashed corridors, bare cement floors, fleets of broken luggage trolleys and a humming sense of below-stairs anarchy.

Ganesham was deep in discussion with the head housekeeper, Reshma Panang.

The two sprang to their feet as she entered, and looked at her with confusion.

'I understand that you were the first person to enter Anjali Patwardhan's bathroom when she was reported missing?' said Poppy, addressing Ganesham.

The old man, smartly trim in his black butler's outfit, gave a bird-like nod of his lacquered head. 'That is correct, madam.'

'And the door was locked?'

'We were forced to break the lock.'

'The windows too?'

'Yes.'

'So, barring a miracle, Anjali could not have vanished into thin air?'

'That is correct, madam.'

Poppy thought about this. 'There has to be a logical explanation.'

'It could be the ghost,' said Panang, suddenly.

Poppy's ears perked up. 'What? What ghost?'

'Mrs Panang misspoke,' said Ganesham sharply. 'There is no ghost.'

Poppy stared at the man, then folded her arms. 'Mr Ganesham. My husband was a policeman for thirty years. I cannot claim to possess his instincts, but I *have* picked up a thing or two in that time. Now, would you like to tell me what is going on?'

Ganesha blinked, his thin moustache twitching above his lip.

'It is an old wives' tale,' he said finally. 'Just over fifty years ago, a woman staying in that suite was murdered by her husband on their wedding night. The man in question was the son of a powerful politician, so powerful that he was never arrested, never charged. Ever since then it has been said that the woman's ghost haunts the suite, waiting for another unhappy bride.'

Poppy's eyes betrayed her incredulity. 'Well, I met Anjali. And I do not think she is the type to be carried off by anyone, ghost or otherwise.'

Ganesham sighed. 'You are right, of course. Perhaps it is not my place to say this, but the most likely explanation is that if Miss Anjali was unhappy with her impending marriage she probably found a way to arrange her own disappearance. She is not the first bride to do so, and I dare say she will not be the last.'

'But she must still be found,' persisted Poppy. 'If only so that her family can assure themselves that she is safe.'

'I agree. But what else can we do? We have discreetly searched the hotel, to no avail. And the family have asked us not to involve the authorities.'

'No,' agreed Poppy. 'That would create a scandal that neither family is willing to countenance. They are hoping that she will return in time for the wedding.'

Ganesham gave a sad shake of the head. 'I have been here for more than half a century. The things that I have seen . . .! Actors and actresses, presidents and princes. I once saw the American saxophonist Miles McGrady shoot jazz legend "Happy" Franklin in the foot for singing a birthday song for his wife. It later transpired that the pair were *involved*. The first year I was here, at the New Year's celebration of 1956, I was in the Mughal Ballroom when the Rani of Cooch Nahin's leopards savaged the French actor Marcelle Maximilien while he was performing his mime act. The poor man was not to know that the Rani had an intense hatred of mime. And then there was that time the magician, Om Shanti Om, wowed the chief minister on the fiftieth anniversary of Independence by climbing into a box and vanishing!'

Poppy had seen this latter event on television. The great magician, India's finest, had locked himself into a steel box – subsequently wrapped in chains, and set on fire – only to emerge unscathed moments later from a second box yards away.

She had always suspected that the first box had held a secret compartment—

Poppy froze.

A thought had just flashed into her mind. Anjali had asked housekeeping to stay out of the bathroom. She had asked them not to clean in there.

Could it possibly be . . .?

'Mr Ganesham, you are a genius!' she said. 'I think I know how Anjali vanished from that room. But I will need your help to prove it.'

Ganesham straightened. The mantra that had become a part of him over the long decades instinctively arrived at his lips. 'I am at your service, madam.'

'You are right,' said Layla Padamsee. 'I *was* in Hollis Burbank's room on the night that he died. After the auction, Adam and I fought. We fought because of Burbank, because of the obscene offer he had made at the after-party. At the time we had both reacted with horror. As you know, Adam took a swing at Burbank. For my own part, I was shocked, but I let it pass.

'The trouble started when we got back to our room later that evening.' Her lips quivered and tears welled in her eyes. 'Adam . . . Adam began to speculate. He . . .' She hesitated, then plunged on, 'he started to imagine what we could do with that much money. You see, Chopra, we are in debt, deeply in debt. Two years ago Adam took out a loan to set up a business venture with some partners, a modern art studio where I could sculpt, and we could nurture young artists. Unfortunately, his partners turned out to be crooks. Adam began to see Burbank's offer as a way of getting us back on our feet.

'Of course, he was drunk, I understood that, but sometimes, when a person is drunk, they speak what is in their heart. I know that he feels trapped by our financial problems. Here was his chance.' She took a deep breath. 'At some point, he stopped circling the matter, and just said it. *What if . . .?* What if we took Burbank at his word? What if I, his *wife*, went to Burbank's room, delivered the . . . *goods* and collected my payment?' Her voice had become hard and brittle. 'That was when I snapped. I couldn't believe that he had asked this of me. We got into a furious fight. In the end, I told him that if he really wanted to sell his own wife, then I would do it. I would do it, and whatever happened after that would be on his head.'

'And that is when you went to Burbank's suite?'

She nodded, sadly. 'I don't know why I went. I think it was just to spite my husband, I was so furious with him.

'Burbank was still awake. I remember how he seemed unsurprised to see me. I suppose he must have made such advances before. I found myself standing in front of a mirror. And suddenly I was overcome by a feeling of such utter self-loathing that I knew I could not go through with it. Burbank appeared behind me. I told him that I wished to leave, that it had all been a mistake. I tried to slip past him, but he grabbed at me – that's when he crushed the bangle, cutting my wrist. I slapped him, hard across the face, twisted out of his grasp and ran from the room.

'That was the last I saw of him. I was barely with him for five minutes. And that is the truth.'

Chopra turned to Padamsee. 'And you?'

Padamsee found it difficult to meet Chopra's eyes. 'I was drunk—' he began, defensively, but Chopra raised a hand. 'I mean, where did you go after your wife left your room?'

The critic drew himself up. 'I went to Burbank's suite. I pounded on his door until he opened up. I told him that if he had touched a hair on my wife's head I would kill him.' He seemed to deflate. 'But Burbank just looked at me irritably, and told me that Layla had already come and gone. He told me that if either of us bothered him again he would call the authorities. And then he shut the door on me.'

'Why didn't either of you tell the police about this?'

Layla Padamsee spoke up. 'Because I felt guilty. The next morning we were told that Burbank had died; the rumours said that he had killed himself. I started to think that perhaps it was because of me, because of what had happened. That possibly he believed I would create a scandal, and this caused him to do what he did.'

'Burbank does not strike me as the sort of man to suffer greatly from a conscience,' said Chopra.

'Perhaps you are right,' said Layla. 'But I wasn't thinking straight. I was still upset by everything that had happened. It's only since this morning, when Adam apologised and told me how much I mean to him, how afraid he is of losing me, that I have begun to recover myself.'

Chopra considered the Padamsees' testimonies.

Both husband and wife had lied to him. Both now

admitted going to Burbank's room just prior to his death. Both had reasons for wanting to cause him harm.

Could he trust their pleas of innocence?

On his way back from the interview Chopra received a call from Rangwalla. 'I have some information.'

Rangwalla had been busy.

Having tasked him to dig up background on the deceased American billionaire, Chopra had sent his associate private detective to visit Shakti Holdings Ltd, the Indian subsidiary of Burbank's organisation.

The fruits of Rangwalla's labours raised more questions than they answered.

'Firstly, Burbank,' he began officiously. 'I spoke to Kishore Dubey, your journalist friend, and he made some enquiries with colleagues of his in America, not that it got us very far. The consensus is that Burbank has managed to keep his past exceedingly private. He seems to have emerged onto the scene some twenty-five years ago, made a fortune, and since then has had a happy knack of investing in the right industries at the right time. He has never given an interview, and stays in the background, employing others to run his various companies while he pulls the strings from above.

'What we *were* able to discover is that he claims to have been born in a place called Texas, and grew up there. Attended university in the same place, and obtained a degree in chemical engineering. His early career is hazy. In an article written a couple of years ago – written without Burbank's cooperation, I should add – a journalist stated that Burbank's claim to having worked in various engineering companies in the southern United States didn't pan out. He couldn't find any record of the man. He appears to have fallen off the map. He resurfaced in 1990, which is when he set up Westland Industries. He married a couple of years later, had a child, a daughter, and then divorced. He has never remarried, and is estranged from his wife and child.' Rangwalla paused. 'And that, frankly, is all I could discover about the man.'

Chopra knew that this was strange. A man as wealthy as Hollis Burbank – he would have expected more information to be in the public record. But then, wealthy men often had the power to reveal as much or as little of themselves as they deemed judicious. He had only to think of innumerable Indian politicians who routinely behaved atrociously in private, and yet somehow managed to maintain a glistening public profile.

'What about your visit to Shakti Holdings?'

'That's where it gets interesting,' said Rangwalla, perking up. 'The man in charge, Gavaskar, tried to give me the runaround, but I told him that if he didn't cooperate he could expect an imminent raid. I didn't say exactly what sort of raid, but he almost dampened his trousers there and then. It is funny how the word "raid" seems to terrify grown men in this country.' Rangwalla cackled evilly. 'It turns out that Shakti Holdings has been very active in the Indian market, not to mention very aggressive. It has made some formidable enemies. In fact, Gavaskar told me that they are about to be taken to court by one of their main rivals – the news is going to break in the media in a few days, so he didn't mind sharing it. He was in a big sweat about it. It's the real reason Burbank is in town. He didn't come here just for an art auction. He came here to sort out the mess his underlings were making of his big Indian venture. He may be a private man, but one thing everyone seems to agree on – Burbank hates to lose.'

'Who is the rival company taking Shakti Holdings to court?'

Rangwalla told him the name.

Chopra's moustache twitched in surprise.

He knew the name. He knew the company.

And he knew the man who ran it.

HOW TO ESCAPE FROM A LOCKED BATHROOM

'So let me get this straight,' said the engineer, staring at Poppy with a frown that corrugated his forehead into a series of deep trenches, 'you want me to *dismantle* this bathtub? Even though there is absolutely nothing wrong with it?'

They were standing in the bathroom of Anjali Tejwa's suite: Poppy, Huma Dixit, the butler, Ganesham, the engineer – whose name tag declared him to be one R. Swadhesh – with Irfan and Ganesha crowding in behind. Swadhesh, Poppy had been mildly surprised to discover, was the same man she had seen earlier perched atop a ladder fiddling with the giant celebrity cut-outs in the wedding hall.

'Yes,' she said firmly.

Swadhesh looked at Ganesham. 'And you agree with this?'

'Please do as madam asks.'

The engineer sighed, puffing out his cheeks in a gesture that suggested the whole world had gone mad.

He took the screwdriver that appeared to reside permanently behind his ear, and lowered himself to his knees in order to remove the panel that made up the side of the tub. The panel was covered in mosaic tiles, with a complex pattern of Egyptian hieroglyphs.

Ganesha shuffled closer, curiosity edging him forward.

'Stand back, little one,' muttered Swadhesh, 'this could get dangerous.' A moment later his grimace turned into a puzzled frown. 'Wait a minute. Something's not right here.'

'What is the problem?' asked Ganesham.

'This panel is usually affixed to the side of the tub with a series of screws. The screw heads are covered over with putty, to give a smooth finish, and to blend into the pattern of the mosaic. But I've just removed the putty and there are no screws.'

'Then what is holding the panel to the tub?'

'Good question.'

He levered the tip of his screwdriver into the hairline crack between the panel and tub, and wiggled it around until the panel came loose. Using his hands, he ripped the panel away to reveal the naked bowl of the tub and the ten-inch cavity below; the cavity between the bottom of the bowl and the tiled bathroom flooring.

He set down the panel, and looked at its reverse side.

Two flat handles were visible down near the foot of the panel. The engineer peered at them with an expression of bewilderment.

'I am guessing those handles should not be there,' said Poppy.

Swadhesh scratched his moustache with his screwdriver, lost in thought. Finally, he said, 'No. The panel seems to have been held to the frame of the tub by a high-strength adhesive, rather than the usual screws. But I have no idea what these handles are here for. This is all very unusual.'

'I think I have an explanation,' said Poppy. 'This is how Anjali vanished from your locked bathroom.' She turned to Huma. 'Tell me, after you broke in here, were Anjali's clothes missing? The ones she removed to take her bath?'

'No. They were right there, on that chair.' Huma pointed to a bamboo bathroom seat.

'And did Anjali ever visit this suite *before* the wedding party arrived?'

'Well, of course,' said Huma. 'Once it was decided the wedding would take place in the Grand Raj, we came here to check out the rooms.'

'And did you arrive here before the rest of the wedding guests?'

'Yes. We checked in two days ago. Anjali wanted to get the feel of the place.'

Poppy nodded as if this was the answer she had expected. 'Then this is what I think happened. I believe Anjali must have planned her escape well in advance. I don't believe she was certain that she wanted to run away, but she had decided to prepare for such an eventuality, just in case she couldn't go through with the wedding. She checked in early, unscrewed the panel on the bathtub, attached those handles to the inside of the panel, then affixed it again, using just an adhesive instead of the screws, possibly one of those spray ones – I've seen my husband using them,' she explained. 'She then placed putty over the screw-holes so that no one would notice. It's hard to pick up among the Egyptian patterning.'

'That's why she asked housekeeping not to bother cleaning the bathroom!' said Huma. 'She didn't want them to see what she had done.'

Poppy nodded, then continued. 'On the day she went missing, she entered the bathroom, locked the door, ran the bath, then removed the panel. I think she must have placed a change of clothing in the cavity under the tub. She put on these clothes, sprayed adhesive onto the frame of the tub, then slid into the space below, manoeuvring the panel back into place using the handles she had attached to it. It must have taken a bit of juggling, and it wasn't perfect, but the illusion didn't have to last long. When you broke into the room, no one really took an interest in the bathtub itself. Anjali had vanished from a locked room – that was all that mattered.

'She waited until the noise died down. Once she felt certain the suite was empty, she pushed out the panel, wriggled out from below the tub, glued the panel back into place, then left the room.'

They all stood in silence, absorbing her words.

'But why?' said Huma. 'I mean, why go to such lengths? Why not just walk out of the front door?'

'That I am not sure about,' said Poppy. 'But I can hazard a guess. My understanding is that a great deal of pressure has been placed on Anjali's shoulders to go through with this marriage. If she had simply walked away it would have put an end to the whole thing, not to mention created a tremendous scandal. This way no one could say for sure that she had fled. She has, after all, vanished from a locked room.'

'But this is worse!' cried Huma. 'Her father is on the verge of calling the state's chief minister. The Tejwas may be all but bankrupt, but they are still a royal house.'

'Yes,' agreed Poppy, sadly. 'I don't believe Anjali really thought *that* part of her plan through. But sometimes, when a person feels trapped, they do not consider the consequences of their actions.'

Huma's face fell. 'I'm to blame,' she said. 'Her grandmother asked me to follow Anjali around, to stay by her side. I think she knew Anjali's heart wasn't in this.'

'It's not your fault,' said Poppy, patting her on the arm. 'When I spoke to Anjali, I am certain she herself was undecided on her best course of action. It might well be that my conversation helped make up her mind. In which case, the blame lies with me.'

'What do we do now?'

'The real question,' said Poppy, 'is where has Anjali *gone*?'

CLASH OF THE TYCOONS

Avinash Agnihotri was pacing the carpet angrily as Chopra entered the business suite. 'I was on a conference call with Tokyo, Chopra,' he said irritably. 'Business is war in Japan and you pulled me off the battlefield. Your message said it couldn't wait.'

Chopra paused before replying. 'You have not been entirely candid with me in the matter of your relationship with Hollis Burbank.'

Agnihotri froze, his face growing still. Something passed behind his eyes and was gone. 'I dislike your use of the word "relationship",' he said eventually. 'One does not have a *relationship* with a man like Burbank.'

'Even hatred is a form of relationship.'

'I've met many people in my life, Chopra, many businessmen. I understand that when people meet me they have an agenda. Even you, standing there with your good intentions, a seeker after truth. You want something from me and you will do what it takes to get it. But most people know how much they can get away with before the scale tilts too far. Well, Burbank was one of the few people I have met who I believe to be wholly without a conscience. I believe he was someone who would do anything, say anything, *be* anything to get what he wanted. And so, yes, I hated him.'

'Why?'

'Surely you know. Isn't that why you are here?'

'I wish to hear it from you.'

The silence spun itself out. Finally, Agnihotri spoke. 'A few years ago Burbank set up his Indian subsidiary Shakti Holdings Ltd. He had decided that he wanted a slice of the outsourcing action that has made India so wealthy of late. It didn't bother me. My company has been around for years; we were established, and we had a strong reputation with our overseas clients. The trouble is that Burbank doesn't fight fair. Within a year of setting up, Shakti Holdings had poached most of my top staff. Burbank offered them ludicrous salaries, well above the industry norm, topped up by lavish bonuses. It made no sense to me, but, having seen him in action at the auction, I now believe this kamikaze approach is his personal hallmark. Of course, *his* organisation can afford to throw money down the drain.

'In the period that followed he began what I think of as phase two of his attack. A dirty tricks campaign. My staff began to be harassed. Shakedowns by the cops. My female staff – many of whom work late to match timings in America – were intimidated, followed around by shady characters on motorbikes. Planning permissions for new ventures suddenly mired in red tape. And then there were our clients. Anonymous letters about dubious practices in our Indian workplaces. Tip-offs to trade magazines about flaws in our flagship software products.' Agnihotri's face darkened, as his tone became angrier. 'We began to lose clients, especially in America, our most profitable market. It didn't take me long to work out that Burbank was behind it. His guerrilla warfare campaign has cost me hundreds of millions of dollars over these past few years. When I discovered that he was coming to India, I leapt at the chance to confront him face to face.'

'Is this dirty tricks campaign why you have initiated court action against him?'

'We have filed a case against Shakti Holdings for patent infringement, and a separate case for corporate espionage,' confirmed Agnihotri. 'It is my belief that Burbank paid staff from my company to steal technical designs from our line of software products – core algorithms that took years to develop. Some of those designs have shown up in software that Shakti Holdings now claims as its own.'

'Do you have a strong case?'

Agnihotri pursed his lips. 'Our evidence is highly technical, or based on witnesses who might easily be threatened or bribed. Given the state of our court system I have little confidence of a favourable result. Even if there is one, it may take so long that I doubt I will be around to see it.' Chopra could well understand his cynicism. The Indian court system was so slow it had been likened to a man stuck on the toilet with a case of terminal constipation.

'Then why are you pursuing the action?'

'Because it is time to draw a line in the sand. I despise bullies. And Burbank was a bully of the worst kind. If nothing else the case will blow a hole in his organisation's reputation. Once the media get hold of some of the things I intend to say, there'll be nowhere for Shakti Holdings to hide.'

'Some might say that all this points to a motive for you to harm Burbank.'

'We're back to that?' said Agnihotri angrily. 'Have you even managed to prove that his death was not suicide? And even if Burbank *was* killed, *I* had nothing to do with it. I want to destroy him in court. I want to reveal him for the thug that he is. I cannot do that if he is dead.'

'You have no alibi for the time of his death.'

'Why should I need one? What evidence do you have that I was anywhere near his room when he died?'

Chopra had to admit that he had no such proof. But Agnihotri was a man who ran hot on anger. It was not inconceivable that he had gone from his suite to Burbank's that night, to confront him a second time, after the altercation in the VIP toilets.

Agnihotri checked his watch ostentatiously. 'I have to get back to my meeting. The next time you want to accuse me of a crime, let me know in advance. I'll make sure to have my lawyers present.'

Chopra watched the businessman stalk back into the conference room.

THE LAUGHING INDIAN

The restaurant was packed.

Chopra followed the waiter to a table out on the balcony overlooking the harbour. Dusk had fallen, and the lights from a thousand seagoing vessels – from dhows to oil tankers – twinkled on the water.

Lisa Taylor rose to greet him, a dazzling vision in a red evening gown. Her bare shoulders glimmered in the soft exterior lighting. 'What do you think?' she said, twirling the lower half of her gown. 'I've managed to get myself invited to a society party. Hobnobbing with the rich and shameless.'

'It is, ah, very nice,' said Chopra, tripping over his tongue. 'A fine fabric, and very functional for the occasion.'

'You really know how to make a girl feel special,' said Taylor. 'Join me for a drink?'

'I would prefer to discuss the matter of the sketch.'

'And we shall. Over a drink,' said Taylor firmly. As she saw him continue to hesitate, she flapped her hands. 'Oh, come on, don't be such a stuffed shirt.'

Chopra lowered himself carefully onto the seat, as if perhaps an explosive had been attached to it. He glanced around the restaurant, but no one seemed to care that he was sitting here, with an attractive foreign woman, in a distinctly unprofessional setting.

He removed the sketch and set it onto the table, then coughed loudly to reassert his sense of mission. 'What did you discover?'

Taylor leaned over. 'Okay, so I sent a photo of the picture over to a colleague in Delhi. He's an expert on Indian art.'

'I thought *you* were an expert?'

'To a certain extent. Though my colleague thinks I'm just a glorified saleswoman.' She shrugged. 'He's not the easiest man to work with.' She tapped the sketch with a manicured nail. 'This is a preparatory composition for a much larger work. Artists sometimes create these when they are considering a large canvas, but don't want to draw a full-sized outline directly onto it. The sketch itself – and I should have realised this myself, I suppose – is very reminiscent of a series of paintings by Shiva Swarup at the beginning of his career. I'm sure you know who he is, right?'

Chopra nodded. 'Yes. I met with him earlier.'

'Really? What did you think of him?'

'He is an interesting man,' said Chopra primly.

'Well, until this auction, he's never really given me the time of day. His paintings sell well enough, of course, and he's a household name, at least, here in India. But a very prickly persona. Which isn't always a bad thing. Creates a bit of mystique. A bit like you, I suspect.'

'I do not have a prickly persona,' said Chopra. 'I have principles. There is a difference.'

Taylor put up her hands, as if surrendering. 'I meant it as a compliment . . . Anyway, back to the sketch. Some thirty years ago, Swarup launched his career with a series of paintings called the Laughing Indian cycle.' She tapped on her mobile phone, and turned it to Chopra. The screen displayed a single canvas of an old, naked Indian man, propped against the wheel of a handcart, a grotesque smile on his face.

There was a distinct similarity between this full-blooded canvas and the black-and-white sketch discovered in Hollis Burbank's suitcase.

Taylor scrolled through a series of similar paintings, until Chopra sat back.

'What does this mean?'

'I don't know,' admitted Taylor. 'All of *these* paintings have Shiva Swarup's signature on them. But your sketch is initialled K.K. Neither I nor my art-expert friend have any idea who that might be. Of course, it *could* be a dedication to someone else, someone important to Swarup at the time.'

'If Swarup *did* draw this thirty years ago, then how did this sketch come to be in the possession of Hollis Burbank? My understanding is that he had never visited India prior to this trip.'

'Not to my knowledge,' agreed Taylor. 'And I certainly never sold him that sketch. Funnily enough, Swarup has never left India either.'

'Swarup denied knowing anything about it when I

showed it to him. Why would he do that if he was responsible for it?'

'Beats me. He's a real man of mystery, Swarup. Never gives interviews. Hates talking about himself. He's a lot like Burbank in that regard.'

Chopra considered this, recalling his meeting with the enigmatic artist. 'Tell me more about him,' he said eventually.

'Well, that Laughing Indian series is what first got him noticed. After those paintings came out he was offered an internship with Zozé Rebello, who, at the time, was just about the most famous artist working in India. After that, the sky was the limit for Swarup, though personally, I've never much cared for his work. The truth is, I've seen dozens of artists who are better painters. But that stint with Rebello made him famous – or perhaps I should say *notorious* – and in this crazy business that's all you need.'

'How do you mean "notorious"?'

'They had a huge bust-up. Rebello threw Swarup out on his ear. Banned him from his studio. Refused to say why. But the notoriety meant that Swarup's next exhibition was a runaway success – the *enfant terrible* who even Indian art's wild man Rebello couldn't stomach. It cemented his reputation.'

'Where are the Laughing Indian paintings now?'

'At the National Gallery of Modern Art, in Delhi. Swarup donated them to the gallery years ago. I've always wondered why he never sold them at auction. They're worth an absolute fortune.'

Chopra was silent once more.

A waiter arrived, and Taylor ordered a martini, but Chopra waved the man away. He rarely consumed alcohol, particularly not while on duty.

'We come back to the question of why Burbank had this sketch hidden in his possessions.'

'It's a mystery,' agreed Taylor. 'But then Burbank preferred to keep everything about himself shrouded in an air of intrigue. To be completely honest, I don't think I ever knew the real Burbank. It was as if he deliberately hid himself from the world.'

Chopra pondered this. 'You didn't really care for him, did you?'

'He was my client, Chopra,' said Taylor. 'Nothing more. Should I feel embarrassed for being good at my job? Should I feel bad because his death means a lost commission to me? And not just one commission, but all the future commissions I would have earned from him. He wasn't a likeable man. I haven't lost a good friend. I've lost a key component of my economic livelihood. And so, yes, I am angry. I am royally pissed off, in fact. And if you ever find out who did it, I would like five minutes with that person, just so I can show them how I feel.'

Chopra saw the fury roil across Taylor's beautiful features.

'I *will* find out who did it,' he said. 'It is what I do.'

He rose to his feet, picking up the sketch and tucking it back into his pocket. 'I shall keep you informed of my progress.'

Taylor beamed at him. 'Are you sure I can't convince you to stay for a light supper? Or to come with me to my bash?

Might be nice to walk in with a charming, intelligent man on my arm for a change.'

'I cannot,' said Chopra, flushing. 'I have work to do.'

'Don't you ever stop working?'

'I, ah . . .' He felt himself floundering. 'It is what I do,' he repeated, feebly.

As he left the restaurant he failed to notice Poppy standing in the shadows, watching him leave, a thunderous look on her face.

A FLASH OF INSIGHT

Chopra spent the next hour in the hotel's business suite, sitting at one of the computer terminals, trawling the Internet for background on Shiva Swarup. His earlier meeting with the artist now came sharply into focus.

What was the connection between the sketch in Burbank's possession and Swarup's Laughing Indian paintings? Burbank speaking to Swarup on the night of his death could no longer be dismissed as a casual conversation, as Swarup had led him to believe. But if there was a link between the two men, what was the nature of that link? And who was this mysterious K.K.? What did that individual have to do with Hollis Burbank, a man who had never even visited India? The Laughing Indian paintings were thirty years old. Did that mean Burbank's sketch was similarly ancient? How had it ended up in his possession?

Questions, questions, and no answers.

Finally, tiring of his fruitless speculation, Chopra headed towards the hotel lobby, and home.

And then he stopped, remembering the suite Poppy had wangled – a suite now paid for by Gilbert and Locke – and that they were both due to spend the next few days there.

The thought bothered him.

In truth, he had no wish to stay at the Grand Raj Palace, to his mind a glorified crime scene. It felt somehow unprofessional, a wrong note in an otherwise familiar piece of music.

Nevertheless, he found his feet trudging their way up to the suite. It was the least he could do, having upset Poppy's plans for their anniversary.

Contrary to his wife's belief, the occasion meant a great deal to Chopra; it was simply the *pageantry* that Poppy had planned that gave him heartburn each time he thought about it. He had never been a man who believed in making a drama of life. He felt what he felt, and that was good enough for him.

The world did not need – and never had needed – histrionics from Inspector Ashwin Chopra.

He found his wife tucked up in the four-poster Queen Anne bed, reading a book. It was *Gitanjali*, the famous book of spiritual poetry by Rabindranath Tagore, Bengal's Nobel Prize-winning poet. This was a bad sign.

Poppy only retreated into the comforting embrace of *Gitanjali* when she was upset.

'Where are Irfan and Ganesha?' asked Chopra.

'Irfan has gone to settle Ganesha into one of the gardens,' said Poppy, without looking up. 'He will be back soon.'

Chopra detected a stiffness in his wife's tone. He hesitated, then sat down on the edge of the bed. 'I am sorry about all of this, Poppy,' he said. 'But you must understand that I have to follow this through.'

She set down the book, and looked at him with an expression that, for once, he found inscrutable. 'Yes,' she said. 'I understand. It is who you are.'

Chopra attempted a laugh, but it came out as the strangled death-cry of a hyena, and so he lapsed into silence again. A sense of acute discomfort had overcome him, something he rarely felt in his wife's presence.

'I shall get ready for bed,' he mumbled, and stumbled his way to the bathroom.

Here he brushed his teeth, gargled and slipped out of his clothes. He discovered two bathrobes – his and hers – on the towel rack. The monogrammed robes instantly turned his thoughts to Hollis Burbank, the American's body draped in a similar robe, on his bed, eyes staring at the ceiling. Something about that image, about Burbank's robe, stirred uneasily in Chopra's mind. A stray thought flashed a fin at him, then swam away . . .

When he returned to the bedroom, he saw that Poppy had turned off the lights, set her sleeping mask over her eyes and dropped into what appeared to be a deep slumber.

Somewhat put out, he wandered back out to the living area.

He switched on the TV, flicked through channels. An

alabaster horse's head – the Rani of Jhansi's stallion – stared at him down its long nose with an expression of mild opprobrium. Unable to relax, he turned off the TV, got up, went back into the bedroom, dressed, then went downstairs.

He found Irfan in one of the smaller gardens, stretched out on the grass beside Ganesha, who had collapsed onto the ground in readiness for sleep. The night's sticky heat was alive with distant voices and the buzzing of mosquitoes. An empty steel platter lay beside the little elephant. Ganesha appeared to have eaten the pachyderm equivalent of a king's banquet, and seemed distinctly the worse for wear. Chopra knew that elephants could suffer from indigestion just as readily as humans – Ganesha's appetite would soon become a matter for concern at this rate.

And to think, when the elephant had first arrived in his care he had been malnourished and off his feed!

'He is depressed,' the vet Lala had declared, only half-joking.

That was when Chopra had first begun to learn about elephants, about their extraordinary intelligence, their emotional range, their ability to feel pain, affection, grief. His appreciation of *Elephas maximus* – otherwise known as the Indian elephant – had increased exponentially in these past months.

And yet there was still so much about his young ward that he did not know.

The mystery of his origins, for one, and why his Uncle Bansi had sent Ganesha to him in the first place.

One day he would have to get to the bottom of it, but for now, he had no idea where to even begin. Bansi had been missing for years. And, in the vastness of the subcontinent, attempting to search for him would be akin to searching for a needle in the biggest, most unruly haystack in the cosmos.

He realised that Irfan was asleep.

On a sudden whim, Chopra lay down beside Ganesha, put his hands behind his head and looked up at the stars. The drowsy elephant reached out with his trunk and petted his face.

'Human beings are strange creatures, aren't they, Ganesha?' he mumbled. 'We can build a whole world, create societies, invent maths and philosophy, medicine and art. And yet, at heart, we remain no better than animals. Some might say worse. At least when an animal behaves savagely it is instinctive. But we humans are, supposedly, intelligent.' He sighed. 'Everything is illusion, and no one is really who we believe they are—'

He stopped, then sat up.

An idea had just flared through his mind, leaving a trail as bright as a comet's.

Illusion.

He recalled Lisa Taylor's words from their earlier meeting: *'I don't think I ever knew the real Burbank. It was as if he deliberately hid himself from the world.'* And Rangwalla's enquiries that had confirmed how little was known about Burbank's past.

A past shrouded in mystery.

Chopra's eyes gleamed in the lamplit dark.

Could it be *that* simple?

He did not know.

But he knew how he might discover the truth.

Ronald Loomis opened the door to his room in a pair of boxer shorts and a Rolling Stones T-shirt. He stared blearily at Chopra. 'Do you know what time it is?'

'I need your help.'

Loomis hesitated, then turned and led him inside. 'I'd say excuse the mess, but frankly I don't care what you think.'

Chopra glanced around. The room was as dishevelled as Loomis. A half-consumed bottle of whisky sat by the bed. Clearly, the young PA was still coming to grips with the death of his boss.

'Is it possible that Burbank had another identity?' said Chopra, getting straight down to it. 'That, at some point in the past, he changed his name?'

Loomis stared at him. 'What makes you say that?'

Chopra took out the copy of the photograph found in Burbank's suitcase, the one marked with the names Faulkner, Murthi, Sen and Shastri. Loomis studied it. 'The police showed me this. I don't know these people.

'Yet there was a reason Burbank kept it with him. A thirty-year-old photograph taken in India. My instincts tell me that these people were important to him in some way. Why would that be? Unless, perhaps, he knew them? And the simplest way for him to have known them was if he had been here, with them, in India, thirty years ago.'

'That's a big leap.'

'Perhaps. But Burbank's past is shrouded in mystery.'

'He was an intensely private person,' Loomis conceded. 'He never talked about his past.'

'Didn't that ever strike you as strange?'

Loomis snorted. 'Mr Burbank didn't tolerate anyone prying into his personal life. Not even his personal assistant.' He sat down on the bed. 'They're going to release his body tomorrow. I'll be flying it back to the States. To give it a proper burial. I spoke to Burbank's daughter today, on the phone. I tried to tell her what a great man her father was. That, in his own way, he loved her. It was the hardest thing I have ever done. Do you know what she said? "He's just a stranger to me."' He shook his head, a man without a rudder. 'You ask me if Burbank could have been someone else, once upon a time? The answer is "yes". He could have been anyone he wanted to be. But for me he will always be the father I never had.'

THE FOREIGNERS REGIONAL REGISTRATION OFFICE

The next morning Poppy Chopra awoke to discover that her husband had already left, and that the feelings of existential anxiety that had infected her the evening before had settled in, like an unwanted visit from a mother-in-law, sniffing and opening cupboards, running a finger over her mental mantelpieces and generally being an unwelcome nuisance.

Poppy considered herself an optimist, by nature.

She rarely dwelt on problems for too long, preferring to 'lance the emotional boil', as she always put it. Sometimes those emotions got the better of her, and that was fine, for what were human beings if not the subtle equation of their thoughts and feelings?

Yet it was rare for her to feel so . . . so . . . *subdued*.

Seeing her husband in the restaurant with Lisa Taylor the night before had left her like a bullock caught in a swamp. She found herself unable to shake off the image; her emotions seemed suddenly heavy-footed and gloopy.

And yet she knew, with an iron-clad certainty, that there was no fire to this smoke.

She trusted her husband implicitly. They had weathered too much together for her to begin doubting him now.

Nevertheless, little weevils of . . . *disappointment* gnawed away at the edges of her heart. Did her husband really need to spend so much time in the company of that woman while dashing around on his investigation?

That *beautiful* woman, the little demon sitting on her shoulder hissed into her ear.

Beautiful and exotic.

Last evening Poppy had been keen to get her husband alone so that she could tell him about her moment of inspiration, how she had worked out the mystery behind Anjali Tejwa's vanishing act from a locked bathroom. It was something they might have shared.

She admonished herself for being so maudlin.

After all, she was staying in a suite in the grandest hotel in the country!

A picture of the Rani of Jhansi looked down on her from the wall of the bedroom, the Rani clutching a sword and damascened shield, her chin thrust forward at a poetic angle. She could practically hear the woman telling her to buck up, to get on with it and stop being such a . . . such a . . . Well, whatever it was she was being.

Poppy finished dressing, then helped Irfan get ready before the pair of them went down to the restaurant for breakfast, picking up Ganesha along the way.

In the restaurant, the little elephant was greeted lustily by the waiters and other patrons – he had become something of a celebrity around the hotel. Some of the foreign tourists insisted on taking pictures with him, which Ganesha did not mind in the least. He had a peculiar vanity when it came to being photographed, Poppy had discovered. If an elephant could take pictures she was certain he would be as obnoxious as any teenager armed with a mobile phone and a selfie stick.

Halfway through her meal, she looked up to find Lisa Taylor bearing down on her, in a figure-hugging dress that left little to the imagination.

Flushing, she stood to face the woman.

'Hello Mrs Chopra. You haven't seen your husband around, have you?'

'No,' said Poppy stiffly. 'Actually, I have not seen him around very much at all. He seems to be very much occupied with your case.'

'Hollis Burbank was my client, and now he's dead,' said Taylor mildly. 'I'd really like to know what happened.'

'Well, I am certain my husband will get to the bottom of it,' said Poppy. 'He is very good at that.' She could not help the trace of bitterness that edged her words.

'If you see him, do let him know I'd like to talk to him. He doesn't seem to be picking up his phone.'

'He gave you his phone number?'

'Yes. So that we could keep in touch. About the investigation.' Taylor gave Poppy another dazzling smile. 'I must say that really is a lovely sari you're wearing.'

'Thank you,' said Poppy, automatically. 'And that is a lovely bikini you are wearing.'

'What? Oh no, this isn't a bikin—' Taylor stopped. 'Oh,

I see. Ha ha. Yes, I suppose you're right. It is a little revealing, isn't it? But I have a client flying in from Singapore and, just between us girls, he's a bit of a letch. A dress like this, well, it gets me halfway to the sale. I'm sure you understand.'

Poppy hesitated.

She hated the way Lisa Taylor made her feel unsure of herself. And then she hated herself for feeling that way. 'I will let my husband know that you wish to speak with him.' Another thought flashed into her mind – before she could stop herself the words had tumbled from her mouth. 'I will be speaking to him soon to remind him to take his pills. I will tell him then.'

Taylor's perfect brow crunched into an elegant frown. 'Pills?'

'Oh, yes. Did he not tell you? He is suffering from a heart condition.'

'God, no! Is it serious?'

'Very. He almost died from it. That is why he retired from the police force. He has been told by his doctors to avoid stressful activity. He could drop dead at any minute.'

'You're joking!'

'I am not joking. This is not a matter of joking. He is an old man. His body is breaking down.'

'Well, you could have fooled me. He looks in great shape. And I wouldn't have pegged him a day over forty. He's got great skin. And that hair . . . Personally, I think he looks like one of your Bollywood movie stars, a mature one, maybe.'

'He is not forty,' snapped Poppy. 'He is in his *late* forties.

And he has the heart of a sixty-year-old. You must not over-excite him.'

'I shall bear that in mind,' said Taylor coolly. 'Probably a good thing he didn't see me in this dress then, right?' She gave a breezy grin, and Poppy flushed, wondering if perhaps there had been a disguised barb in the Englishwoman's statement.

Ganesha reached up with his trunk, tapped Taylor's dangling hand.

She smiled at him and patted his skull, earning a waggle of his ears in return.

Et tu, Ganesha? thought Poppy, grinding her teeth.

Meanwhile, some four kilometres away in the Dhobi Talao district of south Mumbai, the man at the centre of this uncomfortable discussion was standing in the reception of the Foreigners Regional Registration Office, Mumbai, attempting, with a growing sense of impotence and frustration, to make another man understand exactly what it was that he required.

That man, a civil service bureaucrat called Balaji, appeared to have been, in the distant past, nailed to the chair on which he now sat. Somehow, from his seated position, he contrived to look down upon Chopra.

'Let me see if I understand you correctly, sir,' said Balaji. 'You wish me to locate records for an American gentleman you say *may* have worked in India thirty years ago, and yet you do not even know his name?' He said this in a tone that indicated to the others waiting in the reception that this was possibly the most ludicrous of the many ludicrous things that he had heard in all his years of wearing out the seat to which his backside was attached.

Someone sniggered, emboldening the martinet. 'Perhaps you would also like me to eat fire, and run over hot coals?'

Chopra realised that, in the interminable drudgery of Balaji's existence, here was a moment of unexpected glory, one to be grasped with both hands.

'I did not say that I do not know his name,' he said, through gritted teeth. 'What I said was that I believe this man may have changed his name since he worked in India. It really is quite important.'

'Well, why did you not say, sir? I shall, of course, drop everything else and focus my sole attention on you. Please give me a moment to inform all these good citizens –' he swept an arm lavishly at the crowded waiting room '– that their petty concerns are of no importance when a man such as yourself barges his way in here and makes demands of us little people.'

Little people!

Chopra stifled the urge to reach out and put his hands around the idiot's throat. Instead, he took out his wallet and showed him his identity card. 'This is police business,' he said loudly, then leaned over and whispered: 'And if you don't help me, you will have to answer to the chief minister himself.'

The man shot to his feet, suddenly as nimble as a ballet dancer.

If there was one thing Indian civil servants feared more than death itself, Chopra knew, it was the wrath of a politician.

As Balaji led him deep into the bowels of the FRRO building, he spoke quickly, suddenly as loquacious and helpful as a blue jay. 'You say this man was in India in 1985?'

'That is my belief.'

'Well, sir, at that time there were only two FRRO offices in the country. In fact, it only became mandatory for foreigners staying in the country to register themselves in 1984. Any foreigners who came to work in India would have been registered in either Mumbai or Delhi. You are certain that the man you are looking for was working in Maharashtra?'

'I believe so,' Chopra repeated. The writing on the back of the photograph that had been found in Burbank's possession had said Chimboli, Feb. 1985. The Chimboli region was in the state of Maharashtra.

'Then his records must surely be here in our Mumbai office. We have records stretching back to the very beginning. You will not believe me if I tell you that our record-keeper also stretches back to the very beginning. Ha ha. His name is Laxman. He began work here in 1984, and he is still here. He is a most interesting character; you will surely love to meet him.'

Chopra was certain that his forthcoming encounter with the legendary Laxman would be anything but pleasant, but he forbore from commenting.

They arrived at a dark door, entered and walked down a flight of steps into a cramped anteroom. A single lightbulb threw shadows around the musty-smelling gloom.

Balaji banged an old-fashioned bell sitting on a

splintered wooden counter, and whispered, 'We have no space upstairs. All our records have been placed down here, in Mr Laxman's safekeeping. The authorities keep making noises about computerising everything, but Mr Laxman is very opposed to this.' He suddenly clammed shut as a figure materialised noiselessly behind the counter.

Chopra stared at Laxman.

He had heard that people who worked for years in a particular role sometimes took on the contours of their profession. Indian policemen, for instance, often became jaded and cynical, their legs bowed by the weight of the petty human connivances and malfeasances they carried around with them for years. This Laxman, with his pallid complexion, ashen hair, watery eyes and starved look, had taken on the tragic aspect of a phantom, having haunted this dark, musty hall of records for three decades. Chopra supposed that something of the bloodlessness of his work had settled into the man's soul.

Quickly he explained his request. 'I am looking for a man whose name I do not know. But I believe he may have been working here in India in 1985. And he was American. It is possible that he had a colleague here, a man named Faulkner, though I cannot tell you which nationality this Faulkner is.'

Laxman continued to stare at Chopra. The only indication that he had heard was the almost imperceptible twitching of a nostril.

'It is official police business,' piped up Balaji, then instantly piped down again, as Laxman turned his vampire's gaze upon him.

'Please come with me,' he said finally, and turned away.

Chopra followed the record-keeper through a maze of wooden shelving that loomed over them, each shelf crammed with red manila folders. The whole place was sunk in a Stygian gloom, with the old pressed air of a tomb, and seemed to whisper with the scurrying of mice, and the gentle crunch-crunch of invisible mites eating their way through decades of yellowing paper.

Finally, Laxman ghosted to a standstill, so noiselessly that Chopra almost walked into him.

The record-keeper waved at the shelf behind him with an anaemic hand. 'Here you will find all the files for the year 1985. There are a great many of them. This was a time of industrial liberalisation in India. Major reforms by the Delhi government enticed foreign companies into the country, bringing with them employees of all nationalities.'

Laxman recited this as if delivering a lecture. Chopra got the feeling that beneath the man's waxy, corpse-like exterior there beat the heart of a historian. In some ways, Laxman *was* a historian; or, at the very least, a custodian of a tiny slice of time in that monolithic past that continued to define the country even as she marched confidently into the future.

'I will leave you to it,' said the record-keeper, and turned on his heel.

Chopra had been expecting the man's help, but he didn't bother to call Laxman back.

He decided to start at one end of the lowest shelf before him. He pulled out a file – coughing loudly as the dust tickled his nostrils – untied the fraying string holding it together and opened it.

The yellowing paper at the front of the file held a faded colour photograph of a white woman called Marie Bouhana, French national, born in Paris in 1958. The remaining documents comprised Bouhana's official papers and employment visa – to work with a Mumbai-based textile firm named Sunrise Textiles Private Limited.

Chopra closed the folder, retied it and slotted it back into place.

He looked up and down the length of the shelving, then sighed.

This was going to be a lengthy and unpleasant task.

Poppy looked around Anjali's bridal suite. It seemed even larger than when she had last been here, now that the only ones in the room were herself, Huma Dixit, Irfan and Ganesha.

She had decided to take matters into her own hands. The fact that the search for the missing bride within the hotel had proven unsuccessful only confirmed that Anjali Tejwa was a very resourceful young woman. She would not have prepared such an elaborate escape, only to allow herself to be discovered so swiftly. With little else to go on, Poppy had decided to employ a technique that she knew her husband favoured – a close examination of the crime scene.

Over the course of the following two hours she proceeded to go over every inch of the suite.

Confronting the missing woman's personal effects, she asked Huma's permission before diving into the suitcases. The morose young girl simply shrugged. 'Do what you like. It hardly makes a difference now, does it?'

Anjali had brought along an entire wardrobe for the wedding, including her astonishing bridal dress, a shimmering silk lehenga in traditional red, embroidered with gold and encrusted with jewels. It was the single most beautiful garment Poppy had ever seen. Her own wedding outfit had been a humble creation, handed down to her by her mother and altered by the village tailor back in Jarul, who had tut-tutted his way through the alterations, as if it was Poppy's fault that her proportions were not as generous as her mother's had been at that age.

Unable to resist, Poppy held the dress against herself and took a quick glance in the mirror while Huma was distracted on her mobile phone. The dress seemed to *breathe*, shimmering with a life of its own. She could almost hear it whispering, reminding her that her own anniversary was just two days hence . . .

She realised that Ganesha was staring up at her with a quizzical expression.

Irfan had draped a colourful Kashmiri shawl around the little elephant's shoulders; it glimmered faintly in the sunlight pouring in from the room's latticed windows. The mischievous boy had also painted lipstick over the tip of Ganesha's trunk.

Poppy smiled. 'Don't we both look absolutely fabulous?'

she whispered, then put the wedding dress back into the wardrobe and continued her search.

Methodically, she worked her way through the rest of Anjali's luggage, finishing with a small travelling case, clearly an item handed down through the generations. The brass plaque on the case declared it to be the handiwork of Taylor Brothers of Cavendish Square 1860; it was inlaid with purple velvet, and the outer carved wooden shell was inset with mother-of-pearl handles. Various compartments provided sanctuary for make-up, and other essentials for the woman-about-town.

In one of these compartments Poppy discovered a wad of receipts wrapped in a rubber band.

She leafed her way through them. Most were for items of clothing Anjali had purchased recently for the wedding. With a pang of envy she saw that Anjali had been shopping at some of the most exclusive stores in Mumbai. A smile touched her lips as she came across a receipt from a famous Mumbai tailor, Lightning Lala. She recalled Lala's adverts from the television; the self-proclaimed 'fastest tailor in all of India'.

Ganesha moved up behind her and poked at the inside of the travelling case. The aroma from the bottle of perfume that Anjali kept inside was probably playing havoc with his hypersensitive trunk. Poppy knew, from her husband, that an elephant's trunk was one of the most sensitive organs in the whole of the animal—

She froze mid-thought and then sat back, staring at the sheet of paper in her hand, at the typed lettering that had halted her search.

'Well,' she muttered to herself. 'This is unexpected. Most unexpected, indeed.'

Chopra found what he was looking for in the 167th file he took from the shelves.

By this time he had sunk down onto the floor, his back slumped against the shelving, the small bones of his neck aflame with cramp, eyes fatigued from reading in the dim light, his nostrils raw from the constant sneezing brought on by the clouds of dust released each time he opened a new file.

Many of the files had cursory information, and no photographs, so were useless for the purposes of his investigation.

Cursing silently to himself for the umpteenth time, he had opened this particular file and immediately found himself staring at an image of the white man in the photograph discovered inside Hollis Burbank's suitcase, the man he assumed was Faulkner.

He excavated the photograph from his pocket and compared the images.

There was no doubt.

It was the same man.

His full name was Jared Faulkner, American national, born in 1952 – making him thirty-three years old in 1985 – in Beaufort, South Carolina, and an employee of Fermi Engineering India Private Limited, a joint American–Indian company operating in India at the time. Faulkner's stated purpose for being in India was given as 'Chemical Engineer', which meant little to Chopra. His proposed address while in the country was listed as a corporate guesthouse in Pune, which, again, was of little use.

He took a picture of the documents on his mobile phone, then returned the file.

He called Rangwalla, sent him Faulkner's details via his phone and asked him to dig up what he could. In truth, he thought, it was a hopeless task. Assuming Faulkner was still alive, he would be in his sixties by now. And he might be anywhere in the world.

Nevertheless, Rangwalla could start by attempting to trace him in his home town in the United States. Chopra knew this task would inspire dread in his former sub-inspector, so he told him to make use of Kishore Dubey again. He needed more information about Faulkner; he felt certain this would bring him one step closer to Burbank, the *real* Burbank.

Chopra finished going through the rest of the files. He did not find anyone in there who might have been Hollis Burbank. Then again, with so many files missing that all-important photograph, it was possible that he had held a file with Burbank's true identity in his hands and not recognised it for what it was.

Instead, he decided to focus his attention on the company that Jared Faulkner was listed as having worked for, Fermi Engineering India Private Limited. It was a good bet that Burbank had a link to the same organisation.

A quick online trawl using his mobile phone revealed

nothing. Clearly, in the thirty years since Fermi Engineering had set up in India, it had either ceased operations or changed its name.

Yet there *was* a way for Chopra to peel back the veil, and find out more about the company. It would necessitate a visit to another of India's ubiquitous administrative agencies, a thought that did not immediately fill him with enthusiasm.

The Western Region office of the Ministry of Corporate Affairs in India was located in the ambitiously named Everest Tower on Marine Drive, only a few hundred yards from the artist Shiva Swarup's studios that Chopra had visited the previous day.

Once again, he parked his van and made his way along the crowded promenade, the heat of the midday sun shimmering from the asphalted pavement. A man stepped in front of him holding an enormous knife.

Chopra reared back, but the man just grinned at him. 'Coconut, sir?'

He thrust the brown fruit at the former policeman.

It was almost lunchtime, and Chopra found his stomach suddenly rumbling. He bought the coconut and, further along the promenade, three freshly fried samosas, ignoring the flapping semaphores of alarm from his panic-stricken brain. The samosas, smeared in mint chutney and squashed between two floury baps, tasted better than he remembered, though he was willing to concede that there might be a bill to pay later on.

The Ministry of Corporate Affairs – or MCA, as they preferred to be styled in Hip New India – was on the sixteenth floor.

Chopra crowded into a busy elevator.

On the third floor, a man in a brisk business suit squeezed in, dragging a goat by a leash. Chopra resisted the urge to enquire as to the reason for this surreal sight, but by the eleventh floor he could stand it no longer. The goat had begun nuzzling at his shoe and, when he tried to surreptitiously toe it away, had become offensive and belligerent, attempting to bite his ankle.

'I am sorry,' he blurted out. 'I have to know. Why do you have a goat with you?'

'You mean Guru?' replied the man. 'He is a mascot. For my company. Guru Goat Products Incorporated. We produce goat's milk. And goat cheese. Goat yogurt. Goat chips. Goat ghee. Goat pickle. Goat salami. Goat cake . . .' Chopra listened, regretting having asked the question, as the man launched into a long-winded and passionate extolling of the virtues of goat-based merchandise. The goat, meanwhile, continued to stare coldly at Chopra, like a spurned lover.

'I have an elephant,' Chopra said, more to get the man to stop talking than anything else.

The man gave a thin smile. 'I considered that,' he said. 'But it's bloody hard work milking an elephant.'

Contrary to Chopra's expectations, the offices of the MCA were a world apart from the underground murk of the FRRO records bunker.

He was pleasantly surprised to discover a well-lit, neatly laid-out space, decorated with blown-up pictures of top Indian businessmen – from steel czars, to dot-com entrepreneurs, to private space rocket visionaries – accompanied by inspiring, if somewhat schmaltzy exhortations to corporate endeavour: 'I dragged myself up from the slum, you can too'; 'Make India great again!'; and a rather dubious contribution from the founder of a national e-retailer: 'If at first you don't succeed . . . do something else.'

There was even a picture of Gandhi – a man Chopra greatly admired, but not one he had ever considered a 'businessman', unless one viewed him as a man in the business of helping redefine a nation. The quote beside Gandhi's picture was one of his favourites: 'It is difficult, but not impossible, to conduct strictly honest business.' During his years in the Brihanmumbai Police, Chopra had had a plaque with this same quote installed in his office. It had been a constant reminder that, even in an organisation routinely accused of venality, it was still a simple matter for each individual to set his or her shoulder squarely to the wheel of diligence and incorruptibility.

One need only decide to be honest, he had always felt, and it could be so.

Chopra was attended by a youngish man in a suit and tie, and designer spectacles. A cloud of expensive aftershave preceded his entry into the little waiting room in which Chopra had been parked.

The young man introduced himself as Rangoon, and briskly asked Chopra to explain what it was he was looking for.

'I require the employee list of a company that operated in India some thirty years ago,' Chopra said. 'I am fairly certain that it was active in 1985, but I can find no record of it now.'

Rangoon picked an imaginary piece of fluff from his perfectly creased shirt. 'That should be very simple, sir,' he said, in a condescending tone. 'Assuming you have the proper authorisation to view such records.'

Chopra showed Rangoon his identity card.

'Very well,' said the young man, in a more cooperative tone. 'Please follow me.'

They walked through to a bank of computer terminals.

Rangoon slipped into a chair, flexed his fingers like a concert pianist and then attacked the keyboard.

Moments later he stopped, a puzzled frown on his features. The Olympian self-confidence had slipped from his demeanour. 'Well, this is curious,' he said.

'*What* is curious?' said Chopra, hovering at his shoulder.

'The records of the company that you mention – Fermi Engineering – have been sealed.'

'What do you mean "sealed"?'

'I mean that they have been placed under restricted

access. Which means that I cannot access them,' he added helpfully.

'Well, who can then?'

'That's just the thing,' said Rangoon. 'The level of access is listed as Classified. Which means that no one at this office can help you. The records have been sealed by New Delhi. I am afraid that you are out of luck, sir. Only someone in the government can authorise the release of these records.'

PONDICHERRY BLUES

Poppy found Anjali Tejwa's grandmother – the woman known as Big Mother – in the Banyan restaurant.

She had manoeuvred her dreadnought of a wheelchair to the restaurant's counter, employing it like a medieval siege engine laying onslaught to a castle, as she berated the cowering maître d' for the shortcomings of the meal she had just been served.

The poor man, prematurely stooped and grey, appeared to wilt further with each lash of her tongue.

Poppy stepped forward. 'Big Mother, may I speak with you? It is about Anjali.'

The woman turned to Poppy, giving the maître d' the opportunity to slink away, a look of grateful relief shuddering over his face.

'Ah, the woman who worked out how my granddaughter vanished from a locked bathroom,' said Big Mother. 'Poppy, isn't it?'

'Yes,' said Poppy. 'And I have found something else.' She

held out the sheet of paper she had discovered in Anjali's valise.

Big Mother took the sheet, scanning it with her quick, dark eyes. 'This is a travel itinerary. A train to Pondicherry, first-class reservation. Leaving yesterday afternoon.'

'I found it inside Anjali's luggage.'

Big Mother drew in a sharp breath. 'Was the ticket there too?'

'No.'

'Which means that Anjali has already gone.'

'It seems that way.'

Big Mother's lips compressed as she lapsed into thought. 'What else was missing from her room?'

Poppy glanced behind her to Huma Dixit.

'A small rucksack, Big Mother,' said the girl, miserably. 'A few clothes. Some cash she had brought with her.'

'What is a "rucksack"?' said the old woman suspiciously.

'A bag that you put on your back.'

'Strange place for a bag,' muttered Big Mother. 'Bags are usually on the backs of servants.' The index finger of her right hand tapped the arm of her wheelchair. 'There is no mention of a hotel in this itinerary.'

'No,' said Poppy.

'Pondicherry is a big place. I went there once, when I was a girl. For a wedding, in fact. The Maharaja of Yanam was marrying his twenty-eighth wife. The man was in his seventies by then, as big as a house. He was a real glutton, and not just for food. A connoisseur of every excess imaginable. The old royal families were never paragons of virtue, but most had an unspoken agreement with the people they ruled. Part of that agreement was never to push them beyond the limits that human dignity should be forced to endure. Old Iyengar didn't give a hoot for that sort of thinking. He was a royal of the old school. Blood and Guts, they called him. Used to go out shooting tigers. If there weren't any tigers around he'd settle for putting holes in a few peasants. Of course, it didn't help that he was a notorious opium fiend. Dedicated swathes of his realm to cultivating it. Once charged a herd of elephants armed with nothing but a blunderbuss.'

Behind Poppy, Irfan placed a hand on Ganesha's skull, patting him gently. Irfan usually enjoyed hearing stories about the old maharajas of India, but he didn't appreciate this story of a royal who went around shooting at elephants.

Ganesha's ears twitched.

His trunk snaked up onto the table of the diner nearest to him – who was avidly following the conversation between Poppy and Big Mother – and lifted off a pastry, which he smartly tucked into his mouth. Comfort food.

'But that is our past,' said Big Mother. 'Our future . . . our future is in our genes. All we have is our children.' Poppy saw for the first time just how old the woman was, but in that magnificent way of ancient monuments. In a way Big Mother *was* a monument, to a vanishing way of life.

'But what do we *do*, Big Mother?' asked Huma, plaintively.

'The real question, young lady, is why did Anjali choose to go to *Pondicherry*. Does she have friends there that I am not aware of?'

'I-I don't think so,' replied Huma. 'She never mentioned anyone like that. But I can't be sure. I mean, it's so easy to make friends these days. On Facebook, and Twitter, and—'

She stopped as Big Mother held up a gnarled hand. 'You are talking about the computers again. Haven't I warned you about that? It makes my head hurt.'

'But it is a fact of modern life, Big Mother. And Anjali may have made a friend that way. Someone who invited her to Pondicherry.'

Big Mother gave a grudging sniff. 'Can you find out if Anjali has such a friend?'

'I can try,' said Huma, uncertainly.

'In the meantime, there is something else we can do,' said Big Mother firmly, turning to Poppy. 'You seem to be a woman with a good head on her shoulders. If you still wish to help, then perhaps you can accompany me to Victoria Station.'

'But why?' said Poppy. 'Anjali's train left yesterday.'

'Yes,' said Big Mother. 'And there is something about that I would like to check.'

A commotion behind Poppy diverted the attention of the restaurant.

A thickset man had stood up from his chair. Red-faced, he was holding his hands to his bald pate. 'My hairpiece!' he bellowed, glaring accusingly at Ganesha.

All eyes turned to the little elephant.

Resting atop Ganesha's skull was, indeed, the incriminating presence of a glistening black toupee.

'Ganesha!' scolded Poppy. She turned to Irfan. 'I suppose you are going to tell me this wasn't him either?'

'But it wasn't!' protested the boy. 'I know he wouldn't do that.'

Poppy plucked the hairpiece from Ganesha's head, and held it out to the irate gentleman.

He snatched it from her, and slapped it back onto his skull. It sat there, looking like a small furry animal that had just died.

She glanced back down at Ganesha, at the distressed way the little calf was flapping his ears. A worm of doubt gnawed into her anger. She turned back to the thickset man. 'Did you actually see him take it?'

'What do you mean?' said the man, belligerently. 'It was snatched from my head while I was looking the other way. When I turned around there it was on *his* head.' He jabbed a finger at Ganesha. 'If your elephant cannot keep his trunk to himself he should be locked up. You know, in some parts of the world they cull them so they don't become a nuisance.'

Poppy folded her arms. 'Cull them?' Her voice had become dangerously low.

'Yes,' said the man firmly. 'In Kenya, for instance, they shot a load of them a few years back. Elephants lay waste to the land, you know, make it unliveable for everything else. It's fashionable these days to go around talking about saving the elephant, but, as far as I'm concerned, they're just big ugly eating machines.'

'*You're* a big ugly eating machine!' shouted Irfan, from behind Poppy. Ganesha had huddled up close to him, his head down, ears flat against his skull, a sure sign of distress. The little elephant always understood when he had become the object of ire.

'Irfan!' said Poppy, as a nervous titter ran around the restaurant.

'Hah!' said Hairpiece Man, waving a hand in the boy's direction. 'Is it any wonder the elephant is such a thug when you cannot even teach your child basic good manners.'

Poppy had had enough.

Her chest heaved as she opened her mouth to annihilate the bad-mannered buffoon— but she was stopped short by the sound of Big Mother's voice booming out across the restaurant. 'You oaf,' said the old woman, powering her wheelchair forward. 'Just when I think I have met every manner of fool in my life, an even bigger dolt comes along. So the elephant took your hairpiece? Who cares! It is a child and children get up to mischief. But you, you are an adult. A malicious, wicked man, so stuffed with your own self-importance you think the world revolves around you. What gives you more right to live on this earth than that elephant?'

'But-but—' spluttered the man.

'*They* were here thousands of years before us,' continued Big Mother, relentlessly. '*We* stole *their* land. I tell you, if there is to be a cull, then the best place to start is with the likes of you.'

'But what's an elephant doing parading around a hotel anyway?' whined the man.

'I could ask the same of you,' said the old woman, poking a finger at his ample belly. 'It seems to me you've done a good job of laying waste to the land yourself.' She turned to Poppy. 'Let us go. We have work to do.'

Poppy led the little band out of the restaurant.

As they neared the exit, she caught sight of the

golden-furred monkey she had seen in the hotel garden the day before, the film star's pet. It was perched on a child's high chair at the rear of the restaurant, surrounded by the film star's minders. She observed it, as its beady eyes tracked the despondent Ganesha.

Poppy's own eyes narrowed, recalling how Irfan had been certain the monkey had been responsible for the fracas with the priest's robe. Could it be . . .?

FERMI ENGINEERING

During his thirty years as a police officer Chopra had become used to hitting brick walls.

Such was the nature of a police investigation, particularly on the subcontinent, where the service lagged behind in the technology that in other parts of the world appeared to solve cases at the click of a mouse. As a younger man, this had frustrated him, and he had thrashed about trying to make things happen. But, as time went by, he had learned that there was only so much that could be done. The wheels of justice sometimes became stuck in a muddy rut, and it took time, effort and – more often than it would be prudent for the public to know – a slice of good fortune to get the cart moving again.

The revelation that the records of Fermi Engineering had been sealed was a disappointment.

And yet, at the same time, Chopra's nose was tingling. Questions elbowed themselves to the forefront of his thoughts: why had the records of a seemingly ordinary company – now defunct – been sealed by the government? What was the link between Fermi Engineering and Hollis Burbank?

He knew that if he were to progress the investigation into the American billionaire's death, he must seek answers to these questions.

But his reach did not extend to the marbled halls of power in New Delhi.

Fortunately, he knew someone whose influence did.

Chopra had recently earned the undying gratitude of the British government by helping to recover the legendary Koh-i-noor diamond. The great jewel, once the world's most valuable stone, had originally been mined in India and had passed through a succession of kings and emperors before the East India Company had shipped it off to Britain to offer as tribute to Queen Victoria. The British monarch had instructed her master jewellers to incorporate it into the Crown Jewels, and that was where it had remained ever since.

Until the Crown Jewels had been brought to Mumbai's Prince of Wales Museum as part of a special exhibition and the Koh-i-noor subsequently stolen in a daring heist. When Chopra's old friend had been arrested for the crime, he had felt duty-bound to investigate.

Ultimately, he had been successful, though his role in the return of the great diamond had been kept a secret. The British government had expressed its gratitude through the medium of the High Commissioner to India, a diplomat based in the suburbs of Mumbai.

It was this man who Chopra now called.

At their first meeting Robert Mallory had struck Chopra as an eminently practical man. He supposed that the post of High Commissioner to India could easily be considered a poisoned chalice. On the one hand, it was a high-profile posting, a seat at the table in the world's newest superpower. On the other, the commissioner would be forced to deal with the office-bearers of the Indian government, a task marginally less conducive to personal well-being than being thrown into a pit of spitting cobras.

Nevertheless, from what he had learned of Mallory, he seemed competent, and unafraid of the task he had taken on.

'How's that little elephant of yours?' Mallory asked, having answered Chopra's call to his mobile.

Chopra could hear a cacophony of bleating noises in the background.

'He is fine, sir,' he answered. 'I-ah-I require your assistance.'

'Give me a second. Let me get inside. Can hardly hear myself think with all these camels.'

Chopra wondered for a second if he had misheard.

When the commissioner came back on the phone, he briskly explained: 'I'm in Jaipur. There's some sort of camel festival going on, and the chief minister insisted I attend. He's got this hare-brained scheme of exporting baby camels to Britain. Thinks there'll be a big market for it, just like the alpaca craze a few years back.'

Chopra had no idea what an alpaca was, but he sincerely doubted that the good people of England would wish to keep camels. While humans believed they had domesticated the camel, no one had actually told the camels that. Camels were large, smelly, surly and extremely obstinate. Not to mention dangerous. With their plate-sized hooves, a kick from a camel could easily break a man's back.

'Anyway, camels aside, what can I do for you?'

Chopra quickly explained the circumstances surrounding the death of Hollis Burbank, and his subsequent investigation.

Mallory fell momentarily silent as he considered the matter. 'Even if I could help,' he said, eventually, 'the issue here is why should the British government care? I mean, Burbank is an American. It's bad luck that he's been killed, and worse luck that it might raise a stink. But it's not our stink, is it? I've learned not to meddle in the affairs of others. Bad smells have a way of clinging, if you're not careful.'

Chopra had been prepared for this. 'My instincts tell me that there is something here. We *must* get to the truth.'

'The truth?' said Mallory, chuckling down the phone. 'My God, Chopra, you are priceless! A true man of faith. I, on the other hand, don't really believe in the "truth", not in the way you mean it. Wasn't it Nietzsche who said that there are no facts, only interpretations?'

'I have a quote of my own,' countered Chopra. ' "Morality is the basis of all things, and truth is the basis of all morality." Do you know who said that?'

'Elvis Presley? Mickey Mouse?'

'Gandhi,' said Chopra stonily.

Mallory sighed. 'I am really not sure how I can help you.'

'What if I told you that Burbank was in India at the express invitation of a British company, Gilbert and Locke, the world's largest auction house? It would be a shame if the media got the wrong end of the stick, and were to embroil Gilbert and Locke in the controversy. I expect that with Anglo–Indian trade being part of your portfolio you might find the press beating a path to your door.'

Mallory hesitated, then gave another chuckle, though one that was less generous this time. 'I see that you're picking up some of the arcane skills of statecraft. However, your scenario is far-fetched, to say the least. I doubt that anyone will care about Gilbert and Locke's involvement in this American's death. Even should they, it is hardly a matter for the British government.' He sighed. 'Nevertheless, I am a man who likes to hedge his bets. I've got enough on my plate already without having to wade into another PR disaster between our nations. I'm still trying to smooth ruffled feathers over the whole Koh-i-Noor fiasco. I'll see what I can find out. I make no promises though. I know everyone who matters in Delhi, but it doesn't mean they'll dance to my tune. Your politicos, I'm afraid, are a law unto themselves.'

'Thank you,' said Chopra, and ended the call.

Mallory called back two hours later, as Chopra was finishing a hurried lunch snatched from a roadside vendor, a simple meal of steamed rice cakes. 'So,' began the commissioner, 'the chap running the Ministry of Corporate Affairs is a friend. Given how closely we have to work together to promote Anglo–Indian trade, that's only to be expected, I suppose, but it just so happens that we are in the middle of negotiating a multi-billion-pound trade deal in the armament sector. I implied to my friend that the wicket could become decidedly sticky if he didn't help me out.

'Of course, he was mystified as to why I was interested in a defunct company from the eighties. I had to make up a story. I rather believe I gave him the impression I was some sort of amateur historian, writing a book on foreign trade in India during that period. Not that he bought a word of it.

'But he's a smart man. He's gained a little leverage over me, and that has made him eager to cooperate. He's emailed me a file of scanned documents. I'm going to forward them to you.' He hesitated. 'I have to warn you. There's a lot of black ink in there – and there is absolutely nothing I can do about that. If my friend has access to the unredacted versions of these records, he didn't admit it to me.'

Half an hour later Chopra was sitting in the business centre of the Grand Raj Palace printing out the documents that Robert Mallory had emailed him.

The British High Commissioner had not exaggerated.

Much of the information in the records had been blacked out. It was impossible for Chopra to determine if that information had been redacted recently, or in the past.

In particular, details concerning the dissolution of the company had been all but eliminated.

All that he could make out – reading between the lines of blacked-out text – was that the company had been wound up abruptly in late 1985, following a special resolution of its board. This had been in response to an incident whose nature was not clear to Chopra – largely because it had been redacted from the reports. Whatever had transpired, it had not only been serious enough to lead to the winding up of the company, but had also led to the sealing of the firm's records.

Chopra leafed through those scant records that had escaped the censor's pen.

The company's financial accounts appeared to show a healthy trading profit for the four years the firm *had* been in operation. Boisterous statements from the company's chairman – a Mr Dharmender Gill – introduced the annual reports, embellishing a tale of solid performance and above-average growth. The company's future seemed bright.

And then, overnight, it had all come to a shuddering halt.

What had happened? Why had Fermi Engineering shut down? And what had any of this to do with Hollis Burbank?

Chopra found himself one step closer to the answer in a document titled 'Personnel Roster'.

This was what he had been looking for, and he was relieved to discover that here the redactor's zeal had been curbed. Inside the roster – which contained employee information from the company's inception through to 1985, the year it had ceased operations – he found profiles of the organisation's key employees, each profile accompanied by a small photograph.

Quickly, he ran his finger down the pages, examining the pictures, until, three pages in, he discovered Jared Faulkner.

There he was, staring out from the white sheet, a half-smile on his handsome lips. The accompanying profile declared him to be the company's Deputy Chief Engineer. A short background puff stated that he had obtained a Bachelor's in Chemical Engineering from the University of Stanford in America, and had previously worked for an American firm called Titus Engineering Solutions, a mining outfit based in Colorado.

Somehow, he had ended up in India.

Chopra continued through the document.

Just two pages later he froze.

The photograph facing him was of a dark-haired man, in his thirties, blue-eyed, with a hard, almost hostile expression. The hair was slicked back, the eyes piercing and the jaw set square. The face, like something familiar seen through water, triggered a motor inside Chopra's brain. He had never seen this man before, and yet he knew him. The ravages and attritions of time could erode much, but the basic essence of an individual would always remain, like a ghostly echo of what had once been.

In that echo Chopra recognised the man he had come to know as Hollis Burbank.

And yet, this younger version of Burbank went by a different name.

The profile attached to the photograph stated that this man was Roger Penzance, Chief Engineer for Fermi

Engineering India Private Limited. Like Faulkner, Penzance had been born in the States, had obtained a degree in Chemical Engineering – his was from Baylor University in Texas – and had subsequently worked for a number of engineering firms in America.

Chopra's gaze lingered on the photograph.

Could this be the vital breakthrough? Could the real motive for the American's murder lie in the mystery behind his connection to Fermi Engineering? One thing was now certain. Hollis Burbank – and Chopra found it easier to continue thinking of the man as Burbank, rather than Penzance – had gone to great lengths to conceal his past. He had changed his name, possibly even changed some aspects of his physical appearance – the face of Roger Penzance was subtly but noticeably different to the face of the American billionaire, different in a way that could not be explained simply by the effects of ageing.

Why had Burbank changed his identity? What had happened in India that he had felt compelled to eliminate Roger Penzance, and don the guise of Hollis Burbank?

At least this explained Burbank's rabid commitment to protecting his privacy.

Clearly, the American wished to draw a veil over his past.

Indeed, Chopra strongly suspected that Burbank had fashioned a false past for himself – he must have realised, as his wealth and fame grew, that it would be impossible for him to remain completely beyond the reach of those who wished to pry into his background. By putting out a false trail he had successfully managed to keep the fact of his true identity as Roger Penzance a secret.

Once again, it all came back to why? Why would Burbank have taken such a drastic step?

Chopra continued to work his way through the Personnel Roster.

In short order, he found two of the three other individuals in the photograph discovered inside the lining of Burbank's suitcase. There had been four figures in that photograph, their surnames scribbled on the reverse: Faulkner, Murthi, Sen, Shastri.

Narayan Murthi was now revealed as another engineer employed by Fermi. His background profile stated that he had qualifications in advanced chemical synthesis, and had worked in southern India for two decades before joining Fermi Engineering. Further down the same page was Ravinder Shastri, a chemical scientist, recently graduated from the University of Baroda in the state of Gujarat. He had joined Fermi Engineering only one month prior to the photograph being taken.

There was no Sen, the only woman in the photograph – assuming that the name on the back of the picture did indeed refer to her – listed.

Chopra's eyes lingered on the photograph.

Why was she missing from the roster? Had she simply been omitted? Or, as seemed more likely, did this mean that Sen was not an employee of Fermi Engineering? In which case, why was she wearing a white lab coat like the others? What was she doing with them in this photograph?

He completed his trawl of the documents.

There was nothing else that immediately caught his eye – or at least nothing else that hadn't been blacked out. His palms itched at the fact that the information he needed was possibly right before him, yet there was no means by which he might access it.

And yet, all was not lost. He was not without a lead to follow.

If Narayan Murthi and Ravinder Shastri were still alive, there was a good chance they were in India. And if that was the case, then Chopra might be able to find them, and through them discover more about Jared Faulkner and Hollis Burbank.

THE HANGING GARDENS

Desk research had never been one of Chopra's strong suits.

During his years on the force, he had always maintained an image of himself as a man of action. This image had been harder to sustain after he had been promoted to run the local station in Sahar and, as a consequence, found himself tied to his desk for more hours than he would have cared to admit.

And yet, even then, he had managed to engineer opportunities to get out into the streets, to visit crime scenes and get his hands dirty in the interviewing of witnesses and suspects. As time went by, he realised that real police work – in contrast to the bullets-and-bash-em-up police method so beloved of Bollywood – was often made up of hours and hours of dull, painstaking and methodical effort, chasing up minor leads and sifting through stacks of routine information.

And yet, as tiresome as this was, time and again Chopra had found that it was this method that ultimately led to success, the discovery of a seemingly inconsequential thread of evidence that turned the key and broke open the whole investigation.

Now, as he sat in the business centre of the Grand Raj Palace Hotel, he found his old instincts awakening.

His task, on the face of it, was simple: locating Narayan Murthi and Ravinder Shastri, the two men who he could, with a degree of certainty, link to Hollis Burbank's secret past as Roger Penzance.

To a man without Chopra's unique experience, the job of locating two Indians in the midst of a billion might have seemed daunting to the point of impossibility. But the former police officer had spent a lifetime finding those who did not wish to be found. Even in a place as congested, as seemingly disordered as modern India, it was still difficult to remain invisible. And, at this point, there was no reason to suspect that either Murthi or Shastri were attempting to conceal themselves.

Chopra's starting point was official records.

The one thing India had imbibed from her colonial overlords that had persisted long after they had been hounded from the subcontinent was the rabid adherence to record-keeping. The British – in their desire to ensure that not a single nugget of plunder escaped their attention – had kept meticulous records. In some regions, particularly the richer pocket kingdoms of India's regal families, British record-keepers had been deputed by the colonial capital in Calcutta to note down every single rupee that was taxed, collected and spent in the region. Enormous hide-bound ledgers could still be found in old record rooms, itemising every possession and detail of each family in the kingdom, listing their contribution to the local tithes and thus, ultimately, permitting an assessment of the region's contribution to the British coffers.

The administrative organs of modern India had kept alive this tradition of meticulous bureaucracy, something Chopra had been thankful for on numerous occasions. Census records, election records, birth, death and marriage records, land and property deeds and now, in the modern era: phone records, utility records, computer records and even social media footprints . . . To the seasoned investigator there were a plethora of means to track down elusive individuals.

Chopra began with a basic Internet trawl.

Although the trawl turned up nothing about Murthi or Shastri – other than a seemingly endless list of possible Murthis and Shastris, which were common enough Indian surnames, after all – when Chopra added the words 'chemical engineer' to the search, at the top of the page, in the paid adverts section, was a link to the website of the Indian Institute of Chemical Engineers, the country's leading professional body for the industry. According to their website, any chemical engineer worth their salt in India was a member, or had been at some point in the institute's illustrious seventy-year history, stretching back to its inception in the very year of Independence.

The institute's headquarters were in Kolkata, on the far side of the country, though there were branches across the subcontinent.

Chopra phoned the HQ.

He had decided against presenting himself as an investigator. He knew that, particularly with larger organisations, this sometimes led to a wall of silence being erected against the perceived intrusion. Instead, he claimed to be a senior editor for a topical news programme wishing to commission a documentary on chemical engineering in the country, cataloguing the way the industry had helped shaped modern India. As part of this glowing tribute he was keen to interview a couple of stalwarts from the eighties, whose names he had been given by an expert. A Narayan Murthi, and a Ravinder Shastri. They had worked for an organisation called Fermi Engineering, among others.

He was shunted between departments at the institute until he ended up with Alumni Records. A keen young woman asked him to hold the line while she delved into the records.

When she came back on the line, her voice carried both sadness and a hint of excitement. The sadness came from the fact that she was forced to report, with great regret, that Shri Narayan Murthi had passed away in 2004, at the age of seventy-five. The institute had published an obituary in its monthly journal.

Her voice brightened.

With Murthi's demise dealt with she could now report the good news: her search for Ravinder Shastri had been successful. He had retired just two years earlier after an illustrious career with one of India's largest petrochemical companies. The institute had run a piece on him following his retirement, felicitating him for his achievements.

Chopra asked her if she had contact details for the great man.

She was delighted to report that she did. (Chopra guessed that life in the Alumni Records section of the Indian Institute of Chemical Engineering was not quite all it had been cracked up to be. His enquiry was possibly the most exciting thing that had happened to the young woman in a long time.)

He noted down the details, thanked the girl, then looked at the address she had given him with a sense of things finally falling into place.

Ravinder Shastri lived right here in Mumbai, not half an hour from the Grand Raj Palace.

THE STATION FORMERLY KNOWN AS VICTORIA TERMINUS

There were many things that the British had been guilty of during their long stay on the subcontinent. Profiteering, exploitation, systematic abuse; even, on occasion, government-sanctioned murder. And yet there remained, dotted about the vastness of the subcontinent, innumerable monuments to the British legacy that were still viewed with something approaching fondness by many in India. Among these cherished institutions was the vast railway network that the British had overseen – at the expense of thousands of Indian lives – and which had provided the foundation for a colonial system of governance and looting, but later served as a springboard for India's own progress towards modernity. Love them or loathe them, the British had left their mark, and the great Indian railway system was now the country's biggest employer, as well as one of the world's largest and busiest rail networks.

And the very first train of that mighty network had, on 16 April 1853, departed what would become the station known as Victoria Terminus.

VT Station – as many locals continued to refer to it, despite the fact that it had been renamed back in 1996 after the Maratha warrior-king Shivaji – was one of the busiest railway stations in the world, frenetically shunting more than three thousand trains a day. A grand building designed in the High Victorian Gothic style, the station's spires, turrets, pointed arches and signature dome concealed a bewildering internal layout that, to the uninitiated, became a frantic maze designed to grind down the human soul.

As Poppy entered the station, moving swiftly to keep pace with the wheelchair of Anjali Tejwa's grandmother, she glanced up at the statue of Progress atop the dome, a female figure holding aloft a flaming torch and a spoked wheel. It was her favourite monument in the whole of Mumbai, and never failed to lift her spirits.

As it did her fellow Mumbaikers, VT Station held a special place in Poppy's heart.

Not only had it become one of the earliest symbols of Mumbai – as opposed to the old colonial outpost of *Bombay* – it was also the one place that almost every citizen of India's dream city could identify with. It was the common man's meeting point, a watering hole shared by Indians of all castes, creeds and classes, the backdrop to countless Bollywood films, the starting point of innumerable friendships, and a million Mumbai stories.

Poppy remembered the shock she had felt when, a few years earlier, terrorist gunmen had targeted the station, killing fifty-eight luckless souls. She recalled the terrible images of station platforms smeared in blood, platforms that she had navigated countless times in her younger days when she had first arrived in the city, jostling her way through the riotous commuter crowds, the Western tourists, the snack vendors, the coconut-water sellers, the station beggars and bootboys, the gewgaw salesmen and runaways.

And yet, the very next morning, the trains were running again, a testament to the indomitable spirit of the subcontinent's greatest city.

They sped through the station's grand concourse, the Panzer-like wheelchair scything a path through the commuters, scattering startled rush-hour refugees in all directions. Poppy wasn't clear exactly why they had come to the station, but Big Mother was a woman after her own heart, a no-nonsense matriarch who trusted her instincts implicitly.

In short order, they found their way to the station's administrative offices, where the terminus's chief superintendent Mayank Kejriwal was just sitting down to lunch.

In the two decades he had worked at the station, Kejriwal, a dark, squat man with a comfortable belly and a bald spot that had only recently begun to bother him, had seen everything. Derailed trains, flooded tracks, marching strikers, fire, accidents, super-dense crush loads and, latterly, the horror of the terrorist attack. Day in and day out for twenty years he had marshalled his team to ensure that the trains kept running, that the blood of the city kept pumping around its glistening copper and steel veins. So adept had he become at navigating the trials and tribulations of managing the station that his days were now distinguished only by the sense of order and contentment that he felt in a job well done.

And yet, as he unscrewed his steel tiffin box and breathed in the heady aroma of his wife's ladyfinger and potato curry, and subsequently opened his eyes to find himself face to face with a severe-looking woman in a wheelchair, bearing down on him like a runaway Konkan Express, he sensed that his halcyon contemplation of his own good fortune was to be rudely, and possibly terminally, interrupted.

'My name is Shubnam Tejwa Patwardhan, the former maharani of Tejwa. I am looking for my granddaughter. Are you the person in charge of this madhouse?'

Kejriwal slowly lumbered to his feet. For some inexplicable reason he felt unable to remain seated in the woman's presence. Her general demeanour had the same effect on him as his childhood schoolmistress, the inimitable Mrs Wadhwa.

'Yes, madam,' he said. 'How may I be of assistance?'

'For a man with such big ears you seem to be hard of hearing. I have just told you: my granddaughter is missing.'

Kejriwal blushed. He had always been sensitive about his ears. 'Madam, how old is your granddaughter? I will inform my staff immediately. A missing child is our top priority. Rest assured we will find her.'

'She is not a child,' said Big Mother sharply. 'Not in the way you seem to believe. She is a young woman.'

Kejriwal's brow furrowed. 'A grown woman has gone missing in the station? Surely, you can simply phone her. Or she will find her way to the exit.'

'She does not wish to be found.'

'But that makes no sense.'

Big Mother moved her wheelchair menacingly closer to the superintendent. 'Let me see if I can translate this into sentences simple enough even for *you* to understand: my granddaughter is due to be married. She has run away. We believe that she may have come to this station to travel to Pondicherry. Yesterday evening. Ergo we have come here to find out if she did indeed board her train.'

Kejriwal's mouth hung open. 'But, madam, there is no system to monitor exactly who does or does not board a train. Our ticket inspectors merely verify that those who are boarding are in possession of a valid ticket.'

Big Mother gave a slow smile.

It reminded Kejriwal of the cobra-like smile of Mrs Wadhwa when he had provided an incorrect answer in class. This was invariably followed by humiliation and, on occasion, the painful administering of a cane to his rump. He sincerely hoped the old woman was not carrying a length of bamboo with her.

He would not have put it past her to employ it.

'There *is* another way of determining whether my granddaughter boarded that train,' she said. 'I am surprised that you have not thought of it yourself. But then, what else should I expect from a grown man who spends his days playing with trains?'

A SECRET TAKEN TO THE GRAVE

The drive to Ravinder Shastri's residence took Chopra once again around the curve of Marine Drive, past the bustling promenade of Chowpatty beach, where each year thousands came to submerge clay idols of Lord Ganesh during the annual festival of Ganesh Chaturthi. Shastri lived in the elite district of Malabar Hill, in the exotically named Alexander Graham Bell Tower, a dazzling twenty-storey apartment building that speared up from the landscape like a rocket bound for the moon.

Outside the building Chopra was confronted by a platoon of armed security guards. It was only after he waved his identity card at them that they permitted him into the building.

Shastri's apartment was on the nineteenth floor.

Chopra rang the buzzer, and stood back.

The door swung aside to reveal a small, emaciated woman in a sari: the housemaid.

Shastri was not at home. The maid informed him that

the master of the house was in the nearby Hanging Gardens, where he went each day after his lunch.

Chopra left his van outside the tower, and walked the five minutes to the gardens.

The Hanging Gardens of Malabar Hill – officially the Pherozeshah Metha Gardens – had been built back in the late 1880s. Some said the terraced gardens had been designed to overlay the reservoir that sat beneath them, to protect the water from the potentially contaminating effects of the nearby Towers of Silence where dead Parsee bodies were laid to rest.

Though 'rest' was not a term Chopra would have used.

Parsees consigned to the Towers of Silence were left to be disposed of by the city's carrion birds, in line with Zoroastrian belief. He imagined that, even in the afterlife, being pecked to shreds by vultures was probably not the most restful of experiences.

It was late in the afternoon now, though the sun was still strong and unforgiving. Outside of the van's air conditioning Chopra found his collar swimming around his neck, sweat stinging his eyes.

The gardens were surprisingly busy.

Indians – mainly older citizens, and determined joggers in Lycra – propelled themselves around the manicured space. There was the occasional foreigner standing about looking lost. Chopra supposed they had been fooled into believing that the gardens were worthy of a visit. If they were expecting some sort of wonder of the world, a modern-day version of the mythical Hanging Gardens of Babylon, they were sorely disappointed. Aside from a few decorative bushes chopped into the shape of animals, there was little to see or do in the gardens other than wait for the sun to set majestically over the Arabian Sea, or contemplate one's own navel.

He found Shastri sitting on a granite bench, staring out to sea, hands clutched around a polished cane. A book lay beside him: Vikram Seth's *A Suitable Boy*.

'Mr Shastri?'

The old man – and he *was* old now, Chopra saw, white-haired and hoary, with sunken cheeks and a dark, volcanic gaze – swivelled his head to look up at him.

'My name is Chopra. I am a detective investigating the death of an American named Hollis Burbank. You may know Burbank by a previous identity – Roger Penzance. It is this that I wish to talk to you about.'

A light flared in Shastri's eyes, and then he swung his gaze back out to sea. 'I have not heard that name in many years.'

Chopra sat down on the bench. 'I need to know what happened at Fermi Engineering, back in 1985. I need to understand why Roger Penzance became Hollis Burbank.'

'I cannot speak to you about that.'

'Why?'

'If you have discovered Fermi, then you already know why.'

'Because the records have been sealed by the Indian government,' said Chopra.

Shastri did not respond to this.

'My guess is that all those who had anything to do with whatever happened at Fermi Engineering were forced to sign an official secrecy oath.'

Again, the retired engineer said nothing, but Chopra was sure that his arrow had found its mark. He had suspected that this might be the case. After all, it would have been pointless for the government to seal Fermi's records if they had not also sealed the lips of those who knew what had taken place there.

'That was thirty years ago,' he continued. 'Isn't it time the truth came out?'

'The truth is overrated,' said Shastri. 'And besides, a truth told out of its time is meaningless, can even do more harm than good.'

'Something happened at Fermi Engineering,' persisted Chopra. 'Something that led to a government cover-up, and to Roger Penzance changing his identity. Now Penzance – Burbank – has been murdered. I cannot be certain but it may be that his death is linked to his past. The truth can only help.' He took out the photograph and held it out to Shastri, tapping it with his finger. 'That's you. And that is Narayan Murthi and Jared Faulkner. Who is the woman?'

Shastri's hands seemed to shake on the handle of his cane. 'You found Murthi?'

'Yes. He passed away some years ago.'

Shastri blinked. 'He was . . . my friend. My mentor. He recommended me for the position at Fermi.'

'As a chemical engineer?'

'Yes. Without Murthi's recommendation I would never

have got the job. I had a few years' experience, but this was a plum posting, working on a major government project.'

'What *was* the project?'

'That I cannot tell you.'

Chopra shifted on the warm stone seat. 'Then tell me about Faulkner.'

'He is dead,' said Shastri flatly.

'How do you know that?'

'Because I saw him die.'

Time seemed to waver and shrink around the two men. An overweight jogger panted past them, a look of panic wobbling over his face, faint music streaming from his headphones.

'How did he die?' said Chopra eventually.

'I cannot tell you.'

Chopra tried another tack. 'Tell me about *him* then.'

'He was a charming man. Smart, handsome, outgoing. He made friends easily. He was an American, but there was nothing brash about him. He immersed himself in India – it was his first time here. He took an interest in everything, our culture, our history, our food – he even learned to play cricket, after a fashion.' A smile played over Shastri's lips as the past replayed on a screen in his mind. 'He was a man of integrity. We all looked up to him.'

'And the woman in the picture? I assume her name is Sen. Did she work for Fermi too?'

Shastri became still, the shadows of his face deepening. 'No. She was never an employee of Fermi. She was a doctor. Her practice was close by Fermi's base of operations, and so they hired her, on a part-time basis. She administered to us. That's how she and Faulkner met. I suppose you could say they fell in love, though neither came out and said it. But we knew. Frankly, at the time, it was a source of angst for a number of us. Radhika Sen was a handsome, intelligent woman. It wasn't just Faulkner who was captivated by her charms. The strange thing was that none of us begrudged them their happiness. They were both good, honest people.'

'Where can I find her?'

'You cannot,' said Shastri. 'She is dead.' And abruptly, as if struck by a bolt of lightning, the old man bowed his head and began to weep. His shoulders shook, and tears fell onto his gnarled hands, curved around the head of his cane.

Chopra sat there, momentarily stunned.

He realised that the old man was helpless before the tide of memory engulfing him.

When he finally recovered himself, Chopra asked: 'You obviously cared for this woman. Tell me about her.'

'She was one of the bravest human beings I have ever met,' said Shastri. 'She stood up for what she believed in. Humanity, goodness, charity, truth. She didn't deserve to die. Not like that.'

'How *did* she die?'

Shastri shook his head mournfully. 'I cannot,' he said, the words hitching in his throat. 'I have already said too much.'

'What are you afraid of? These events are thirty years in the past. Surely, it is now time to reveal what really took place at Fermi.'

'The past is a country no one wishes to visit,' said Shastri sadly. 'It is a land that contains only regret and sorrow.'

Chopra changed course. 'Tell me about Roger Penzance.'

Shastri stiffened, as if he had been bitten by a snake. An expression of loathing had overtaken him. 'Penzance was the polar opposite of Faulkner. If Faulkner was Lord Ram, then Penzance was evil Ravana. It is not often in life that people are so black and white, but, in this instance, it was true. Penzance was arrogant, rude, stand-offish. Yes, he was a brilliant engineer – the most brilliant among us – but he had no skill in dealing with people. He was a driven man, furiously ambitious. For him everything led back to his own advancement. Achieving our goals was important to him only insofar as they tied in with his own agenda.'

'You hated him,' said Chopra softly.

'We *all* hated him.'

A short silence passed. 'What else can you tell me about him?'

'Only that if he is just now dead, as you say, then he has lived thirty years too long.'

'What does that mean?'

But Shastri would say no more.

Realising this, Chopra swung himself to his feet.

He had learned much, but not enough for him to consider the visit an unqualified success. He could sense that Shastri wished to say more, but would not. He doubted that it was just the confidentiality agreement stopping the old man from speaking. He suspected that a large part of what held the engineer's tongue was guilt.

But guilt for what?

That was the crux of the matter.

A great knot of guilt into which was wrapped the past of Hollis Burbank.

For Chopra to make further progress, he would need to pursue another road.

And he thought he knew just where to begin.

AN OBNOXIOUS MOVIE STAR

While Poppy went with Big Mother to Victoria Terminus, Irfan and Ganesha had chosen to stay behind at the hotel. Poppy had had her reservations but, as Irfan pointed out to her, he was used to staying with Ganesha at the restaurant each night on his own anyway.

She extracted from him a solemn promise that he would stay in his room, and out of trouble.

Ten minutes after Poppy left, Irfan found his feet itching.

Ganesha, curled up in front of the television watching a show about a man who ate cars for a living, seemed content to lie around until Poppy returned. But Irfan had never been inside a five-star hotel before. Every minute that he stayed in his room seemed like a lost opportunity.

'I think you're getting restless, aren't you, Ganesha?' he said loudly.

Ganesha looked up. His trunk and face were smeared with ice cream. Irfan had ordered a dozen tubs, assorted flavours – in the interests of scientific discovery – from room service, and now the empty cartons were strewn about the carpet like wounded soldiers in a battle.

'Yes, I can see you are itching to explore.' He got up and opened the door.

Ganesha flapped his ears, looked quizzically at the boy, then lurched to his feet and wandered over to the door. Irfan prodded him into the corridor. 'Oh, look,' he said. 'You have left the room. It is my duty to accompany you and make sure you do not get into trouble. It is what Poppy would want.'

Ganesha mopped up some ice cream from his face with his trunk.

'I suppose we should clean you up first,' said Irfan, thinking how Poppy always insisted on wiping his own face when they were set to go out.

He led Ganesha into the bathroom, and the walk-in shower. 'Come on.'

He turned on the shower, then watched as Ganesha bundled inside, his bottom sticking out of the entrance. The power shower jet cascaded off the elephant's flanks, running in rivulets down his squat legs to his square-toed feet. Ganesha twirled his trunk and flapped his ears with happiness – elephants, Irfan had learned, loved water. It kept their sensitive skin hydrated, and seemed to fill them with a sense of euphoria. Certainly, Ganesha was always at his most playful when being hosed down in his courtyard at the restaurant.

After the shower, they headed downstairs, making their way out into the gardens, where they saw that the film crew had once again set up for a shoot.

Irfan looked around for the pretty actress they had seen the day before. Like Poppy, he adored the movies, but didn't recognise the actress. Then again, he was a Mumbaiker, a Bollywood aficionado – he didn't know much about cinema from the south.

There was no sign of her.

Instead he saw, once again, that stupid golden-furred monkey, in its stupid waistcoat, lounging in a deckchair.

The langur caught sight of them and stood up on its hind legs, teeth bared, eyes narrowed malevolently, hissing at them.

'Come on, Ganesha,' said Irfan. 'Let's go find somewhere else to play. I don't like the company around here.'

They turned and went back into the hotel and into the grand ballroom where the giant cut-outs of famous personalities had been set up, in readiness for a wedding that now looked as if it might never take place.

Halfway through the deserted room, a shriek turned their heads.

Boy and elephant looked up.

The golden-furred langur was perched above them on an enormous chandelier, holding what looked like an orange in its hand.

'Go away!' shouted Irfan. 'I know you've been trying to get Ganesha into trouble. You're a bad monkey!'

The langur bared its teeth and launched the orange at them. It struck Ganesha on the top of his knobbly skull, and bounced off towards the feet of a cut-out of a famous soap star. Ganesha gave a little bleat of distress and hunkered behind Irfan, hoping to ward off further aerial bombardment.

Irfan's eyes narrowed.

He scampered to the orange, picked it up and, in one swift movement, hurled it back at the monkey.

The langur's eyes widened. At the last instant it leapt from the chandelier, landing on the shoulders of the cut-out of Sachin Tendulkar. The momentum of the leap rocked the cut-out from its moorings; it swayed forward, causing the langur to scrabble furiously at Sachin's neck, wrapping its tail around his cardboard head. This served only to further push the cut-out downwards, teetering it on its base. For one brief second it seemed as if it might realign itself . . . but then, as the monkey leapt away towards the safety of another cut-out, pushing off with its hind legs, the added thrust sent the great cricketer toppling forward, to crash into the cut-out of a well-known local politician just yards away. The politician, caught in a pose of transcendental self-congratulation, hands raised aloft, fell instantly forwards, seeming to clutch lustily with his outstretched arms at the sari-clad screen siren before him.

Irfan and Ganesha watched in thrilled horror as the giant cut-outs began a ceremonial procession of destruction around the room, crashing to earth like giant dominoes, taking with them the meticulously laid out lighting and flower arrangements and shattering vases and glass ornaments from tables.

When the last tinkles of broken glass had stuttered into silence, a deathly quiet descended upon the grand ballroom.

Irfan and Ganesha looked at each other with round eyes.

'*What* is the meaning of this?'

They turned to see a large, red-faced man in a navy suit descending on them. The man's vertiginous head of hair swayed atop his skull like a roosting chicken. A brass tag on the breast pocket of his suit declared him to be Sreedhar Pillai, deputy assistant general manager. 'You have wrecked the ballroom!'

'It wasn't us,' said Irfan. 'It was him!' He pointed at the langur . . . or at where he had thought the monkey was, except that it was now conspicuous only by its absence. 'It was the monkey,' he said.

'Monkey?' Pillai raised himself up. 'You wish me to believe that a *monkey* caused all this? And what monkey are you talking about anyway? There is no monkey here.'

'But it's true,' protested Irfan.

The man folded his arms. 'I may only be the deputy assistant general manager,' he said, 'but you cannot make a monkey out of me. You two are in serious trouble.'

'Wow! What happened in here?'

They all turned to see Gautam Deshmukh, Anjali Tejwa's prospective groom, approaching. His stunned gaze took in the destruction of the ballroom. 'Did we get hit by an earthquake?'

'I must apologise, sir,' said Pillai. 'It is these miscreants who are responsible. But you need not worry. We will have the ballroom back in shape in no time at all. And, rest assured, these two will be severely punished.'

'Punished?' echoed Gautam.

'Severely!' Pillai nodded.

Irfan avoided looking up at the big man, his face red with embarrassment. Ganesha shuffled his toes, and hung his head.

Gautam crouched down and looked Irfan in the eye. 'Did you really cause all this damage?'

'It wasn't our fault,' mumbled the boy. 'There was a monkey.'

'They are talking nonsense, si—' began Pillai, but Gautam cut him off with a wave of his hand.

'You know, when I was young, I once destroyed my father's favourite car. A brand-new Bentley. My feet could barely reach the pedals and I ended up driving it into a lake.' He winked, then stood up. 'I don't think punishment will be necessary, Mr Pillai.'

'But, sir! What will your father say? He has ordered that everything must be perfect for your wedding.'

'Mr Pillai,' said Gautam, 'it is *my* wedding, not my father's. And as there is nothing here that cannot be fixed I do not think we need trouble him about this, do you? He has enough on his plate at the moment.'

Pillai blinked. 'Very well, sir.'

Irfan stared at Gautam in amazement. He realised that perhaps the unhappy groom wasn't quite the oaf everyone was making him out to be. Certainly, anyone willing to help out an unjustly accused elephant must be a decent person. He hoped they found his runaway bride soon. Irfan would be sure to tell her about how Gautam had come to their aid. Perhaps she'd have a change of heart about marrying him once she realised he was basically a good person. And maybe everyone would pat Irfan on the back for bringing the two of them together. There might even be a reward in it, from the grateful fathers . . .

He felt a tug on his arm.

He looked down.

Ganesha was pulling at him with his trunk.

He watched as the little elephant trotted away, his trunk in the air.

'Come on,' said Irfan. 'I can prove that we weren't responsible for this.' He knew that Ganesha's sense of smell was extraordinary. There was nowhere for that devious monkey to hide.

As it turned out the monkey in question had made no attempt to hide.

It was back in the hotel garden, lounging in its deckchair.

As they approached, it gave them a brazen stare, lips bulging with insolent menace.

Irfan flung an arm at the langur. 'There! *He* did it!'

Pillai stared from the monkey back to Irfan, and then said, '*Him*?'

'Yes.'

Pillai's mouth twitched. 'Have you any idea who that is?'

'The pet of some famous movie star from the south,' said Irfan. 'She is probably around here somewhere.'

'He is not the pet of some famous movie star from the south,' said Pillai hotly. 'He *is* the famous movie star from the south. *That* is Rocky, the Wonder Langur. The star of such blockbuster films as *Rocky's Revenge, Rocky goes to Tollywood, Rocky and the Seven Ninja Buddhists* and, of course, *Boom 1* and *Boom 2*. He is one of my favourite actors.'

Irfan stared at the man as if he had lost his mind.

'You do not seriously expect me to believe that one of the south's biggest stars wrecked my grand ballroom?' continued Pillai, practically frothing at the mouth.

Irfan tuned the man out. Instead, he turned and glared at the langur.

Rocky.

The monkey pulled back his lips, and bared his teeth.

'Okay,' muttered Irfan. 'If that is how you wish to play it. No one gets away with making fun of me and Ganesha. Not even a famous movie star.'

HOMI HAS THE ANSWERS

It took Chopra almost an hour to drive back north.

By the time he arrived at the Sahar Hospital, inching through rush-hour evening traffic, he was almost regretting his impulse. It would have been simpler to call his old friend, Homi Contractor, the senior police medical examiner stationed at the hospital.

Then again, Chopra knew that Homi was a queer old bird.

Though they had worked together for years, the old Parsee was possessed of a streak of bloody-mindedness that, if handled improperly, could make him as recalcitrant as a rhino with toothache. Besides, now that Chopra was no longer dealing with him in his capacity as the officer in charge of the local police station, it behoved him to show his friend a little consideration.

He quickly navigated his way through the bustling corridors of the hospital. When he reached the morgue, it was to discover that Homi was in the operating suite.

Chopra made his way back up to the ground floor, peered through the portal of Operating Theatre Four, then pushed open the door and stuck his head inside.

He was immediately confronted by the sight of Homi's round, perennially flushed face, with its bulbous, whisky-drinker's nose below a blue surgical cap. Homi, like the six students around him, was resplendent in scrubs, but had pulled his face-mask down below his rubbery chin so that he could articulate his displeasure. On the operating table was a cadaver, the flesh peeled back from the sternum in the familiar Y-shaped autopsy incision, though the 'Y' appeared to Chopra – who had seen more than his fair share of post-mortems – rather erratic in design.

'Mr Sarnath,' growled Homi, 'you are a disgrace. By God, man, even Frankenstein's monster would refuse to let you near him!'

'Sorry, sir,' mumbled the offending Sarnath, eyes downcast. 'I was very nervous.'

Chopra knew that his old friend was a hard taskmaster.

As well as performing autopsies for the local police cantonments, the old Parsee was also the Chair of the College of Cardiac Physicians and Surgeons of Mumbai, a responsibility he shouldered with utmost seriousness. Homi was a gregarious, outspoken and highly intelligent man, but one with a short fuse that seemed to be perpetually lit.

Chopra coughed.

Homi turned. His expression of anger instantly melted into one of welcome.

'Chopra? What are you doing here?'

'I need some information.'

'Can it wait? I'm a little busy.'

'Of course. I'll be down in the morgue.'

Homi arrived half an hour later, flopping down into his customary seat behind his overloaded desk.

'It's exam week,' explained Homi. 'My interns are busy practising. Just pray that your corpse doesn't come before this lot one day,' he added grimly.

Usually Chopra would indulge his friend, listening to Homi rant on about the shortcomings of the 'modern generation', but today he cut him off before he could work up a head of steam.

'I need your help with something.'

'You usually do,' said Homi, archly. Modesty, Chopra had long ago realised, was not among his friend's many sterling qualities. 'I presume this is to do with the Burbank investigation? As I told you yesterday, I cannot say for sure that the man killed himself.'

'That's not why I'm here,' said Chopra. Quickly, he laid out for Homi the trail that had led him to the engineer Ravinder Shastri. He took out the photograph of Shastri, Murthi, Faulkner and Sen. 'I need your help to identify this woman,' he said, tapping the picture. 'Her surname is Sen, and she was a doctor, in or around Pune, back in 1985.'

'With so much information to hand, I'm surprised you need my help.'

'Normally, I wouldn't ask,' said Chopra. 'But time is of the essence here. The senior echelons of the police department are keen to label Burbank's death a suicide, sweep it all under the carpet.'

'But you've convinced yourself there is more to it?'

Chopra hesitated. 'My instincts say yes. And if it *was* murder, I must explore every avenue.'

Homi rapped his knuckles on his desk. 'Well, in that case, consider it done. I shall wave my magic wand, and you shall have your information, Cinderella.'

'What? Who is Cinderella?'

Homi rolled his eyes.

He was a man who prided himself on his literary knowledge, but sometimes felt that it was wasted on his friends. Chopra was a bright man, but the minutiae of Western fiction was not his strong suit.

He took out his phone and made a call to the President of the Medical Council of India.

In Homi's capacity as Chair of the College of Cardiac Physicians and Surgeons of Mumbai, he had run into the man on numerous occasions. Homi covered the phone with his hand. 'The man's a buffoon,' he revealed. 'About as much charm and personality as a crushed slug— Ah, Prabhakar, how are you, old chap?'

Chopra listened to Homi making pleasantries – a task he knew ill suited his friend – before getting down to business. Homi quickly explained what he needed. He was given a number for the head of the council's record-keeping section. He made the call, and engaged in another lengthy conversation, in which, it seemed to Chopra, he was given the runaround. By the end of the call he felt certain Homi was about to hurl his phone at the wall.

When he eventually did hang up, he wilted into his chair. 'I am learning to manage my temper better,' he explained. 'Rekha signed me up for classes with a well-known spiritual guru.'

'Oh, really?' said Chopra, intrigued. 'How is it going?'

'Very well. In our first session I threw him out of the window.'

Chopra stared at his friend.

'Relax, Chopra. We were on the ground floor. The old charlatan started talking about the mystical energy of the cosmos, and whatnot. You know what that sort of talk does to my blood pressure. Mind you, I haven't felt this good in years, since chucking him out of that window.' Homi beamed. 'At any rate, the Medical Council will get back to me shortly. You can wait, or I can call you.'

Chopra stood up. 'I should be getting back to the hotel. Poppy will be waiting.'

'You know, my great-grandfather knew the man,' mused Homi as he escorted his friend to the door.

'Who? Burbank?' said Chopra in confusion.

'No, of course not. I'm talking about Khumbatta. He met him when he was a boy. Khumbatta was knocking on a bit, by then, of course, but he was still sharp as a tack. You know he used to do card tricks? He was notorious for pulling out a fifth ace in the last knockings of a poker game.'

Chopra smiled.

There were a million anecdotal stories about the legendary Peroz Khumbatta, founder of the Grand Raj. It didn't surprise him that Homi's great-grandfather had bumped into him. The Parsee community of Mumbai had always been a small, highly select bunch; in many ways, the Parsee industrialists of the nineteenth century had shaped the city. Mumbai owed them a debt, even as their voices dwindled away to just an echo in the great slipstream of time.

'Call me as soon as you know,' he said. 'And try not to throw any of your students out of a window.'

'I make no promises,' said Homi, with a grim smile.

'Well, there you are, then,' said Kejriwal, sitting back with a shimmer of nervous relief. 'She is not there.'

Big Mother hunched forward in her wheelchair, staring at the bank of monitor screens before her.

They were gathered in the control centre of Victoria Station, a state-of-the-art facility that had been recently installed to much fanfare and speech-making. Kejriwal had spent his earliest years on the rail network out in the Maharashtrian hinterlands, when the system was still mechanical, and stationmasters in the smaller outposts still rang a cymbal to alert dozing rural passengers to the arrival of each train. And now they had this abundance of technology, the precise workings of which often caused his head to throb when the junior technicians took it upon themselves to explain it to him.

Yet this was modern India, he supposed. Hurtling forward with unstoppable abandon like the *Flying Ranee* of his youth.

They had spent the past hour examining the CCTV footage for Platform 15, from which the Mumbai to Pondicherry express train departed, focusing on the narrow window of time when Anjali Tejwa should have been boarding that very train. They had pored over the faces of those making their way into the carriages, a patience-sapping endeavour in the company of the ill-tempered old woman. Kejriwal felt quite drained.

'We may have missed her,' said Poppy. 'Some of those passengers were wearing hats, or headscarves. It was difficult to make out their faces.'

'She is not on the train,' announced Big Mother.

She wheeled her chair sharply around, requiring the stationmaster to jerk backwards or risk losing his knees.

'How can you be so sure?' said Poppy.

'Because I know my granddaughter. Did I not tell you that she is a highly intelligent woman? She has orchestrated this whole thing. Do you think that after planning her escape so cleverly from that bathroom, she would be so careless as to leave the details of her onward journey for us to find?'

'You think she left the travel itinerary there on purpose?' said Huma.

'Almost certainly,' said Big Mother. 'She knew someone would search her belongings. If not her family, then the police, at some stage. She knew we would conclude that she has made off for Pondicherry.'

'I had a look at her computer,' said Huma. 'I couldn't find any friends in Pondicherry that she had made through social media. That's not to say she didn't have them, but . . .'

Big Mother waved her concerns away. 'Anjali is not in Pondicherry, nor anywhere near it.'

'Then where is she?' said Poppy.

The old woman's certainty wavered. 'I don't know.'

'What do we do next, Big Mother?' asked Huma.

'Perhaps it is time to involve the authorities?' suggested Poppy.

'No,' said Big Mother. 'We cannot risk the scandal. And besides, I do not believe that Anjali is in any danger. She knows exactly what she is doing.'

'What *is* she doing?' said Huma. 'I mean, if she doesn't want to get married, then why not just come out and say so? What's the point of putting us all through this?'

Big Mother sighed. 'Anjali is very smart,' she repeated. 'But even the smartest of us can become lost in the maze of emotions that make us human. Perhaps she doesn't want to marry Gautam; perhaps she doesn't want to marry at all. On the other hand, she understands what is at stake here. She feels responsible for the rest of us; we are her family, after all. She has no wish to see us destitute. She knows that the wrong decision could signal the end of the Tejwa royal heritage, such of it as now remains. It is a great burden for one so young.'

'And if you did find her,' said Poppy. 'What would you say to her? I mean, ultimately, is she free to make her own decision?'

'As free as any of us truly are in this world,' said Big Mother cryptically. 'I am no tyrant. Anjali means more to me than you could know. But I am a pragmatist. I see the greater good that can come from this union.'

'But if she were to return, having decided that, in spite of the consequences, she would rather not go through with the wedding?'

Big Mother regarded Poppy with a measured look. 'That moment has not yet arisen. I will worry about it when it does.'

ANOTHER LOOK AT THE PAINTING

Darkness had fallen by the time Chopra reached the hotel.

A sudden fatigue gripped him as he entered the lobby. The day's revelations swirled around his mind, like mice on a wheel. He felt a tension inside himself, a confusion that he was unused to. The complexities of the investigation, the pressure to find quick answers, were beginning to take their toll. He rubbed his face with his hands, trying to resurrect his sense of mission, knowing, at the back of his mind, that what he really needed was a brisk shower and a meal.

A few hours of sleep would not go amiss either.

And yet, somehow, he found himself punching the elevator button for the Grand Raj's topmost floor.

Moments later he was walking past the guards stationed outside the Khumbatta suite, and into the room in which Hollis Burbank had met his fate.

Why had he come here?

It was an old habit, seeking inspiration from the crime

scenes he had attended during his years on the force. Of course, usually he was certain that a crime *had* been committed. In the present instance things were not so clear cut.

His instincts told him that Burbank's death was not by his own hand. Someone had murdered the American. Yet the motive for that murder might lie in the present or in the distant past.

There was insufficient information for him to make a clear leap of deduction.

He felt like a high diver, poised on the edge of a cliff, looking down into murky waters, unsure of exactly what lay beneath the waves.

He found himself standing before the painting above Burbank's bed, *The Scourge of Goa* by Zozé Rebello.

Once again he was struck by the nature of the image, the torment depicted on the faces of the individuals, the sense of outrage and injury coalescing, like a wild storm of human angst, into a grand vision of hell. A crucible of pain and terror trapped within the frame of Rebello's canvas. He understood, in the abstract way of most people with little knowledge of the domain, that the purpose of art was to move the beholder, but he did not understand art like this. Its only purpose seemed to lie in leaching vitality from the soul, in rendering inert the very things that allowed the human spirit to triumph over the baser desires that lay waiting in the darkness.

What had possessed Rebello to create such an image?

'Ah, there you are!'

Chopra turned, startled out of his contemplation, to find Lisa Taylor framed in the doorway.

She was dressed in a finely cut designer trouser suit, her hair piled up in a golden ball, diamond earrings glittering in the lobes of her shapely ears. It occurred to him that the Englishwoman looked more attractive in this seemingly simple attire than the glamorous and revealing outfits she often favoured.

Less, he had always felt, was usually more.

'What are you doing here?' he coughed out.

'The lift porter told me you'd come up here,' replied Taylor. 'I'm after another progress report. My boss is foaming at the mouth.' She shuttled closer and he caught the heady scent of her expensive perfume. 'You look tired. How are you feeling? Your wife said you're a bit of an invalid these days.'

Chopra coloured. 'I am quite fine, thank you,' he said, his shoulders automatically straightening. 'I have never felt better.'

She stared at him with her cool blue eyes, then smiled. 'Well, you look pretty robust to me. She's a lucky woman. It's a hard thing finding an honest man these days. I meet a lot of rich, successful men in this industry. The kind who wouldn't hesitate in drowning their own mothers for a Caravaggio pencil sketch. There's no honour in the art world, and integrity is a word few have ever heard of.'

Chopra had no response to this.

He would never admit it, but Lisa Taylor exuded a sense of feminine charm that appealed to him. This, in itself, left him simmering with a sense of low-flying guilt, though he knew that it was unwarranted.

'So, what news?'

Relieved to focus on something else, he brought Taylor up to speed on his recent efforts.

'I knew it!' she said, when he had finished. 'I knew there was something about Burbank. He was always cagey about his past, and now I know why. Do you really think his death could be tied up with something that happened all those years ago?'

Chopra shrugged. 'It is too early to say.'

'Did I mention the clock is ticking?' said Taylor, pointedly. 'My boss, Gilbert and Locke's managing director, is flying in from London. This whole thing is causing heartburn in the firm's senior echelons.'

'But Burbank's death has nothing do to with your auction.'

'It doesn't matter. We're tainted by association. Remember what I told you: everything in this business is smoke and mirrors. One of our wealthiest clients dies after making a major purchase at an auction we organised? The press coverage, once the full details of Burbank's death are released, will be brutal. And Gilbert and Locke's name will be front and centre. You have no idea of the palpitations that is giving the stuffed shirts back home. They want the facts, Chopra. Then they can work out how best to spin them to their advantage.' Taylor checked her watch. 'I'm going to have some dinner. Would you care to join me?'

Chopra hesitated. 'I should get back to my room.'

'Do you always do what you *should*? Sometimes it can be fun to break the rules.'

Chopra glanced sharply at Taylor. The hint of amusement in her eyes only increased his discomfort. 'I, ah, have some notes to make.' Why had he said that? He sounded like a seventeen-year-old boy again, back in cadet school, tongue-tied in front of the statuesque Sergeant Fonseca, the female trainer in charge of imparting to her wards the minutiae of the Indian Police Service rulebook. A vision in khaki, and the focus of many a pubescent dream. The sound of Fonseca detailing subsection 2.1 (a), Rule 8 (i) on the requirements of cadet officers to engage daily in 'brisk and invigorating physical exercise' still gave him shivers.

Taylor allowed him to dangle on the hook for a moment, then smiled. 'As you wish.' She turned, then paused at the door. 'By the way, did anything come of that sketch? The one you found on Burbank?'

'I have discovered nothing further.'

'So no idea who this K.K. is? I confess, it's got me intrigued.'

'If I find out I will be sure to let you know.'

'You're a good man, Chopra. It's a shame we didn't meet under different circumstances . . .'

With that she sailed from the room, leaving Chopra feeling more at sea than before he had entered the suite.

He took one last look at the Rebello. 'What in the world were you trying to say?' he murmured, before turning to leave the room.

Back inside their suite Chopra was mystified to discover that he was alone.

He wondered briefly if Poppy and Irfan had gone down for dinner, but then saw a small card propped up against a vase of fresh flowers on the coffee table.

He picked up the card and scanned it.

It said, simply: *I am on the roof. P.*

Quelling his alarm at the image of his wife up on the roof of the grand old hotel, Chopra made his way out of the suite and towards the stairs.

He walked out onto the Grand Raj's roof terrace into a bubble of evening heat, leavened only slightly by a warm breeze rising from the sea. The space was lit by glow-lamps, each surrounded by a roiling cloud of mosquitoes, intermittently zapped into oblivion by electric ultraviolet insect killers.

A pianist in a tux played a grand piano in the corner, while couples milled around a fountain garden laid out over the terrace. At various points on the edge of the space, brass telescopes had been set up to allow guests to enjoy the 360-degree views.

Chopra spotted Poppy by one of the telescopes and made his way over. A nervousness he was unaccustomed to fluttered through his stomach.

'Poppy, what are you doing up here?' he asked as he reached his wife.

Poppy stepped away from the telescope and bade him look.

Mystified, Chopra put his eye to the instrument.

The image took a second to focus, and then he saw himself staring at the entrance to the nearby Regal Cinema. The Regal was one of the city's oldest cinemas, built in the thirties, an art deco masterpiece that had changed little in the eighty years since it had first opened its doors.

'Do you remember, when I first came to the city, on our first anniversary you took me to the Regal to see *Geethanjali*? It was a special midnight showing. They served rose ice cream in the intermission.'

Chopra did remember.

It had been a special evening, one that had stayed with him long afterwards.

'It is those memories – memories of you and me, together, in good times and bad – that have made my life rich beyond measure. I have adjusted to every disappointment because I knew you were there by my side. Today we are no longer that newly married couple. But my feelings for you are stronger than they were then. Because now I know who you *are*. And that is a man I love, trust, respect, and admire.'

'Poppy—'

'Let me finish. I am not saying these things to upset you, or to berate you. I accept that you must do what you must do. Your work is a part of you, and I would never take that away because I know it would change you into someone I would no longer recognise. I am saying these things simply for myself.'

Chopra sensed the melancholy in his wife's voice. He found himself struggling to find the words to reply.

'Poppy, the investigation is not as important as our marriage.'

'No,' said Poppy, but without enthusiasm.

'Is it about Lisa Taylor? She is my client. That is all.'

'Yes.'

'Nothing more.' Chopra felt himself kicking around in a bog of emotional quicksand. In spite of his wife's words, he sensed her simmering anger.

'I mean, really,' he added desperately. 'She is just a client.'

'Yes,' repeated Poppy, woodenly.

His phone rang. He let it ring until his wife said: 'Answer it. It may be important.'

'Not as important as you,' said Chopra, but it sounded feeble, even to his own ears.

Poppy gave a small smile, and turned back to the telescope.

Chopra answered the phone.

It was the hotel's deputy assistant general manager. 'Sir, we have a problem with your elephant. There has been an incident.'

FIRE IN THE HOLE

Irfan and Ganesha lurked by the edge of the double doors leading out towards the Grand Raj Palace's swimming pool, Ganesha partially concealed behind a marble statue of Emperor Akbar astride a war elephant, brandishing a sword. Irfan peered around the doors, scanning the poolside where the film crew had set up a shoot. A sign by the door prohibited use of the pool for the coming hours.

Nevertheless, many guests had gathered to watch.

After all, this too was an authentic slice of life in Mumbai, the home of Bollywood.

Irfan's eyes narrowed as he spotted Rocky. A make-up artist was brushing the fur around his face, fluffing it up into movie-star handsomeness. The assistant's hand slipped, and he tugged accidentally on the little monkey's hair.

Rocky shrieked and clubbed the poor man across the ear with a leathery paw.

'What the hell are you doing?'

Irfan watched as a heavyset man wielding a bullhorn bore down on the make-up artist. The man wore a safari jacket with the word DIRECTOR stencilled on the back. He put the bullhorn to his lips and roared into the hapless make-up artist's other ear: 'How many times have I told you not to upset him before a shoot!'

'I'm so sorry, sir!' mumbled the make-up artist, holding his hands to his deafened ears.

'Get out of my sight!' yelled the director.

He watched his beleaguered underling scurry away, then bellowed. 'Right! We go in five minutes!'

Exactly five minutes later the director was sitting behind the principal camera, the lighting rigs ablaze, the actors in position.

Having asked one of the crew, Irfan knew that this was one of the film's most critical scenes.

The movie's villain, a foreign spy, had stolen important documents from the government. He was now meeting with his handler in the Grand Raj Palace. Unbeknownst to him, Rocky's owner, a suave secret agent, had been deployed by the Indian security services to recover the documents. But the hero had been put out of commission, and it was now up to Rocky to save the day.

Again.

This was Rocky in the role of a primate James Bond, the third in a very successful franchise. In this pivotal scene, the villain, being chased by undercover agents, was due to burst into the swimming pool area – where a barbecue was taking place – and race for the doors on the far side. However, halfway through his mad dash, Rocky was to leap on him from behind, clap his paws over his eyes and send him hurtling into the pool.

Another evil plot foiled courtesy of the subcontinent's most dynamic monkey movie star.

Irfan had other plans.

He hefted the wooden catapult in his hands. He was a master with the weapon, and could hit the eye of a pigeon from ten yards. 'I'll teach you to bully my friend,' he muttered, as he fitted a small rubber ball into the leather pouch.

On the set a hush had descended . . . and then a voice called out 'Action!'

The actors playing hotel guests milled around the pool, their voices rising in conversation, as the director's rig moved slowly along a dolly track. Suddenly, the main doors to the pool deck burst open, and a tall, broad-shouldered man in a black tux clattered into the space. He stood, breathing heavily, clutching a leather attaché case, and looked around wildly. Loud voices rang out from behind him.

Cursing, he charged forward, pushing a well-dressed man and woman out of his way and into the pool. The woman shrieked, and now screams echoed from around the pool as the man plunged his way through the crowd.

And then, a flash of fur . . . and now Rocky was on the fleeing villain's back.

Irfan raised his slingshot and unleashed his projectile.

A satisfying twang accompanied the rubber ball as it speared across the pool and struck Rocky on the back of the head. The monkey yelped and fell off the actor's shoulders, directly onto the flaming coals of the barbecue.

Instantly, the langur leapt up, shrieking at the top of his lungs.

'Oh my God!' someone shouted. 'He's on fire!'

Irfan blanched.

It was true – Rocky *was* on fire!

He could only watch in horror as the little monkey bounced around by the side of the pool, slapping away at his burning waistcoat.

A blur of grey shot past Irfan.

Seconds later, Ganesha reached the hapless monkey, wrapped his trunk around his flailing tail and bundled into the pool.

Elephant and monkey vanished beneath the blue surface.

More screams echoed in the night.

And then Ganesha's trunk appeared above the water, dragging the monkey to the surface.

One of the actors leapt in and fished Rocky out of the pool, setting him down on the tiles. A crowd instantly gathered around the stricken langur.

Ganesha, meanwhile, remained in the pool, only his trunk protruding above the water.

Irfan dived in, and swam out to the little elephant. He ducked his head and held his face next to Ganesha's, a foot below the water. Ganesha's eye rolled up at him, but the elephant's efforts were engaged in holding his trunk up like a snorkel.

Irfan surfaced, and looked around desperately. He needed help. Ganesha couldn't keep his trunk up for ever.

'Help!' he shouted. 'We need to get Ganesha out of the pool!'

'That elephant is going to drown!' shouted a female voice. 'Someone do something!'

Ten minutes later, the fire service arrived.

And shortly after that, Poppy and Chopra reached the pool in a breathless rush.

Chopra listened patiently to the deputy assistant general manager, Pillai, as he explained how the hotel had had to call out the fire service to rescue Ganesha from the pool, winching him out using a crane on the back of a fire truck.

A loud round of applause had accompanied Ganesha's emergence from the water.

'Your elephant risked his life to save Rocky's,' said Pillai. 'It was the most courageous thing I have ever seen!'

'He is a brave boy,' said Poppy, giving Ganesha a hug. The little elephant gave a soft bugle. All things considered, he seemed none the worse for wear.

'However,' said Pillai, his tone turning stern, 'the incident would not have occurred in the first place if it were not for your boy here.' He pointed at Irfan, who was sitting huddled in a bath towel, staring at his feet. 'I am afraid that the director of the movie is considering pressing charges. Not only have you ruined his shoot, but your son's actions almost cost the life of his star. Thankfully, the fire only caught Rocky's waistcoat, and he has escaped permanent injury. But the mental scars . . .' Pillai shuddered.

Chopra turned to Irfan. 'Why did you do it?'

Irfan continued to stare at the ground.

'Irfan, I have always told you that the only acceptable course of action – in any situation – is the truth. That is what I expect from you now.'

Irfan looked up, tears in his eyes. 'I wanted to stop him from bullying Ganesha,' he blurted. 'I never meant to hurt him.'

Chopra sighed. 'Come on,' he said.

Together, they made their way through the hotel to Rocky's suite.

Here they found the room packed with the star's entourage, including his chief minder – the beautiful young woman Chopra had assumed was a film star. Her name was Shreya and she listened quietly as Chopra explained the situation. 'I think I understand what has happened,' she said, eventually. 'Three years ago, Rocky starred in a movie where elephants were involved. In one of the scenes he was supposed to ride on the back of an elephant. Unfortunately, for some reason, this elephant went into a rage that day, and stampeded off into the city. Poor Rocky somehow became trapped in the elephant's headdress and couldn't jump off. It was three hours later before we could rescue him, and by that time all the bouncing around had broken nearly every bone in his little body. Ever since that day he has harboured a hatred of elephants.' She gave Ganesha a sympathetic smile. 'Come with me.'

She led them into the master bedroom, where Rocky was sitting in a large padded cot strewn with fruit. As he saw Ganesha he stood up on his hind legs, nostrils flaring, teeth bared.

Shreya began to speak to him, supplementing her words with hand signals. Chopra caught the word 'friend'.

Finally, the monkey seemed to understand.

He looked at Ganesha through his black-button eyes, then extended a paw.

Ganesha glanced at Chopra, then extended his own trunk.

'There,' said Shreya, giving a delighted clap. 'Friends! What a wonderful story this will make. And you don't have to worry about the director pressing charges. He's a bit of a blowhard, but now that Ganesha and Rocky are friends he wouldn't dare upset him by taking things any further.'

Chopra's phone rang.

It was Homi.

He excused himself and stepped out of the room.

'Radhika Sen,' said Homi. 'Born in 1958 in Maharashtra. She qualified as an MBBS at the B.J. Medical College in Pune with top grades. Then, surprisingly, went to practise back in her native village, a place called Ramgarh, out in Chimboli. She died in 1986, a car accident.'

Chopra breathed silently down the phone. 'Family?'

'Well, she never married, and no children, not officially anyway. Next of kin records cite an older brother, Gajendra Sen, resident of Ramgarh.'

'Thank you,' said Chopra, and ended the call.

He looked back and saw that Irfan, Ganesha and Poppy were all engaged with the monkey.

A coldness settled into the pit of his stomach.

He knew that tomorrow he would go to Ramgarh.

He could only hope that what he would find there might bring him closer to the truth behind Hollis Burbank's death.

POPPY RETURNS TO FIRST PRINCIPLES

Early the next morning, not long after her husband had left on the errand she knew would occupy him for much of the day, Poppy found herself back in Anjali Tejwa's bridal suite.

She had awoken with a renewed sense of purpose.

In part this was due to the conversation she had had with Chopra the previous evening, following the incident with Irfan. Although they had not resolved things completely – she still felt a simmering anger towards him for his lack of sensitivity regarding their anniversary – she *had* discussed her efforts to help find the runaway bride.

His reaction had been thoughtful, and measured.

Instead of urging her to go to the authorities, he had considered the situation and said to her, simply: 'Go back to first principles. Ask yourself why she has left. What is she hoping to achieve? What is her real motive in all this? Usually, when I am stuck on an investigation, I go through everything that I have discovered again, with the finest-tooth comb. I look for that one piece of information that doesn't quite fit.'

Poppy had heeded her husband's advice.

She had gone over everything she thought she knew about Anjali's disappearance, writing each item down on a notepad, as she had often seen Chopra do. When this failed to reveal anything significant, she had returned to Anjali's room. Something was nagging away at her, tickling the back of her mind . . .

She stood in the bathroom, thoughtfully staring at the tub.

Nothing.

She walked back out into the bedroom.

Huma Dixit, whom she had awoken for the room key, hugged herself by the bed as she watched Poppy circle the suite.

Finally, she stopped in front of the wardrobe.

The little alarm bell inside her had begun to ring loudly. It was something she had seen the last time she had searched Anjali's possessions.

But what?

As she began to rifle, once more, through the missing bride's paraphernalia, Poppy found her thoughts drifting back to the matter of her own upcoming anniversary. She had realised, soon after speaking with her husband the previous evening, that it wasn't so much the fact that the celebration she had planned hadn't gone to, well, plan; it wasn't even that Chopra was both indisposed and not particularly engaged . . . The realisation had come to her that it was the event itself that was the source of her disquiet.

Milestone. Landmark.

Words that had settled inside her like lead weights, making her feel as if she had completed some sort of marathon. She almost felt obliged to hurl her weary body over an imaginary finish line.

Yet this was exactly the opposite of how she wished to feel!

She had always been a creature of spontaneity. This anniversary was simply a joyful marker, a sign of the wonderful years she and Chopra had shared. When had the whole thing turned into such a gruelling—?

She stopped.

She had been searching Anjali's valise, going over the bundle of receipts and papers where she had discovered the travel itinerary, the itinerary that now appeared to have been planted by Anjali to throw them off the scent. In her hand was the receipt from the tailor called Lightning Lala.

There was something incongruous about the receipt, something she hadn't picked up on before . . .

And then she had it.

She stood up from the bed, held the receipt out to Huma. 'What do you see?'

The girl examined the little slip of paper. 'It's just another tailoring receipt. Anjali did a ton of shopping for the wedding. So what?'

'Look at it again.'

Huma's brow furrowed as she scrutinised the receipt once more . . . and then her expression dissolved into surprise. 'Oh.'

'Yes,' said Poppy, triumphantly. 'Exactly!'

IN THE VILLAGE OF RAMGARH

The journey to the village of Ramgarh would take at least three hours. As a consequence, Chopra had set off early, soon after dawn had broken over the city.

Before leaving he had checked on Ganesha, downstairs in his garden 'suite'.

Since his heroics of the previous evening he had become the centre of attention. Chopra hoped it hadn't gone to his young ward's head – he knew how much the little elephant enjoyed the limelight.

He found Ganesha dozing beside a mound of fruit and assorted foodstuffs. The offerings included, incongruously, a basket of fresh fish.

Elephants, as far as he knew, did not eat fish.

The little elephant had a contented smile on his face, dreaming his elephant dreams.

Chopra patted him on the head. 'Do you know what Gandhi said, young man? "The best way to find yourself is to lose yourself in the service of others." You are truly his disciple.'

Ganesha stirred, and passed his trunk dreamily over Chopra's face.

'I wish I could take you with me,' he murmured. 'But I think Poppy needs you more than me right now.'

Chopra drove his Tata van out of Mumbai via the Eastern Freeway, then over the Vashi Bridge, and onto the Mumbai–Pune highway. He made good time through Panvel and Rasayani, slowing down only as he ascended the low-lying mountain pass of the Bhor Ghat into the tourist town of Lonavala. At this elevation, the air was cooled by a rare freshness, and Chopra found himself rolling down the windows and allowing the breeze to strike his face, ruffling his moustache.

By the time he had descended down into the Deccan plain, the temperature had climbed back into the low thirties.

It was going to be another sweltering day.

About an hour out from Pune, he left the highway and struck out northwards, passing fields of flowing wheat, their tops waving sinuously in the morning sun. Bullocks stood around, mired in low-lying pools of water, resembling postmodern sculptures. Rural women swayed through fields of lush grass, clay pots at their hips.

Thirty minutes later, he arrived at the village of Ramghar, situated on the banks of the Indriyani River.

Chopra parked his van on the outskirts of the village – in reality, a small town now – then walked inwards, passing a curious goatherder steering his flock towards the river. A group of boys tugging at a kite paused to watch him go by. A number of old men, with the seamed, leathery faces of those who worked outdoors, sat beneath a peepal tree, puffing away on hookahs.

Chopra approached them, and asked directions to the home of Gajendra Sen.

Sen's home was a brick and thatch dwelling in a crowded lane in the centre of the village.

The door was flung open, but Chopra knocked anyway.

A small boy in a white shirt and blue shorts, with a school satchel on his back, peered up at Chopra in curiosity. 'Hello.'

'Hello,' said Chopra. 'I am looking for Gajendra Sen.'

'You mean Grandfather,' said the boy. 'He is in the bathroom. Do you know how I know?'

'No,' said Chopra.

'Because he is singing. He always sings in the bathroom.' The child grinned.

A woman materialised behind the boy. She was in her late twenties, Chopra guessed, dressed in a faded sari, hair pulled back in a bun. 'Yes?' she said, her expression quizzical.

Chopra explained that he was here to see Gajendra Sen.

The woman hesitated, then invited him inside.

The home was compact, three rooms, including the bathroom.

Chopra was parked at a rickety wooden table. He looked around the room. The cracked plaster. The low ceiling. A blast of incense from a small shrine in the corner. And, taking pride of place beside the shrine, the garlanded photograph of a young woman.

Radhika Sen.

She seemed to stare out into some unfathomable distance, a future only she could see.

The woman offered him tea, which he declined. The child sat beside him, wolfing down a breakfast of sanja, a spiced semolina mixture, served with coriander and yoghurt, eyes glued to a small TV.

When Gajendra Sen finally entered the room, towelling his hair, he stopped and stared at the visitor. He was a tall, lean man with greying hair, rheumy eyes and a whiskery moustache, wearing a loose cotton shirt and dhoti.

Chopra stood. 'My name is Chopra. I have some questions regarding the death of your sister, Mr Sen. Radhika.'

It was as if he had physically struck the man.

Gajendra Sen reeled backwards, the towel falling from his grasp. He blinked rapidly, seemingly on the verge of fleeing.

Finally, he stumbled forward, and fell into a seat at the table.

In the bedroom Chopra heard the woman rattling the doors of a steel wardrobe. The TV droned on. The sounds of a pair of men chattering as they passed by drifted in from the alley.

'I knew you would come one day,' said Sen eventually. His voice was hollow, his gaze fastened to the table's pitted surface.

'I am not here to cause you distress,' said Chopra. 'I am merely searching for the truth. A man has died, a man your sister knew many years ago. I am trying to determine if his death has anything to do with his past.'

Sen said nothing. He seemed truly stricken, and Chopra knew that there was something, some hidden truth that sought to peck its way out from inside him. His journey had not been in vain.

'How did Radhika die?'

A great sob erupted from Sen, shocking the detective. He watched as the man dissolved into racking tremors of grief, a thrashing anguish. The woman rushed to his side. 'Father, what is the matter?' She glared at Chopra. 'Who are you?'

Sen continued to weep. Finally, he ran a sleeve over his eyes, got to his feet and looked down at his grandson, who was staring up at him with an expression of astonishment. Chopra doubted the boy had ever seen his grandfather in such a state before.

'Pratima, please take Piyush to school.'

'But—'

'Do it now! I must talk to this man. Alone.'

Chopra waited as the woman finished readying her son for school.

At the door, she turned and gave Chopra a last suspicious look. The boy waved at him, then frowned. 'Please don't make Grandfather cry any more. It is not his fault his singing is so bad.'

'I won't,' promised Chopra.

When the pair had left, Sen went into the bedroom. Chopra heard the sound of a large tin trunk being dragged across the floor and Sen rummaging inside it.

Sen returned, and set down a steel lockbox on the table. 'Everything you need to know is in there,' he said.

Chopra hesitated, then reached for the box, but Sen stopped him. 'But first there are some things I must show you.'

THE FASTEST TAILOR IN ALL OF INDIA

Once upon a time Bombay had been the textile capital of the nation, with more than a hundred mills clustered around midtown, employing a quarter of a million labourers. This was the era of the local tailor, when thousands of workshops catered to the whims of both poor and rich, Indian and British. In the decades since those heady days, the mills had vanished, and the arrival of the ready-made garment industry had decimated the tailoring trade. A brand-conscious younger generation had turned their backs on personally crafted clothing in favour of fancy labels and swishy trademarks.

And yet there remained outposts of sartorial resistance in the city, tailors who had not only survived, but continued to thrive.

For there would always be those, in a place such as Mumbai, who preferred the personal attentions of a genuine craftsman, someone who could be relied upon to create something *just so*.

The Lightning Lala tailor's shop was located close to the Grand Raj Palace in a quiet corner of Cuffe Parade, fronted by centuries-old cobblestones and a bright facade with a cut-out of a plump and happy-looking tailor standing beside the door. The sign proclaimed: 'Lightning Lala: The Fastest Tailor in All of India.'

Poppy entered to find a brightly lit showroom, a long marble counter running down one side.

Behind the counter, racked from floor to ceiling, were bolts of cloth of all colours and patterns: cottons from Gujarat, block prints from Jaipur, prismatic silks from the south, brocades from Benares. As she looked on, a tailor plucked a roll from the shelving and, with a magician-like flourish of the fingers, unreeled an embroidered crêpe silk fabric onto the counter. The customer – a buxom, older woman with designer sunglasses perched in her hair – seemed unimpressed. 'You call that silk?' she said, with the bass-mouthed firmness of someone who intended to get a bargain even if it killed her. 'I've seen better silk on my maid's underclothes.'

'Welcome, madam!'

Poppy turned to find a reedy young man swaying before her, grinning invitingly. 'How may we help you today?' He took a deep breath. 'We can make for you sari, kurta, salwar kameez, blouse, trousers, jacket suit, skirt, miniskirt, formal dress, summer dress, party dress, evening dress, ball gown, churidaar, lehenga choli. We can make traditional design, modern design, Italian cut, French cut. We can do all customisation that your heart desires: imported fabrics, wool lining, box pleats, side pleats, split yokes, double darts, sweep cut, straight cut, V-cut, high neckline, plunge cut—' He stopped, purple in the face, as Poppy held up a hand.

'I am looking for a girl,' she said, holding out a picture of Anjali Tejwa. 'She came into your store for a tailored outfit.'

The young man, who had been holding his breath, exhaled in disappointment. 'In that case, I must take you to Mr Lala.'

Kashibhai Lala turned out to be a small, round, avuncular man, with bottle-bottom glasses and a tape measure slung around his neck like a stethoscope.

He took one look at Poppy and reeled off a list of numbers.

With a momentary astonishment, she realised that they were her exact physical measurements.

Lala smiled at her. 'It is a skill I learned from my grandfather. I can tell a person's measurements just by looking at them.'

Lightning Lala – Mumbai's self-proclaimed quickest tailor – had been around for five decades, Poppy learned.

His ancestors had been tailors in what was now Pakistan. Following the upheaval of Partition, they had moved down into Mumbai with nothing but the shirts on their backs and the magic in their fingers.

Poppy explained her errand.

She showed Lala the receipt she had discovered in Anjali's valise. The receipt said: *One gentleman's outfit, Rs 3800/-*.

That was the tiny discrepancy, the one piece of information that didn't fit . . . Why would Anjali buy a *gentleman's* outfit? It couldn't be for Gautam, a man she didn't even wish to marry. So why?

'I remember her,' said Lala, and reeled off another set of measurements. 'I tend to recall people by their statistics,' he added, apologetically. 'It was not an unusual request. We have many contracts with big organisations for such outfits.'

'I'm sorry, but I don't know what you mean,' said Poppy. 'Exactly what sort of *outfit* did Anjali buy?'

'I can show you,' said Lala. 'Nowadays, you see, we take a photograph of every piece of clothing we produce and put it onto our computer. My daughter's idea.' He sighed. 'In truth, she runs the business now. I suppose it is useful, as a catalogue of our work. Of course, in the old days, the only catalogue I needed was up here.' He tapped his forehead.

Poppy followed Lala to a computer, then watched him fumble with it.

Eventually, an image appeared on the screen.

She stared at the garment. 'Oh,' she murmured. 'Now *that* I did not expect.'

A TERRIBLE ACCIDENT

They drove along the banks of the Indriyani River, sun dappling the slow-moving water, bullocks wading in the shallows.

Fifteen minutes out from the village Chopra, guided by Sen, steered the Tata van over a narrow stone bridge.

On the far side, they stayed close to the river and then, ten minutes later, turned north along a rutted track that Chopra could see had once been an asphalted access road, now pitted and overrun by weeds.

The road curled behind a screen of trees, their crests flamed by the sun.

Beyond the trees, Chopra brought the van to a halt.

For facing him was an abandoned industrial complex, a collection of derelict buildings, steel unit structures and giant piping arrays. The plant had clearly fallen into ruin, racked by years of neglect, eaten away by rust and overrun by vegetation. A crimson, crackling heat seemed to radiate from the metallic structures.

The entire complex was surrounded by a rusted chain-link fence.

A large signboard stood beside the front gate – but the sign itself had been painted over in black.

Chopra's intuition kicked in. 'Fermi Engineering,' he said.

'Yes,' confirmed Sen. 'This was Fermi Engineering. It was too costly to dismantle, so they just removed anything that could identify it.'

'Why?' said Chopra. 'What happened here?'

For a moment, Sen didn't answer. A crow cawed in the rustling silence. Clouds spun across the sky. 'There is one more thing I must show you.'

They drove a further fifteen minutes along the river, a gentle breeze at their backs.

When they stopped again, it was at another derelict site.

This time, however, the ruins were of a village set by the riverbank. A fire appeared to have raged through the village; what remained of the dwellings – the remnants of brick walls – was blackened and burnt.

'Come,' said Sen.

He led the former policeman into the village.

With each step, Chopra felt the silence wind itself around his throat. There was a distinct texture to the air here, stagnant and motionless. Each breath felt as if he were choking on ashes. Dust devils spun over the parched earth; dry grass crackled underfoot. Time seemed to slow down, flow more slowly around them. He glanced up, saw a hawk floating on an air-pole, a stark sentinel framed against the sun's glare.

The silence pricked the back of his neck and made him feel ill at ease. He had attended untold crime scenes in his time, and had heard colleagues talk of the numen of a place, a spiritual essence that was the residue of a ghastly crime.

If such a thing existed, then it pulsed brightly here.

Sen finally stopped in what might once have been the centre of the settlement.

'My sister was a truly good human being. She was the brightest in our family, in our whole village. She topped her school, and, in time, she went to Pune to become a doctor – it was what she had always wanted. When she qualified, it was one of the proudest days of my life. She could have done anything then, become a surgeon in a private hospital, become a wealthy woman. But she chose to return to us. She wanted to use her training to help those who couldn't afford good medical care. She set up her practice back in Ramghar. Everyone loved her. She was a caring, considerate human being, and this translated into her work as a doctor.

'When the Fermi plant was established they hired her as an on-call medical professional. She would go to the plant regularly to give the employees check-ups. If they were ill they visited her at her clinic. That was how she met Roger Penzance and Jared Faulkner.' Sen paused, a strange expression on his features, at once sad and nostalgic. 'Faulkner and my sister fell in love.

'For a while Penzance expressed his desire for her too,

but she recognised him for what he was: a vain, arrogant, unpleasant man. Faulkner was different. I met him many times – he used to come to our home once he began courting Radhika – and I saw that he was honest in his intentions. Their relationship caused much gossip, but my sister was so well liked, and so indifferent to the rumour-mongering, that it had no effect on them.

'And then, one day, the gods, for their own amusement, decided to undo everything they had made.'

Chopra waited, watching Sen gather himself for whatever it was he was struggling to say. Painful memories that he had long suppressed.

'There was an accident. The plant specialised in chemical engineering. Its core products included pesticides, a new range to help increase the yield of India's crops, in line with the government's bold new five-year plan. Feeding the millions. The accident led to a cloud of methyl isocyanate gas being released, just before dawn, on the night of the fifteenth of May 1985. It drifted down to this village, the village of Shangarh. In the space of a few hours just over two hundred people were killed, fifty-nine families wiped out in the blink of an eye . . .' Sen paused. 'Jared Faulkner was working late at the plant that night. He was killed in the accident.'

Chopra felt the revelation almost as a physical blow.

He had begun to suspect that something terrible lay behind the story of Fermi Engineering's sudden closure, but this was beyond even his darkest imaginings.

Two hundred dead! Men, women, and children, decimated in an instant. And yet . . . he racked his memory.

Why could he not recall reading anything about this? Even three decades on, he felt sure, he would have remembered.

Almost as if he had read his thoughts, Sen said: 'There was a cover-up. Fermi Engineering's Indian plant was a joint venture between an American firm and the Maharashtrian state government. The chief minister at the time had staked his personal reputation on the success of the enterprise. This was at a time when the Indian government had undertaken major economic reforms in the country in an attempt to woo foreign capital. They could not afford a PR disaster. And the death toll – in their terms – was insignificant. Two hundred unknown villagers? It was a price they were willing to pay.

'They immediately put out a story of disease – a sudden, fatal outbreak had claimed the lives of an entire village. The chief minister sent in the troops. They sealed off the site and burned the bodies, and then burned the village. They claimed that this was the only way to ensure that the disease did not spread. It was a plausible cover story.

'Of course, it was impossible for something like that to be completely contained. Dissenting voices – friends and family of the villagers – were silenced, first with money and, later, for those who refused to be bribed, with threats. But some voices could not be silenced.

'My sister was one such voice.

'You see, one of the villagers had been out that night, when the gas cloud hit. He was down by the riverbank, relieving himself. He saw the goats tethered by the bank go into convulsions. The approaching gas began to choke him, and so he ran. He didn't stop until he got to our village, and woke up my sister. She tended to him, but by then he too had begun to convulse.

'Moments later he was dead.

'By the time my sister got to Shangarh a military cordon had been set up around the village.

'When she returned it was to discover that the man's body had been taken from our home. I was in the house that night. I saw the men who took him. Soldiers. Thugs. I tried to stop them, but it was useless. They had their orders.

'The days that followed were the hardest of Radhika's life.

'The morning after the incident, she discovered that Jared Faulkner had died. We were told that his death had been an accident, that the details could only be released to his direct family, and that his body had been immediately cremated as per his wishes. We did not know at the time that Faulkner had no family, no one to hound Fermi for an explanation. No one aside from my sister. And, of course, *her* enquiries were met with a wall of silence.

'And then, later, came the revelation that the entire village of Shangarh had been wiped out. By disease, or so we were told.

'But my sister no more believed this than she believed that Faulkner had died in a simple accident. She had observed the young man's symptoms as he lay dying in our home; she knew it was no disease that had killed him.

'And what the authorities didn't know, couldn't have known, was that my sister had already taken a blood sample from him before the soldiers arrived. Working on her hunch, she sent the vial to a clinic in Pune. When the results came back, she realised that everything we had been told was a lie.

'It was no disease that had wiped out two hundred men, women and children in Shangarh. It was a chemical agent, one that the clinic had identified, and which, my sister knew, could be tied to the Fermi plant.

'Radhika thought long and hard about what to do with this information. Going to the authorities was out of the question – it was evident that they had colluded in the cover-up. She considered approaching the media. But she knew that one vial of blood – belonging to an individual who was now ash – would not be evidence enough against the might of the government. And so she began to collect more information. She began to prepare files on all those who had perished in the disaster. She wanted to create a story for the media based on the lives that had been taken. The files are back at my home. I will give those to you too.'

In the sudden quiet following Sen's revelation, it seemed to Chopra that the man had aged, his tall frame stooped and bent, as if the burden of his secret had hollowed him out from within, and now there was nothing left to hold him erect.

'Fermi Engineering found out what my sister was doing. They sent someone to talk sense into her. That someone was Roger Penzance.

'I was there when he came to our home, sat there in his suit, wiping his forehead with a cotton handkerchief. He told us how awful it was that his friend Faulkner had died, how sorry he was for my sister. He broached the subject of the disaster at Shangarh, calling it a matter of "some delicacy". He made it clear that the authorities did not appreciate my sister's attempts to investigate, her attempts to label it as anything other than the official account of an outbreak of disease. He threatened her, in his oblique manner.

'What Penzance didn't know was that Jared Faulkner had predicted the disaster.

'In the months leading up to the accident he had told my sister that Penzance had begun to cut corners. He had signed orders to install cheaper components, to reduce safety protocols, all in a bid to cut down on operating costs. His bonuses were tied to certain budget targets, and he was willing to do whatever it took to meet those targets. He was reckless, and the result of his recklessness was the accident that killed both Faulkner and the villagers of Shangarh.

'My sister snapped. She accused Penzance of all manner of things, of being a murderer, of being the devil himself. She told him that she had everything she needed to bring him to justice, that she would shout it to the world, make certain that he ended up in prison for his crime.

'Penzance panicked. He warned my sister that any rashness on her part would go badly for her.' Sen paused. 'Four hours later my sister was deliberately run off the road. She died in a fireball that consumed her vehicle. Her killers were never found.'

Chopra could almost reach out and touch the man's grief, it was so palpable.

'I saw Penzance just once more,' continued Sen. 'I went to his quarters, a guesthouse near the Fermi plant. I found a haunted man. He had been packing – I knew then that he was planning to flee. He was talking, to himself, couldn't stop. About the chemical accident, about my sister. He didn't admit it outright, but he seemed to think that those responsible for the cover-up were also behind my sister's death. He seemed truly shaken by it. I think that was when I realised that he loved her. Or coveted her, at least. He'd never understood why she chose Faulkner over him. If he felt any guilt at all, it was over my sister's death.

'He thought that her killers might come for him, to ensure that there were no loose ends left to reveal the truth. I don't know what I expected to achieve by confronting him – whatever it was remained unsaid. You see, I didn't have my sister's courage. Her conviction. I had just had my first child. I couldn't risk harm to my family. In the end, I said nothing. I merely listened to Penzance's mumbled explanations, his veiled threats. And then I left.

'In the years since not a day has gone by without me reliving that encounter. I should have done something then, I should have exposed Penzance and Fermi when I had the chance. But I didn't, and that is a regret that will live with me till the day I die.

'I have kept my sister's files. In her lockbox, you will also find a written statement. She knew that her life may have been in danger so she took the precaution of setting down everything she knew, or suspected. I should have given it to the authorities years ago, but I had no wish to raise old ghosts. I am a coward, and that is my shame. But now, you have come, and I pass the burden to you. Do with it as you will.'

On the way back to Sen's home, Chopra reflected on how

guilt affected people in different ways. Some it warped, damaging them beyond repair. For others, like Penzance/Burbank, guilt was a nebulous thing. Burbank had clearly felt a lifelong guilt over the death of Radhika Sen, a woman he may have loved. It explained why he had held on to those photographs. And yet, at the same time, the death of two hundred villagers had not appeared to weigh heavily on his conscience. There was no real way to reconcile this, except to acknowledge that human beings were more complex than most people assumed. In spite of the engineer Ravinder Shastri's belief, even men like Hollis Burbank were not black-and-white caricatures.

Back at Sen's, Chopra watched the old man remove manila files from a steel cupboard, setting them down on his narrow bed. There were fifty-nine files in all, one for each family. 'She spent months putting these together. It wasn't easy. A lot of the information she took from her own medical records. You see, she was the doctor for Shangarh as well as our own village. It's the reason she took it so personally. She knew every one of those people; they were her wards, her extended family.' He paused in the doorway. 'My sister was my hero, Chopra. I only wish that I could have been half the man she was.'

Chopra sat on the edge of the bed and began to go through the files.

Most had very little in them. The names of the family members, birth certificates, sheets from their medical records. Some contained photographs, and these were the most poignant of all.

His eyes lingered on the faces, the expressions of simple

innocence. No idea of what awaited them around the corner.

He went through each file, not knowing what he could learn, other than the reaffirmation of the gossamer fragility of human lif—

He froze.

The file he had picked up lay open on his lap. The name hadn't registered at first, though it was unusual enough. It was the photograph inside, the family's only child. A twenty-year-old son.

Chopra realised, with a sense of shock, that he knew this man. He knew that face.

And in that instant, he understood that he had found someone with the means, motive and opportunity to murder Hollis Burbank.

Someone who had, hitherto, not even entered into his suspicions.

Chopra shoved the remaining files into a bag, picked up the lockbox and, with a promise to keep Sen updated, raced for his van.

He had to get back to Mumbai as soon as possible.

'We can't really afford this suite, but at a wedding like this, appearances are everything.' Big Mother sighed and wheeled her chair away from the mullioned window overlooking the sea.

She stopped glumly in front of Poppy.

Ganesha trotted forward and ran his trunk over the chair's wheels. The little elephant was inordinately fascinated by the contraption.

'So Anjali had a uniform tailored for herself, a uniform worn by the staff here at the hotel? What does it mean?'

'One of two things,' replied Poppy. 'Either the uniform was simply to ensure that Anjali could walk out of the hotel in disguise with no danger of being recognised . . .'

'Or?'

'Or, she is still here.'

Big Mother nodded glumly, as if she had expected this. 'It makes no sense. Why would she engineer an escape, only to stay here?'

'I'm not sure,' admitted Poppy. 'As you said earlier, Anjali is conflicted. She wants to do the right thing by her family, and yet she feels it may not be the right thing for *her*. And so, perhaps, she wishes to stay close by, to keep an eye on what is happening. Personally, I think she is judging the reaction of Gautam's family . . . and her own.'

'And based on our reaction she will either return or . . .?'

Poppy shrugged. 'I do not know, Big Mother. Only Anjali can answer that.'

Huma Dixit, standing beside Irfan, spoke up. 'She always used to say to me how ridiculous being a royal in modern India was. Nawabs and princes, maharanis and princesses, with their silly airs, their feuds, their jaded pageantry. Stripped of wealth and land, the noble families are just puffed-up goldfish in a bowl. At least, that's what Anjali thought.'

Anger flashed in Big Mother's eyes. She seemed about to

retort, but then thought better of it. She sighed. 'My granddaughter always was bright. Yes, it's true that we royals have been revealed as having feet of clay. But there is still a role for us, even in this modern India of yours. The future may not belong to us, but the past most assuredly does. Love us or loathe us, the royal dynasties of India have shaped this country's heritage. We connect what you are today to what you once were. And that has to mean something or what is the point of anything?' She rested a hand on the head of the inquisitive elephant calf before her. Ganesha responded with a soft bugle. 'What must we do next?'

'I have an idea,' said Poppy. 'Please come with me. We need to see a man who values the past as much as you do.'

WHEN GUEST IS NOT GOD

'Dashputra is an unusual name,' said Chopra. 'Unusual enough to make me take a second look.'

He had arrived back at the hotel, parked his van and made his way directly to the general manager's office. He found the man alone, stealing a moment for himself in another hectic day, a steaming cup of chai set before him, calming music floating in the background.

That calm was shattered as Chopra set down the file he had taken from Sen's home, opened it and revealed the photograph that had brought him back to Mumbai in such haste.

A photograph of a young man called Tanav Dashputra.

Chopra's finger rested on the image. 'You grew up in Shangarh. Your parents were killed in 1985, in the tragedy. You *knew* Hollis Burbank, or of him, all those years ago, when he called himself Roger Penzance.'

Dashputra's eyes seemed to contract, then expand.

He exhaled slowly, and set down his tea.

His hand shook.

He seemed to consider rising to his feet, but his body refused to cooperate and he stayed motionless in his chair.

Finally, he spoke. 'I should have died that night. With my parents, my friends, my village. But I was away, studying in Pune. I, the shining light of Shangarh! The one youngster to escape the cycle of poverty and hopelessness. When I heard what had happened I rushed back, but it was too late. They had already burned the bodies, burned the village. They told me it was disease, a fatal outbreak. That there was nothing else they could have done.

'It was weeks later when Sen, our doctor, told me that they were lying to us. Told me her theory. That the official explanation of disease was a fabrication. That my parents – my entire village – had been killed by an accident at the Fermi plant. A chemical leak. And that they had decided to cover the whole thing up. I had no reason not to believe her. And so I went to the plant to demand explanations.

'I met with Penzance. And I was told, in no uncertain terms, that if I persisted in my attempts to question the official version of events, I would be held accountable. It was beyond his control, he said. Out of his hands. He *threatened* me. And then he offered me compensation, enough for me to swallow the lie, to go away, to complete my studies and never look back.' Dashputra's voice shook with self-loathing. 'And so I made a choice. I took the money. I was young, and ambitious. I thought I knew enough about the world to understand that I couldn't change what had happened. I couldn't bring those responsible to justice. This was India, and I was nobody. A lone voice in the darkness.

'So, yes, I took the money, and I went back to Pune. I completed my studies, and I got on with my life. It was the best way I could honour my parents, the sacrifices they had made for me. At least, that's what I told myself.

'Later, when I heard about Sen's death, about how she had been run off the road, I knew that I had made the right decision. That might have been me.' Dashputra's eyes stared into nothingness. 'And yet, do you know what the funny thing is, Chopra? All these long years I have never been able to sleep soundly. They come to me, in my dreams, in my darkest moments, my dead family, my childhood friends. They demand justice. Guilt has eaten away at me, robbed me of peace. I was a coward, and I have died a thousand times for it.'

Chopra stood in silence.

He had seen this so many times. Men wishing to unburden themselves. It was like sticking a pin into a balloon; all he had to do was stand back and watch everything rush out. First Ravinder Shastri. Then Gajendra Sen. And now Dashputra. Bound together by guilt.

'Did you murder Hollis Burbank?'

Dashputra swallowed. 'I recognised him as soon as he entered the hotel. How could I not? His face had changed, but his eyes . . . they were the same. Cold, indifferent. I wrestled with my conscience. Should I confront him? What difference would it make now? On the night that he died, I could stand it no longer. I was staying at the hotel anyway, as is my usual practice during particularly busy periods. And the auction was the most important occasion we have had in recent years. I couldn't sleep. I had to do something.

I might never get another chance. And so I went to Burbank's room.

'When I got there, I knocked, but he didn't answer. I let myself in with a master key.' He stopped, his eyes glazed.

'Go on,' murmured Chopra.

'He was already dead. Lying on the bed, staring at the ceiling with a knife sticking out of his chest . . . Do you know what I felt then? At that precise instant? Anger. Rage. At the fact that he had escaped. That he had managed to avoid the confrontation I had planned. I stood there, the fury building and building. It was like a fever in my brain! I couldn't just leave, not without some acknowledgement from him of what he had done, what Fermi had done.

'I looked around, and saw a pot of paint and a brush on an easel. I took them – I had just enough sense left to use a handkerchief to handle them, to avoid leaving my fingerprints – went into the bathroom and painted those words on the wall. I AM SORRY. I needed there to be an apology, even if I was the only one who understood it. I cannot explain to you what it means, I cannot explain why I did that, but it is the truth. I didn't kill him, but there are moments when I wish I had.'

Chopra considered Dashputra's testimony.

Did he believe the man? All those years of rage, rage at Fermi, at Burbank, at his own cowardice. It was enough to propel a man to violence, even murder.

'You say you used your keycard to enter Burbank's room? I went through the computerised records. I don't recall such an entry.'

Dashputra had the decency to look away. 'You are right, of course. The police examined the system log for precisely that reason. But before I gave them access, I logged in and deleted that entry. I have a master override.' He blinked. 'I know it looks bad, but I swear to you, I did not kill Burbank.'

As he gazed at Dashputra's sweating face, Chopra could only guess as to how much truth there was in the hotel manager's confession. If he *was* innocent, it would mean that Chopra was back to square one, with Dashputra just another in the gallery of suspects.

He sighed.

He supposed that when Tripathi had given him the assignment even his old friend hadn't realised just how convoluted the trail would prove to be.

And yet if his career had taught him one thing it was this: there was always a way through the maze to the truth that invariably lay at its heart.

'We need your help,' said Poppy. 'You know the hotel better than anyone. You know the staff.'

Aryan Ganesham, the Grand Raj Palace's head butler, stood erect, alone in the staffroom, head tilted to one side as if listening to a music that no one else could hear.

Finally, he spoke. 'Why do you wish to find her? Forgive me,' he went on. 'I do not wish to seem impertinent. But I have seen a great many things in my time at the Grand Raj. I was here, a young boy shining shoes on the street outside, when India declared her independence and crowds gathered beneath the Gateway, Nehru's "tryst with destiny" speech blaring from loudspeakers affixed to the hotel's facade. I was here a year later when Gandhi was shot, and guests poured out of the hotel in grief and shock, an outpouring of sorrow the likes of which I have seen neither before nor since. I was here when Indira Gandhi declared her Emergency, and the hotel was locked down, a fortress in a time of trouble. I was here when the Ayodha riots ignited, and the streets ran red with blood, and people ran into the hotel for sanctuary.' A soft smile played across his lips, like the echo of a distant memory. 'The Grand Raj has played host to thousands of weddings over the years I have been here. In that time, I have seen the pain and suffering that is often caused in the name of marriage, in the name of tradition and honour.'

Big Mother, her cheeks twitching with irritation, wheeled her chair forward. 'I love my granddaughter. I merely wish to know that she is safe.'

'Be that as it may,' said Ganesham. 'If she has abandoned her own wedding there must be a reason.'

'Are you married, sir?' snapped Big Mother.

This comment seemed to arrest Ganesham.

Poppy saw the old butler tense. His eyes became faraway, receding into memory. 'Once upon a time there was a woman, young, beautiful, the daughter of a wealthy man. They travelled often to Mumbai, and stayed in a wonderful hotel, the best hotel in the land. This woman was attended, each time she stayed there, by a young staff member who made it his concern to ensure that her every whim was catered to. Though it was not his place, over the years they became friends. And then, one day, she told him that she was due to be married. Her father had arranged everything. It was to happen in that very hotel. The young man nodded to himself. Yes, of course. It was only fitting. A fine wedding for the finest woman he knew. He took personal charge of the occasion – nothing was left to chance.

'Just hours before the wedding, the woman summoned him to her room.

'She was dressed in her bridal finery – he had never seen anything so beautiful. This woman, this ethereal creature more precious to him than anything else in the world, told him that she loved him. That, if he were to merely say the word, she would give up everything for him, and they would make a new life, just the two of them, cocooned from the world by their happiness.

'The young man smiled. And he bowed, and said, "Madam must not joke. For I am no one. I live only to serve." And then he left, his footsteps taking him quickly away lest she see the pain in his eyes.' Ganesham paused. 'That night, the woman was murdered by her husband in the bridal suite of that magnificent hotel. Perhaps because she told him the truth of her feelings, of her love for another. They say she haunts the hotel still.'

Poppy was stunned.

What grief the human heart was capable of enduring! The thought of lonely Ganesham, the lost love of his life; it was almost too much to bear.

The butler smiled. 'It is just a fairy tale,' he said, his voice strangely hollow.

But Poppy knew that it was not.

The butler turned to Big Mother. 'I will help you find your granddaughter,' he continued, briskly now. 'So that we can be assured of her safety.'

'You must search the hotel again,' said Big Mother. 'This time go room to room.'

Ganesham tilted his head to one side. 'That we cannot do. The guests must not be alerted to this regrettable situation. Discretion is our watchword at the Grand Raj. Besides, we have fifteen hundred staff here, with at least five hundred in the hotel at any one time, spread over eleven floors, three basements and extensive grounds. This is not a problem that can be solved with brute force.'

'Then what do you propose we do?' harrumphed Big Mother.

'There *is* another way . . .' said Ganesham.

WHO IS K.K.?

Chopra sat in the Grand Raj Palace's business suite, the satchel of files and the lockbox at his feet, his notebook open on the glass coffee table before him. A majestic portrait of Peroz Khumbatta, in royal phento turban, buttoned-up coat and frilly-cuffed shirt, looked down at him, his great winged eyebrows gathered together in seeming opprobrium.

Why haven't you solved this yet? the great patriarch of Indian commerce appeared to be saying.

Chopra had no answer.

Hours earlier he thought he had found the solution.

He had diligently followed the trail deep into the past; had uncovered a motive and, with it, the man he thought must surely be the true architect of Burbank's death. But now, having spoken with Dashputra, he could not be certain. By rights, he should hand the man over to Tripathi, let the law take its course.

Yet something was preventing him from doing precisely

that, the little voice in his ear that had been his companion for more years than he cared to remember.

But, if not Dashputra, then who?

The suspects marched past his eyes, like troops at a military parade: the businessman Avinash Agnihotri, the sculptor Layla Padamsee, her fiery husband Adam Padamsee and, perhaps, even the artist Shiva Swarup. All with motives of one design or another.

He sighed, recalling the advice he had given to his wife the night before: go back, re-examine everything.

Well, there was nothing else for it . . .

An hour later, he sat back.

There was nothing in his notes that he had missed, nothing to offer a new thread to pull on. He had reviewed the evidence, reviewed each individual's testimony. He had re-examined the information to hand, searching for that flash of insight.

Nothing.

For some reason, the image of Burbank stretched out on his bed kept intruding into his thoughts. The businessman's glazed eyes, the splash of blood on his white bathrobe. He felt, once again, that earlier vague unease. There was something attempting to flag down his attention . . . Exasperated, he let the thought sink back into the murk.

His gaze fell on the lockbox.

In his haste to return from the village of Ramgarh he had not yet looked inside. There had been no need. Gajendra Sen had told him that it contained a letter from his sister, testifying to her suspicions about the true nature of the disaster that had wiped out the village of Shangarh.

Chopra did not need to read the letter to know that he believed Sen.

He lifted the lockbox onto the table, fumbled for the key Sen had given him and opened it.

No scream from beyond the grave.

Just a brackish mustiness, a dry exhalation.

Methodically, he went through the contents.

Firstly, the written statement from Radhika Sen, sealed in an envelope. He opened the envelope, and scanned the letter.

It was pretty much as Gajendra Sen had said, set down in his sister's words. A chronicle of corruption that had led to the deaths of so many innocents. As he read the letter a cloud of sadness enveloped Chopra. In the deliberate handwriting, the fevered sentences, he sensed a kindred spirit, a woman for whom the battle for truth and justice meant everything.

But in India, the truth did not always set you free.

Sometimes it got you killed.

He finished the letter, set it to one side, then examined the remaining contents.

Papers from Fermi Engineering, purchase orders for components, service orders, engineering schematics, all signed by Roger Penzance. The cutbacks and changes that had led to the accident. Smuggled out by Jared Faulkner and given to his lover Radhika Sen. Faulkner must have known that the plant was untenable; he must have felt the pressure of his own complicity in going along with the changes. He had shared those concerns with Sen, his lover, his confidante.

In the end, it had been for naught.

The worst had happened, and people had died, including Faulkner himself.

A cluster of photographs lay in the box, wrapped in an elastic band. Photos of the site, both internal and external. Photos of key personnel, their names marked in black pen by, presumably, Sen—

Chopra froze.

At the bottom of the box was a drawing. A charcoal sketch, some ten inches on a side. Three figures, clearly identifiable as Penzance, Faulkner and Sen. An angry black cross had been drawn over Penzance's figure.

And, in the corner of the drawing, the initials K.K.

The incongruity of the find held Chopra rigid for a long time. Something brushed the walls of his chest, causing his pulse to quicken. He reached into his pocket and took out the sketch that had been found hidden inside Hollis Burbank's suitcase.

He compared the two.

There was a clear similarity in the styles. More importantly, the initials were identical.

Chopra took out his phone and dialled Gajendra Sen. 'There is a sketch inside your sister's lockbox. It shows Hollis Burbank – Roger Penzance, I mean – Jared Faulkner and your sister. It is initialled K.K. Who drew this sketch?'

'That? That was an artist from Shangarh. Kunal Karmarkar. He came into my sister's clinic one day with a chest infection. Faulkner was there, visiting her, with Penzance – the man you call Burbank. After she treated him, he confessed he couldn't pay, not that my sister ever charged those who could not afford her help. He insisted on drawing the sketch. It remained very dear to her. It was one of the few images she had of herself and Faulkner.'

'Tell me about him,' said Chopra. 'The artist, I mean.'

'There's not much to tell. I didn't know him well. He grew up in Shangarh, went to study art in Pune for a while. Couldn't find work there so returned. Set up a small studio with a fellow student right here in our village, in Ramgarh. We were bigger than Shangarh, you see, just beginning to grow, a few tourists coming through from Pune. Add to that local commissions, murals, that sort of thing. It wasn't a successful operation. They never had any money. And then, of course, he died. In the chemical accident.'

'Who was the other artist?'

'Him? That's the funny thing. Kamarkar's partner was from my own village, from Ramgarh. He went on to become a famous artist. You've probably heard of him. His name is—'

TRIIIIINNNNNNNNNNNNNGGGG!

The alarm pounded through the hotel, jerking Chopra up from his seat.

Within seconds, a hotel concierge came charging through the door. 'It is the fire alarm, gentlemen,' he said breathlessly. 'Please make your way in an orderly fashion to the exits.'

As the alarm continued to sound throughout the hotel, patrons and staff poured out onto the promenade and the

Gateway of India concourse. Within moments the beggars, fakirs, pickpockets and eunuchs inhabiting the concourse had descended upon the hapless newcomers, as if live victims had been thrown overboard into shark-infested waters. The Grand Raj Palace's security guards strived mightily to hold them at bay, swatting at stray hands reaching for the tailored pockets of well-heeled Europeans, or bodily flinging themselves between the unwanted advances of unwashed beggars upon highly strung American dowagers.

Marshalling the chaos was Aryan Ganesham, the hotel's head butler. He, alone of those around him, seemed calm and unruffled, a sergeant-major exhorting his troops while under heavy fire.

Within short order, the guests and staff had all been accounted for, and stood goggle-eyed as the fire service arrived upon the scene.

Ganesham approached the man in charge, and said, succinctly: 'A false alarm, I'm afraid.'

The fire chief gave the butler a suspicious squint. 'We will still have to check it out.'

'You must do your job.' Ganesham nodded.

He left the fire chief to bark orders at his men, and then went to investigate the staff.

By the time he had made his way through the mass, he was certain.

Anjali Tejwa was not there.

Chopra found Poppy huddled with Irfan, Ganesha, Huma Dixit and the woman who called herself Big Mother.

Irfan's eyes were glowing.

Like most children, he was fascinated by the idea of the fire service and its dashing agents. His elephant companion seemed equally dazzled. It was all Poppy could do to stop them from tearing after the firemen who plunged into the hotel as if it were a towering inferno, instead of the staid old building it had always been.

'Are you okay?' asked Chopra.

'Yes,' said Poppy. She lowered her voice, and said: 'It is not a real fire alarm.'

'What do you mean?'

'What madam means,' said Ganesham, arriving on the scene, 'is that *I* set off the alarm.'

'Why on earth would you do that?' growled Chopra.

'It was the simplest way I could think of to get everyone out of the building and in one place. So that we could search for Anjali Tejwa.'

Quickly, Poppy brought Chopra up to speed on developments.

He shook his head, frowning. This sort of thing did not sit well with the former policeman. He had dealt with enough prank calls at the Sahar police station to make him believe that hanging was too good for those who indulged in such hi-jinks.

'What do we do now?' said Big Mother.

Ganesham glanced up at the hotel. 'Perhaps she has really gone.'

'She wouldn't just vanish,' said Huma. 'I think Poppy

was right. I think she's close by, waiting to see what happens, making up her mind.'

A gloomy silence descended on the group.

Finally, the firemen re-emerged, the fire chief casting around with a disgusted look. Chopra watched the man zero in on the hotel's general manager, and engage in a short, terse conversation, before bellowing at his men.

The fire trucks roared off in a blaze of exhaust smoke. Shortly thereafter, the guests began to file back into the hotel.

Chopra turned to his wife. 'I must get back to my own investigation.'

Poppy was about to reply when Lisa Taylor materialised at her husband's shoulder. 'I'm so glad to see you're okay,' she said.

She was dressed in a pair of shorts and a clingy halter top.

'It was a false alarm,' said Chopra, stiffly.

'Well, I was worried for you,' said Taylor. 'Oh, how are you, Mrs Chopra? Didn't see you there.'

'I am fine,' said Poppy, grinding her jaw.

Taylor faced Chopra with a serious expression. 'I am afraid time has run out. Has there been any progress? My boss is arriving shortly. Unless we can tell him something significant I have a feeling he will bring matters to a close. It is becoming impossible to keep the press at bay any longer. A statement will have to be made. Either suicide or murder. One way or the other, things won't look good for Gilbert and Locke. Is there anything concrete we can tell him?'

'There have been some developments,' said Chopra cagily. 'But I need a few more hours.'

'That is probably all we have,' she said grimly. 'Why don't we meet later, and you can fill me in?'

'I don't—'

'Let's say six-thirty. In our usual place.' With that she turned and strode purposefully off into the hotel.

'Your *usual* place?' said Poppy. Had her voice been any cooler it might have solved the problem of global warming there and then.

'Popp—'

Poppy held up a hand. 'I suggest you get on with it. Six-thirty is not far away.' She turned and stalked off.

Big Mother wheeled her chair forward. 'Your wife is a remarkable woman.'

'Yes,' agreed Chopra, with a sigh. He had no idea what had just happened, but knew, with that innate instinct bred into the male species since the dawn of time, that he had done something wrong.

'It's a shame she is married to such an oaf,' finished Big Mother, with a glare.

She powered her chair past Chopra, almost running over his foot.

He stood there, mouth hanging open, obliquely wondering at the unfairness of it all.

A FAKE ARTIST

The cow was gone.

In the lobby of Shiva Swarup's studio Chopra found cleaners shovelling away another mound of excrement. He guessed that perhaps the manifest symbol of the cosmos had pushed its luck too far.

When he reached Swarup's studio it was to discover the dwarf model sitting in one corner, half-moon spectacles perched on his round nose, reading from an iPad. 'If you're looking for Shiva, he's up on the roof,' he said, peering at Chopra from above his spectacles. 'I get the feeling he's a bit suicidal. Wouldn't surprise me if he jumped.'

'Shouldn't you be trying to stop him?' said Chopra, sternly.

'He's an artist. It's their prerogative to be dramatic. Cut off an ear, leap off a building. Can you imagine how much his work will be worth if he splatters himself all over Marine Drive?'

'You don't sound very sympathetic.'

'I'm a silver linings sort of dwarf,' said the dwarf, smiling grimly.

On the roof terrace Swarup was leaning against the railing, smoking and staring out to sea. Light had fallen out of the sky. The sun was now a blood-red ball, dipping into the ocean, a perfect scene for any amateur painter worth his salt.

He glanced up as Chopra approached.

'Kunal Karmarkar,' said the former policeman, by way of an opening. 'You ran an art studio with him in the village of Ramgarh. Do you remember him?'

Swarup's eyes widened. He looked away. 'Yes. He died. There was an outbreak of disease.'

'That is a lie. He did not die of disease. He died in a chemical accident, an accident caused by a man called Roger Penzance. The man who later became Hollis Burbank. The authorities covered up the incident.'

Swarup turned back. His expression was troubled. 'I-I didn't know. I heard rumours, but they made no sense to me. Why would the government cover up something like that?'

Chopra hesitated. Perhaps Swarup really did not know. 'You left the village after Karmarkar's death, became a famous artist. Your Laughing Indian cycle set you on the path to that fame.' Chopra took out the sketch of the old man found inside Burbank's suitcase. 'But those paintings were copied from *this* sketch. A sketch by Karmarkar. A sketch found in Burbank's possessions after his death. Can you explain that?'

Swarup's expression changed. A haunted look came into his eyes. 'Somehow I knew this day would come,' he said eventually. 'Secrets have a way of working their way to the surface, no matter how deep you bury them.' His face seemed to glow red in the sunset. 'Yes, Kunal was my friend. We met at art school in Pune, realised we lived in neighbouring villages. We decided to set up a little studio in Ramgarh. Kunal met Penzance – the man you call Burbank – at our local doctor's clinic, Dr Radhika Sen. Kunal sketched something for her, and it must have impressed Burbank because later he came calling at our studio. He had a keen interest in art even then. He bought some pieces from us – including that sketch you are holding. Or from Kunal, I should say. He dismissed my work, called it amateurish. I overheard him say to Kunal that he should branch out on his own, that I was "holding him back". But Kunal was loyal, a good friend.

'And then he died. In that tragedy. I heard the rumours, about the chemical leak, but, like most people I decided to believe what the government was telling us. I was an artist, not a revolutionary.

'A few weeks later I went back to live in Pune. I set up a tiny studio, but the well of my inspiration had run dry. I'd spend days just staring at the canvas. Kunal had always been my inspiration. It was true what Burbank had said: he was the one with the talent. I had brought some of his work with me. I told myself it was as a reminder, of my friend. It began to whisper to me. I was slowly starving. Desperate. I needed to paint, I needed something to sell, so that I could eat. And so, yes, I began to copy his work. That's when I painted the Laughing Indian cycle. They were all copied directly from Kunal's sketches. I told myself I was doing it as a tribute to him.

'But it was *my* signature I put onto the canvases.

'And then the strangest thing happened, one of those twists of fate that none of us can explain. A famous art critic was visiting Pune at the time. He stumbled across my studio. For some reason the Laughing Indian paintings fired his imagination. He was the one who recommended me for the internship with Zozé Rebello.' A thin smile played over Swarup's lips. 'You know, he was actually working on *The Scourge of Goa* when I went to stay with him. It was incredible, to watch this master craftsman at work. I remember thinking: if only I could capture a fraction of that genius for myself!

'But, of course, talent is a cruel mistress. You cannot train yourself into the Gift. Nevertheless, I learned something important. In the world of art, talent doesn't matter as much as originality. Anyone can draw sunflowers. Anyone can imitate the doodles of a Jackson Pollock. What matters is that you are the *first*! The Laughing Indian paintings were something new, and they made my reputation. I became successful on the back of another man's genius. But once I had run out of things to copy, once I was left to my own meagre talent, I began to churn out rubbish.

'Rebello quickly realised that I was a fraud, of course. That's why he threw me out.

'In the perverse way of things in this country, that made my reputation, so that whatever else I produced afterwards, no matter how bad it was, simply made me more famous. The simple truth is that I have spent my life as an imposter.' Swarup's voice was hollow.

'Tell me about Burbank,' said Chopra.

'I never really knew him. He came to the studio a couple of times, but it wasn't my work he was interested in. I knew that he worked up at the Fermi plant, but I had no idea he was involved in the chemical accident you claim wiped out Shangarh.

'And then, a month ago, out of the blue, he called me. From America. Told me who he was, how he had left India and changed his identity, created a new life for himself. He didn't tell me why. Just told me that he was coming back, to buy Rebello's painting, a work he had coveted for decades. He told me to make sure I was at the auction. He wanted to see me. He said if I wasn't there he would reveal to the world how I had copied the Laughing Indian paintings from my dead friend.

'And so I came to the auction. And we spoke. He wanted me to paint his portrait. Without charge, of course. He showed me that sketch, the one in your hand. Threatened me with it. The proof that my career was based on a lie. He knew that in the hands of the media that sketch would destroy my reputation, everything I had built over a lifetime. An artist can be forgiven many things, Chopra, but not the blatant theft of another's work.'

'Is that why you killed him? To preserve your secret?'

Swarup shook his hoary head. 'I admit I was stunned,

angry, afraid. At first. I spent the night in the hotel – like the other artists, they'd given me a suite, even though I live in the city. I told Burbank that I would sleep on it, and give him my answer the next day. It was a way of stalling, of buying myself time to think, to bring my whirling emotions under control.

'But then, once I had calmed down, I realised that it wasn't Burbank I was angry with. It was myself. You see, the truth is that I *do* feel guilt over Kunal, over stealing his work, stealing the life of fame and fortune that, by rights, should have been his. It has eaten away at me all these years. Burbank's return merely brought those feelings to a head. His death hasn't changed anything. I don't feel relief that he has gone. The mud that he raked up can never settle again. Everywhere I look I see Kunal's ghost. Everywhere I turn I see the spectre of my own self-loathing.'

'Is that why your dwarf friend thinks you are contemplating suicide?'

'It would be a fitting end for an artist, don't you think?'

'There are better ways to make amends. Use your fame, use your wealth. Help others. Dwelling on a past you cannot change is simply self-indulgence.'

Swarup looked back out to sea. 'What happens now?'

'Now?' said Chopra. 'Now I must decide whether I believe you are innocent of Burbank's murder.'

'And there really is no sign of her?'

Big Mother hesitated. 'No. She is gone.'

Prakashrao Tejwa Patwardhan, Anjali's father, slumped down onto a chair in the grand ballroom, his turban clutched forlornly in his hands. The giant cut-outs had been reinstated, and loomed over them all. 'It's all my fault,' he said. 'I have been a fool. I forced her into this. If I'd been any better at managing our finances, we wouldn't need this marriage.' His round body shook with gusts of anguish.

Big Mother said nothing. It was not her habit to offer false solace. The royals of India had weathered greater tragedies than this. And worse was to come. They would need strong hearts, and iron wills, to thrive in the new world order.

To her surprise, it was Shaktisinghrao, the groom's father, who stepped forward and put a hand on Prakashrao's shoulder. 'I have no daughters,' he said. 'I can only imagine what you are going through. My son's happiness means everything to me. He has reminded me that you too are a father. I am afraid that I have been a boor.'

Prakashrao looked up with genuine surprise in his eyes.

He lifted himself to his feet, coughed and stuck out a hand. 'We have *both* acted like children.'

'On that we can agree,' muttered Big Mother.

'The question is: what do we do next?' said Huma Dixit.

'We must find her,' said Shaktisinghrao. 'Whatever it takes. Ensure that she is safe. Perhaps it is time to inform the authorities.'

'But what about the scandal?' said Prakashrao glumly.

Shaktisinghrao grimaced. 'We will weather it together. Come, let us go and think about what we must say.'

Poppy watched the two men walk away, Big Mother wheeling after them.

Huma sat down. 'I should have done more.'

'You could not have known,' said Poppy.

'She is my best friend.'

'Sometimes it is those closest to us who can most easily conceal their true intentions.'

Huma grimaced, tears brimming at the corners of her eyes. 'I miss her. Her intelligence. Her wit. Her common sense. Even that horrible perfume of hers.'

'Perfume?' said Poppy.

'She used to douse herself in it. Some sort of fancy French scent. You could smell it on her, no matter what she was wearing, even when she took off her clothes.'

Poppy recalled the heady scent surrounding Anjali when they had first met. 'Well, they do say a good perfume never fades—' She stopped.

An idea had streaked through her mind. 'Huma,' she said, her voice suddenly urgent, 'do you have the clothes that Anjali took off in the bathroom? Before she changed into the uniform she'd had made?'

Huma blinked. 'Yes. I put them back in the wardrobe in the bridal suite. Why?'

Poppy looked across the room to where Ganesha and Irfan had their heads buried in an enormous flower display. 'I have an idea,' she said.

THE SECRET IN THE STAPLES

'You stood me up.'

Chopra looked up.

He was back in the business suite, head bent once again to his notes, waiting for the scattered papers to whisper to him, something, anything, a glimmer of inspiration.

The investigation had stalled once more.

He had plenty of suspects, and motives multiplying by the second. And yet, that moment of clarity, that singular insight that was the hallmark of a genuine breakthrough eluded him.

He made as if to stand, but Lisa Taylor waved him back into his seat. She threw herself down onto the sofa before him, and crossed her bare legs. Her blond hair cascaded around her shoulders, and her blue eyes glowed with – what? Anger? Acceptance?

'I apologise,' said Chopra.

She waved a hand at his notes. 'And here's me thinking gentlemen preferred blondes.'

'How did your meeting with your boss go?' said Chopra.

'Oh, the usual. He roared. He slavered. As if all this is somehow my fault.' She shook her head. 'He's old-fashioned, you know? Oxbridge education, father is a peer of the realm. The slightest whiff of scandal sets his ancestors spinning in their family crypts.'

'It is unfair to blame you.'

She spread her hands. 'Quite correct. Which is why I quit.'

Chopra's moustache twitched. 'You left your job?'

'Spectacularly,' said Taylor. 'And, for good measure, I threw my wine in his face. A *very* expensive thirty-year-old Montrachet Grand Cru, I might add. But it was worth it. No one treats me like that, Chopra. I have my dignity.'

An awkward silence passed. 'So what will you do now?' said Chopra eventually.

'I'm not sure. I think I'll travel a bit. Take a break. There'll always be a job waiting for me. The art world is a small place, and there aren't that many around with the sort of skills I have.'

Chopra could well believe it.

'When do you leave?'

'I'm booked on a flight out later tonight.'

He nodded automatically, feeling a sudden inexplicable sense of . . . vacuum.

'I do have one regret though,' said Taylor. 'Not staying around long enough to find out who killed Burbank.' She reached into her bag and handed Chopra her card. As he took it from her, her index finger brushed his knuckles, like a moth fluttering against his skin. 'I would appreciate it if you gave me a call once you know the answer. Or even just because you want to.' She smiled. 'I meant what I said earlier – you really are a most intriguing man.'

She rose to her feet, and Chopra rose with her.

'It's funny, isn't it? How some men just inspire hate? I've known Burbank for years but, other than the superficialities, I never really understood him. Why he was the way he was. Why he went out of his way to make people loathe him. I suppose that's just the nature of the beast, right? Some people are just . . . wrong.' She smiled again. 'At least it makes your job easier. Plenty of people out there who Burbank practically hung up a sign for. Come and get me. I'm here.'

Chopra nodded.

Lisa Taylor was correct in that regard. Whatever Hollis Burbank's many faults, fear wasn't one of them. He was a hated man, he must have known that, but it didn't stop him from baiting those who loathed him.

Taylor checked her watch. 'I have to leave. It has been . . . surreal.' Before he could stop her, she leaned over and pecked him quickly on the cheek. 'I hate goodbyes, so I won't bother saying one.'

He watched her bounce out of the suite, feeling as if somehow the lights in the room had dimmed.

An hour later Chopra was sitting in the Colaba police station opposite Rohan Tripathi.

He had presented his findings and together they had gone over every detail, searching for that vital missing link.

'Well, you're right in that you don't have enough for an arrest.' Tripathi sighed. 'Not one that would stick, at any rate. Though I'd like to haul some of these characters into the station and see how they hold up under *my* questioning.' He sighed again. 'I've stalled Gunaji for as long as I could. Unless you come up with something tangible, or extract a confession in the next couple of hours, we're going to have to go with suicide.' He gave a sad shake of the head. 'Rich people. You'd think they'd be well out of it. Too far above the rest of us to ever get caught up in this sort of thing. I mean, you've dug up everything from a jealous husband to a thirty-year-old blood feud. What happened to simply bumping off a rich man for his money?'

Chopra began to nod, then went very still in his seat.

Tripathi's last words echoed in his mind.

What happened to simply bumping off a rich man for his money?

He suddenly realised that in the linear progression of his investigation there was one thing he had failed to consider. That none of the motives he had examined included the oldest motive of all.

Simple human avarice.

Had he made a critical oversight . . .?

He began to go over everything from the beginning. He examined his notes anew, as Tripathi looked on in bemusement. Was there something here, some tiny shred of evidence that he had missed because he had been looking at the murder only from a specific angle, namely, personal hatred of Burbank?

He lined up his thoughts and meticulously reconstructed the American's final evening.

Burbank had come to India to buy the Rebello, but also to shore up his Indian business venture, Shakti Holdings Ltd. He was a man with a dark past, and yet whatever guilt he may have felt over that past had failed to change his basic character. He was as terrible a human being now as he had been then.

The difference was that he had become exceedingly wealthy.

And a rich man had no need to cultivate enemies. They were part and parcel of being rich.

Burbank had triumphed at the auction. He had had the Rebello moved to his room. He had then attended the after-party, before retiring to his suite late in the evening. He had celebrated by ordering a lavish dinner and relaxed by indulging in his hobby, painting. He had donned a bathrobe – and what was it about that robe that kept nagging at Chopra, a revelation quivering just out of reach?

And then, calmly, he had consumed Valium with his Scotch, and put a knife in his chest?

No. It made no sense.

There was no longer any doubt in Chopra's mind that it was murder.

But who? And why?

He went through his notes again, painstakingly checking each fact.

He came across the itemised list of everything that had

been found at the crime scene. His eyes moved down the list . . .

'Staples,' he breathed.

An idea swam close, then flicked its tail and swam away again.

'What?' Tripathi looked at his old friend as if he'd lost his mind.

'Your initial report says that staples were found scattered behind Burbank's mattress, between the mattress and the headboard.'

Tripathi frowned. 'Yes. So what? A man is dead and you're worried about staples?'

'I want to see them.'

Tripathi stared at his old friend, then, shaking his head, picked up the phone.

Minutes later a constable entered and handed Chopra a plastic bag containing five very large, twisted brass staples.

'Staples,' said Tripathi, unimpressed. 'Now what?'

But Chopra's mind was reeling back to the first time he had entered Shiva Swarup's studio, two days earlier, when he had seen workmen unpinning a canvas from its frame . . .

The truth wheeled about him like a giant bird, cawing at him, flapping its wings.

And suddenly he had it.

The revelation. The moment when the mists cleared, and he could see to the other side. This was the moment he lived for. He had always believed that a detective was a traveller, a man who floated between realities. The superficial reality of what *appeared* to be, and the actuality of what *had* been. Somewhere, between those poles, lay the truth, and to get to it took more than reason or intuition. It took experience, of knowing when to trust that little 'click', of knowing when everything had fallen perfectly into place.

He took out his phone, searched his notes and made a call.

'Yes,' came the voice on the other end.

'Adam Padamsee?' said Chopra. 'I need to see you. Right away.'

'Do you really think this will work?' Big Mother looked dubiously at Poppy.

'I don't know,' replied Poppy. 'But it's worth a try, isn't it? Besides, I've seen him do this sort of thing before. Did you know that elephants have a better sense of smell than dogs? It's because of their trunks, you see.'

Big Mother sniffed, and muttered something incomprehensible under her breath.

They were all back in the bridal suite, Poppy clutching the clothes Anjali had discarded in the bathroom when she had vanished. 'Come on, boy,' she said, wafting them at Ganesha.

The little elephant seemed to instinctively understand what was required of him. He trotted forward and buried his trunk in the clothing.

Moments later, he turned smartly on his toes and headed for the door, scooting out with a surprising turn of speed.

They rushed after him as he trotted down the carpeted corridor, the wind in his stern.

A door swung back, and a white man with a towel around his neck stepped out for his supper trolley. As the elephant bounded past, he gaped, and the toothbrush fell to the floor. 'I knew I shouldn't have had that curry for lunch,' he muttered.

At the end of the corridor Ganesha turned into the lift lobby. He shuttled back and forth in front of the elevators as Irfan pressed the button.

When the lift pinged, and the doors slid open, he bundled inside.

'Jesus H. Christ!' bellowed an American voice. 'Is that an elephant?'

'Well, whaddya think it is, dummy? A giant grey marshmallow?'

Poppy stared at the two elderly tourists, a wide-shouldered man in long socks and Bermuda shorts and a red-haired woman in a French beret. 'Ain't he just the cutest?' the woman gushed, gazing affectionately at Ganesha.

'He is clever also,' said Irfan, whose English was coming on in leaps and bounds. 'He is helping us find a missing bride.'

'Is that so?' said the woman, her interest piqued.

The lift reached the ground floor, opened, and Ganesha hurtled out. Poppy, Huma Dixit and Irfan raced after the little elephant, with Big Mother cruising behind in her motorised wheelchair.

The two Americans looked at one another. 'Follow that elephant!' bellowed the woman, and charged after them.

In the illustrious hundred-year history of the Grand Raj Palace, the 'grand old dame of the city' had witnessed many weird and wonderful goings-on. Yet possibly none so surreal as the sight of a baby elephant charging around with a steadily growing band of tourists from around the world in hot pursuit.

A troop of Japanese businessmen joined the fray in the Mughal garden, snapping pictures with a dozen cameras as they ran after the elephant like a single, many-legged beast. In the Nehru Room, a class of uniformed schoolchildren, on a visit to the hotel to view the art exhibition, hurled themselves into the chase, their plump teacher shouting at them to stop, pulling at the hem of her sari as she stumbled after them. A sunburned Australian wearing a turban and a dhoti grinned at his Indian friend as the elephant scooted past. 'Well, Ashok, I've seen kangaroos, wallabies, possums, duck-billed platypuses and more koalas than you can shake a stick at. But I can honestly say I've never seen an elephant charging through a hotel before.'

A trio of Frenchmen, gaping at the incredible sight, turned to one another. '*C'est fou!*' said one, swirling a finger beside his temple in the universal sign of insanity.

'*Non*,' said another. '*C'est magnifique!*'

The third held up a wise index finger. '*C'est Inde!*'

In the pool area, Rocky, the Wonder Langur, re-filming the movie's poolside sequence, leapt onto Ganesha's back as he bundled by, riding him as if he were in one of his own action movies. This set the entire film crew onto the little elephant's tail, the director hollering in apoplexy at the fact that his shoot had been ruined for a second time.

Eventually, Ganesha ended up back at the lifts.

'He's just running around in circles,' harrumphed Big Mother.

'Have patience,' advised Poppy.

They piled into the lift, startling a very tall man in a black-and-white striped football T-shirt. 'Wa-hay, pet, what's all this malarkey then?'

Big Mother squinted suspiciously at the man, wondering what language he was speaking.

Behind them, the crowd attempted to pile into the lift, quickly realising the futility of their actions. 'We'll take the stairs!' someone bellowed.

'But we don't know which floor he's going to!'

'We'll try them all!' said the first voice.

The crowd stampeded away.

On the ninth floor, Ganesha trotted out and headed back along the corridor, towards Anjali's suite.

'You see,' said Big Mother. 'I told you he was just going in circles.'

Poppy bit her lip. Had she had been wrong, after all . . .?

Ganesha bundled past the bridal suite, his feet leaving deep impressions in the corridor's thick carpet. He didn't slow down until he reached the very end of the corridor, and the Jahangir Suite.

He snuffled at the bottom of the door with his trunk.

Poppy, Irfan, Huma and Big Mother caught up.

Poppy knelt down. 'Here, boy?' she asked.

Ganesha continued to root along the bottom of the door.

A loud commotion heralded the arrival of the chasing crowd of tourists. Within moments they had jammed the entire length of the corridor.

'What's going on? Have they caught the elephant yet?'

'They're not trying to catch the elephant! The elephant's looking for someone.'

'The *elephant* is looking for someone?'

'Yes. You know, like Lassie.'

'Who's Lassie?'

'That dog. You remember. She used to go around looking for people. When they got themselves stuck down a mineshaft or something.'

'Bloody stupid thing to do, getting stuck down a mine.'

'The point *being* that this elephant is using its, you know, arcane animal senses to track someone too.'

'Who's it looking for, exactly?'

'I heard it was Tom Cruise.'

'Tom Cruise is here?'

'It's not Tom Cruise, you idiot. It's looking for a lost Indian princess.'

'Hello, have we stopped yet? My heart's about to burst. I shouldn't be racing around at my age, you know.'

'Why were you running then?'

'I don't know. Everyone else was running so I ran too. I thought it was part of the entertainment. I didn't want to miss out, not after what I've paid.'

'Make way, make way! Fathers of the bride and groom coming through!'

A chorus of ‘oof’s and ‘ow, that was my foot’s marked the passage of the two men as they made their way to the door.

Prakashrao Tejwa, round face sheened in sweat, looked at Poppy. ‘I was told that you have found my daughter.’ His voice was full of hope.

‘We shall see,’ said Poppy.

She turned and knocked loudly on the door, a hush falling behind her.

Seconds passed and then, just as she was about to knock again, came the sound of a lock being turned.

She heard Big Mother mutter behind her, sotto voce, ‘This is going to be very embarrassing’, and then the door swung open, to reveal . . .

THE MURDERER IS REVEALED

'What are we doing here, Chopra? I've got a plane to catch.'

Avinash Agnihotri snapped out a left hook and impatiently checked his watch.

They were gathered in the business suite, Agnihotri, the Padamsees, the general manager Dashputra – and Shiva Swarup, slumped spinelessly on the sofa below the portrait of Peroz Khumbatta.

In the corner stood Rohan Tripathi, in uniform, barely suppressed irritation flickering over his features. Chopra knew that the policeman did not approve of this gathering, considering it an entirely unnecessary exercise. 'This isn't a TV show, Chopra,' he had said. 'Why don't you just tell me who did it?'

'Patience,' Chopra had advised his old friend.

Now he checked his own watch, an ancient relic given to him by his long-departed father, a stuttering reminder of the affection they had shared. It was almost time . . .

The doors to the suite opened and Lisa Taylor breezed

in, closely followed by Ronald Loomis, Hollis Burbank's PA.

'Didn't think I'd be seeing you again so soon,' said Taylor, by way of greeting.

'I'm flying out with Burbank's body in a couple of hours,' said Loomis. 'What's going on?'

'Thank you both for coming,' said Chopra. 'I felt you deserved to be here for this.'

Taylor's smile turned quizzical as she took in the others in the room. 'Well, isn't this an all-star cast?'

Chopra turned to the room. 'Four days ago, the man known as Hollis Burbank was found dead in his suite. Contrary to the police's initial belief, Burbank did not commit suicide. He was murdered, a knife plunged into his chest. It is my intention to now unmask his killer.'

A wave of nervous fidgeting greeted this announcement, but no one chose to respond.

'From the beginning this has been a difficult investigation,' continued Chopra. 'Hollis Burbank was a man with many enemies, a man who went out of his way to make those enemies. Each of you here had a reason to wish him harm.

'Avinash Agnihotri.' Chopra turned to the sour-faced businessman. 'Burbank was undermining your business, had cost you millions of dollars with his underhanded tactics. You were taking him to court. To add insult to injury, he outbid you for the Rebello painting. You confronted him on the evening of his death, threatened him.' Agnihotri bristled, but said nothing.

Chopra turned next to the Padamsees. 'Layla Padamsee. You and your husband are in dire financial difficulties.

Burbank made you an obscene offer, an offer that tempted your husband. You went to his room that evening, confused and angry. While you were there, by your own admission, Burbank assaulted you. Did you kill him in self-defence? . . . Adam Padamsee. You followed your wife to Burbank's room, driven by shame and rage. You wanted Burbank's money, but you knew that in suggesting to your wife that she accept his outrageous offer you had committed a grievous error, one that threatened your marriage. You had been drinking. Did you murder Burbank in a rush of blood? Did you and your wife stage the crime scene afterwards, once you realised what you had done?'

Chopra glanced up at the portrait of Peroz Khumbatta, looking down on them with his steadfast iron gaze. 'Hollis Burbank was a man who inspired hatred. In some respects, he actively courted that hatred. Yet, paradoxically, he was also a very private man, one whose past was a closed book. Why? Why did Burbank go to such lengths to shroud his past in mystery?

'It was because Hollis Burbank was not Hollis Burbank. He was Roger Penzance, and thirty years ago Penzance was here in India, working for a company called Fermi Engineering.' A ripple of surprise greeted this revelation. 'Penzance was directly responsible for a chemical leak at the Fermi plant outside Pune, an accident that led to the deaths of two hundred men, women and children. Among the dead were a middle-aged couple by the name of Santosh and Laxmi Dashputra.' Chopra turned to the Grand Raj Palace's general manager, whose dark face swam with fear and self-loathing. 'Your mother and father.

'After the accident Penzance fled India. Afraid that the authorities would one day catch up with him, he changed his identity and became Hollis Burbank. Behind him the state government buried all details of the accident.' Chopra's eyes locked on Dashputra's grim face. 'But you have lived with the consequences of that night, and when you saw the man you knew as Roger Penzance in your hotel, you felt the past come crashing down on you. You admitted to me that you went to Burbank's room that night. You claim that he was already dead, and that all you did was to daub the words "I am sorry" on his wall. Are we to believe you?'

Finally, Chopra turned to the anaemic figure of Shiva Swarup.

'But Santosh and Laxmi Dashputra were not the only ones to die in that accident. A young artist, Kunal Karmarkar, also died that day. Your friend, and the man whose work you stole to launch your own rise to fame as an artist. Burbank knew your secret and tried to blackmail you. Did you kill him to protect your reputation?'

Swarup stared at his feet, unable to meet Chopra's gaze.

The former policeman allowed the silence to stretch, become something tangible and full of shadows.

'All of you had the motive and opportunity to murder Hollis Burbank.' He paused. 'Yet there was only one killer.'

'Why don't you just spit it out?' snapped Agnihotri. 'Tell us who it was.'

'My mistake,' continued Chopra, ignoring the irate businessman, 'was in assuming that the motive behind Burbank's killing was hatred. But the truth is that this murder had nothing to do with Hollis Burbank at all.' Chopra reached into his pocket, and threw something onto the table.

The staples rattled on the glass, the sound unnaturally loud in the silent room.

Agnihotri's brow twisted into an incredulous frown. 'Staples? What have they got to do with anything?'

'These staples led me to Burbank's true killer,' replied Chopra. 'They were found in Burbank's room. These staples were used to bind the canvas of *The Scourge of Goa* to its frame. Hollis Burbank was killed because of a painting worth ten million dollars.'

Chopra's words seemed to rebound from the walls, stunning those gathered before him.

'That night Burbank's killer came to his room. The killer drugged him – with Valium – then stabbed him through the heart. The killer then removed the original *Scourge of Goa* painting from above Burbank's bed, where it was housed inside a protective glass display case. The killer loosened the canvas from its frame – by taking out the staples binding it to the frame, probably with a pair of pliers. This had to be done with some force. For a person not regularly used to it the process proved tricky – some of the staples fell unnoticed behind Burbank's mattress, between the mattress and the headboard. Once the canvas was removed, the killer then substituted a replica of the canvas, and placed the painting back in the display case.

'With the room now set, the killer left.'

'Are you saying *The Scourge of Goa* has been stolen?' barked Agnihotri, incredulously.

'My God, man, is that all you care about?' said Padamsee. 'He's just told us how Burbank was killed. And that someone in this room did it.'

'To answer your question,' snarled Agnihotri, 'yes. That painting *is* all I care about. As for Burbank's killer – it wasn't me, I know that much.'

'You're right,' said Chopra. 'It wasn't you. Hollis Burbank's killer was someone who knew him well enough for him to let them into his room in the middle of the night. Someone he permitted to prepare him a drink. Someone for whom he was willing to lie back on the bed in his bathrob—'

'It was a woman!' exclaimed Agnihotri. 'He let a woman into his room. That randy goat was having an intimate encounter.'

'Yes,' confirmed Chopra. 'Hollis Burbank was known for his roving eye. His killer took advantage of this fact . . . Isn't that right, Miss Taylor?'

Chopra turned to Lisa Taylor, whose eyes widened fractionally, then narrowed, clouding to an impenetrable murk. 'And just when I thought we had something special,' she murmured. She drew herself up with a grim smile. 'I have no idea what you're talking about.'

'You killed Hollis Burbank in order to steal *The Scourge of Goa*,' said Chopra, simply.

Taylor's smile stretched. 'And, of course, you can prove this?'

'You planned this meticulously, for months,' continued Chopra. 'In fact, I believe that as soon as you were given *The Scourge of Goa* to auction you made up your mind to steal it. But you knew that stealing a painting as valuable as Rebello's masterpiece was one thing, getting away with it another thing entirely. You needed a distraction. And what better distraction than the murder of one of the world's richest men, the very man who had bought the painting? You knew Burbank collected Indian art; you knew he coveted that Rebello. You spent months priming him, to make sure he would do anything to get that painting.

'You had to ensure he came to India for the auction, something he had always refused to do. My guess is that you didn't know about Burbank's past on the subcontinent, his time with Fermi Engineering, the fact that he had changed his identity. You could not understand his reluctance. Yet, somehow, you found a way to overcome his resistance. Perhaps you promised him certain favours? A prize that he had been pursuing for years. You are, after all, a beautiful woman.

'After the auction, my guess is that you whispered in Burbank's ear, convinced him to have the painting moved up to his suite. You promised to join him later, to help him celebrate as you both gazed at the canvas that was now worth ten million dollars. The prospect of such an encounter was more than Burbank could resist. He let down his guard. He invited you in. You flirted with him, toyed with him, all the while rehearsing his murder in your mind.

'You see, Miss Taylor, I have no doubt that you planned everything, down to the smallest detail. I know that you chose the Khumbatta suite for Burbank. You knew there was a large knife in the kitchen unit – there would be no need for you to bring a murder weapon to his room. You knew there were two bathrobes in the suite – and that was something that bothered me, subconsciously, from the beginning. Why did the police only find *one* robe in Burbank's suite, when every other suite has two? That missing robe was important. That night, in the suite, you undressed, changed into one of the robes. You poured a drink for Burbank, and mixed in the Valium that you had brought with you. You asked him to lie down on the bed. He complied, believing that he was about to finally fulfil a long-held fantasy. But as the Valium kicked in, he slipped into a stupor. You straddled him, and plunged the knife into his chest. Any blood that may have sprayed from the wound onto your clothes was caught by your bathrobe. Burbank was too far gone to resist, to do anything but pass quickly into the dark.

'Once you were certain he was dead, you got to work. You wiped the knife handle and pressed Burbank's fingers on to it. Then you took down the Rebello painting – you are one of just a few people who have the code to the alarmed display case – and switched the canvas. Finally, you made sure the scene was set. I have no doubt that you wore gloves – but even if your prints *were* found in the room you knew that it would not arouse suspicion. After all, you had already been in the suite many times, to ensure it was ready for Burbank, and to meet with him after he arrived. You changed back into your clothes – the clothes that had not a drop of blood on them, even though you had just stabbed a man to death. You took the painting and the bloodied robe with you, to be disposed of the next day. You didn't think anyone would notice a missing bathrobe, not with the furore raging over Burbank's death.

'And that same confusion was integral to the final element of your plan.

'Because you knew that with everyone's attention on Burbank, it would be a long time before it was discovered that the Rebello was a fake. Had Burbank taken the painting back to America he might well have had it authenticated by his own people. But what if his death was declared a murder? Having spent so much time in India, you knew that murder investigations can drag on for months, sometimes years. And the longer the investigation went on, the longer the painting would be held as evidence. Which would give you the opportunity to dispose of the real *Scourge of Goa* and vanish from the scene.'

Taylor gazed coldly at the former policeman. 'There is a fatal flaw in your theory, Chopra. If I did steal *The Scourge of Goa,* where is it? You can search my room. You won't find it. And without the painting, you have nothing to connect me to Burbank's murder.'

It was Chopra's turn to smile. 'You are correct. We will not find the painting in your room. In fact, we will not find the painting anywhere in Mumbai, or even in India. Because it is no longer here.'

'What!' Agnihotri exploded, but was motioned to silence by the policeman Rohan Tripathi.

'The morning after Burbank's death you visited this business suite. You used the courier service to send an artist's carry tube abroad. On the courier slip – a slip that bears your signature – you stated that the tube contained reprints of famous artworks. There was nothing unusual in this – you had already set the pattern by mailing a number of such tubes out during the past week. The courier had no idea that inside that morning's tube was a painting worth ten million dollars.' A pause. 'The tubes were all sent to an address in the United States. An hour ago, following a tip-off to the Los Angeles police department, that address was raided. *The Scourge of Goa* has been recovered, as has the tube that you used to courier it.'

A gasp escaped Taylor.

Beside her Ronald Loomis stepped towards Chopra, a look of rage flashing over his handsome features. 'That's nonsense!' he said. 'The police can't just barge into my hom—' He stopped as he realised what he had unconsciously admitted to.

'Yes, Mr Loomis,' said Chopra softly. 'The painting is no longer in *your* home.' He allowed a moment's silence, then, 'I am guessing that a maid or a friend has been taking receipt of the tubes for you. I am also guessing that you and Miss Taylor planned this venture together. I have checked with the airlines and I believe you are both booked on the same flight back to L.A. tonight.'

Loomis blinked, rapidly. Chopra could almost see his brain ticking over. 'No,' he said finally. 'It was her plan. All of it. I just went along for the ride.'

'Because you were in love with her,' said Chopra. 'And because she promised to share the spoils.'

Loomis's eyes betrayed nothing. And then his shoulders slumped in defeat. 'It seemed like a good idea at the time.'

Chopra turned to Taylor. 'I checked with your boss at Gilbert and Locke. Nine months ago, after you gained approval for the auction in Mumbai, and knew that *The*

Scourge of Goa would be available, you went to Los Angeles, ostensibly to meet Burbank and other collectors, to pitch the auction to them. You spent three weeks out there. I am guessing that was when you convinced Loomis to join your plan.'

'He didn't take much convincing,' said Taylor, her eyes suddenly flashing with anger. 'He's not quite the innocent he's making himself out to be. He told me he hated working for Burbank. The man rode him into the ground, made his life a living hell. Burbank hired him right out of college, thought he could treat him like a slave. He threatened to ruin him if he tried to leave. I showed him how he could get out from under Burbank's thumb *and* get rich into the bargain.'

'Because you needed him,' said Chopra. 'To help get the painting out of the country. And to keep you updated on Burbank. After going to such trouble setting this all up, you couldn't risk Burbank unexpectedly pulling out at the last second. Loomis's role was to let you know if Burbank started to get cold feet about coming to India, or did anything else that might endanger your plan. After all, he was Burbank's PA. He was your inside man.

'You couldn't anticipate everything, of course,' continued Chopra. 'The fact that Dashputra wrote the words "I am sorry" on the bathroom wall after you had already killed Burbank. That was a stroke of bad luck – it immediately convinced ACP Gunaji that Burbank had committed suicide. But you didn't want a suicide. A suicide would be quickly put to bed. The sale would go through and the painting would be released to Burbank's estate. And that meant there was a risk of it being authenticated before you had had a chance to sell the original.

'No. It had to be murder. That was why you didn't slit Burbank's wrists – that would have looked too much like suicide.

'That was also why you financed my parallel investigation. So that I could convince the authorities that Burbank *had* been murdered. Of course, you didn't believe that I would actually unmask the murderer. You thought you had been too clever for that. But, just in case, you asked for regular reports. You wanted to reassure yourself that I hadn't discovered anything leading back to *you*. I must have seemed quite the fool.'

'Oh, but you are nobody's fool, are you, Chopra?' murmured Taylor, a high colour rising to her cheeks.

'Out of interest, where did you get the fake?'

'An old acquaintance from the art world,' said Taylor. 'One with few scruples, and enough talent to paint a convincing Rebello.'

'One thing I still don't understand,' said Chopra. 'Who would buy such a painting? Once it came to light that it was stolen, it would be impossible to hang anywhere that it might be seen.'

Taylor snorted. 'Where do you think stolen artworks go, Chopra? There's a whole world out there, in the shadows. Collectors who will pay a fortune just to possess something that no one else has. Just because they can.' She drew herself up, held out her arms, hands balled into fists. 'Are you going to put the cuffs on me now?' Her tone was mocking.

'No,' said Chopra. 'I am not a policeman. That would not be appropriate.'

Tripathi stepped forward. 'Miss Taylor, may I have the honour of this dance?'

After Loomis and Taylor had been led away, Chopra found himself staring after them, a flush of mixed emotions coursing through him. Paramount was relief, that the investigation had been successfully concluded. Yet the satisfaction he usually derived from such a result eluded him. A lingering sense of regret gnawed away at him. That Lisa Taylor had proved to be both a murderess and a thief, a cold, manipulative woman willing to do anything for personal gain . . . the thought sat heavily in his stomach.

Guilt.

That was the true nature of his feeling.

He hated to admit it, but he had allowed himself to be momentarily beguiled by the intelligent and beautiful woman. He had not seen her for what she was. Had that clouded his judgement? Would he have resolved the case earlier if he had not been distracted by her dazzling smile, her winsome personality?

It didn't matter now. What was done was done. Hollis Burbank was dead, and his killer caught. What was the point of dwelling on his own fallibility?

'They say the female of the species is deadlier than the male.'

Chopra turned to see the art critic Adam Padamsee at his side.

'Thank you for organising the appraiser at such short notice,' said Chopra. 'I needed to be sure that the painting in Burbank's suite was a fake before accusing Taylor.'

'It was the least I could do,' said Padamsee. He sucked in his cheeks. 'Frankly, I'm amazed she had the balls to go through with it. Not that I'm shedding any tears for Burbank.'

If Padamsee had expected Chopra to agree, he was to be disappointed.

Because, for Inspector Ashwin Chopra (Retd), even a man like Hollis Burbank, a man with the deaths of so many on his conscience, did not deserve the fate that had ultimately found him. Gandhi's words chimed in his mind: 'An eye for an eye will only make the whole world blind.' If, on some cosmic level, justice had been served, then that was between the universe and Hollis Burbank.

It was not a notion Chopra subscribed to.

Perhaps that was what made him who he was.

A man apart.

A FEUD IS BURIED

'Gautam!'

Big Mother's exclamation was mirrored only by Poppy's own gasp of surprise.

Gautam Deshmukh Patwardhan stood in the doorway dressed in a T-shirt and jeans, gaping at the scene before him. His eyes travelled the length of the corridor and back again, finally coming to rest, guiltily, on the eyes of his own father, staring at him from behind Big Mother's wheelchair.

'Son?' said Shaktisinghrao, jaws agape. 'What are you doing here? Whose room is this?'

Gautam opened his mouth to reply, but before he could do so Ganesha bundled past him.

'Hey, wait!' The young man turned and plunged after the little elephant.

There was a moment of perfect stillness as those gathered in the corridor looked at one another . . . and then a stampede ensued, with everyone attempting to cram through the doorway at the same instant. To a chorus of grunts, shouts and the occasional shriek of pain, the invaders steamed into the room, to find . . .

Ganesha pacing in front of the door to the bathroom, Gautam attempting to herd him away by waving his hands as if conducting an orchestra.

And then the door swung back, causing a deafening silence to fall over the jostling crowd.

A tall, slim figure dressed in a green Grand Raj Palace porter's uniform, a turban, thick spectacles and a close-trimmed beard stepped out into the room. The figure surveyed the ranks of people before it, and then looked directly at Gautam, who shrugged helplessly.

The figure gave a rueful smile, then reached up and pulled off the glasses, beard and turban.

Shaking out her hair, Anjali Tejwa faced her audience with a brittle smile. 'Welcome,' she said.

'Anjali!' Prakashrao Tejwa rushed forward and swept his daughter into an embrace. 'You're safe! Thank God!' He stepped backwards, his face quizzical. 'But what are you doing here? And where did you go? If you don't want to marry this boy I won't force you. All you had to do was talk to me.'

Anjali gave a grimace. 'I'm afraid it's a bit late for that now,' she said.

'What?' The old man's face creased in puzzlement.

Anjali and Gautam exchanged glances, but before they could say anything further, Poppy's voice sang out into the room. 'Everyone, can I have your attention please! This is a family matter. Thank you for helping us, but now it's time to leave!'

Grumbling and muttering, the crowd began to leak from the room.

'Well, is there going to be a wedding or not?'

'I was promised a wedding, dammit, and I'm not going home till I get one.'

'Where are the dancing girls? They told me there'd be dancing girls! I didn't come all this way not to see dancing girls.'

'Hah! Kids these days. They have no idea what marriage is. They watch those soppy movies and think it's all roses and chocolates. And then reality drops on them like a herd of elephants.'

'Talking of elephants . . . Wasn't that a clever little thing?'

Once the room had been cleared, Big Mother wheeled her chair forward and glared at her granddaughter. 'I think it's time you explained exactly what is going on here.'

Anjali sighed. 'I wanted to tell you, Big Mother, but I couldn't. When you and my father first told me about the marriage proposal from the Deshmukh family, and how it would solve our financial problems, I was livid. How could you put me in that position? Ransoming my future against our family's good name? I was so angry that I went to see Gautam, to tell him to stuff his proposal, and his money.' She paused. 'But then, once I met him, I realised that he wasn't quite the oaf I had expected him to be. He too lived under the burden of expectations. Yes, he had chosen me, but his choices were limited. His father expected him to marry into another noble family. In fact, he had shown courage in asking for my hand, knowing his family's animosity towards us. I realised that duty binds both ways. I began to consider the sacrifices that you and my father have made, the choices you were never allowed to make, trapped by tradition and responsibility.

'I'm not sure exactly when and how it happened, but Gautam and I fell in love.

'I suppose that was when we might have just gone along with your plans for us, the royal wedding, everything. But there was something holding us back – the ancient feud between our families. The fact that Gautam's father would always believe that he had somehow *saved* us by marrying his son to me.'

Shaktisinghrao blinked, and seemed about to say something in his defence, but a tug on his arm from his wife silenced him.

'And then, as I saw the preparations for the wedding, the ruinous one-upmanship that our fathers were engaged in, I realised that things were worse than I feared. A few weeks ago, Gautam and I both saw them fighting over who would buy us a Rolls-Royce! That was the last straw. There and then we decided that, somehow, we needed to end this ridiculous feud.'

'And your bright idea for how to do this was to *vanish*?' Big Mother glared at her granddaughter.

'We knew that trying to talk sense into our fathers would be pointless. The only thing that would force them to work together was something that affected them both equally.'

'Hah!' said Big Mother. 'These two idiots almost knocked each other senseless because of your disappearing act.'

'But Moth—' protested Prakashrao, but was cut off by a wave of Big Mother's hand.

'You're right, Big Mother.' Anjali sighed. 'Things didn't quite work out as I had thought. I underestimated the enmity between our families. I hoped that my mysterious disappearance from a locked room would help them find common cause; that they would work together to find me – I knew they would not go to the police, not at first, because of the scandal. I hoped that they would realise that this wedding isn't about wealth and power, but about people. About me and Gautam. About two great families becoming one.' She turned to Poppy. 'I am sorry for involving you. I thought it would help to have someone outside of the family to convey my supposed last-minute doubts to them. I couldn't ask Huma to do that. She would have seen through me, known that I was up to something. When we met in the hotel, I sensed that you were the sort of person who would blame yourself for my disappearance, because of the advice you gave me. I had hoped that you would find out about my vanishing act – I knew it would be hard to keep it a secret within the confines of the hotel – and that you would go to my family and give them the impression that I had gone because of my desire not to go through with the wedding. As it turns out, they didn't really need the push.'

'Have you any idea, young lady, of what you have put us through?' said Big Mother. 'The trouble you have caused?'

Anjali looked rueful. 'You told me yourself, didn't you, Big Mother, that you wished for this feud to be ended? Well, now it is. Not artificially, by marrying me to Gautam, but in reality. I think our fathers have finally seen sense. At least I hope so.'

'And if we hadn't found you? Or if these two dolts hadn't buried the hatchet? Then what? Would you have gone through with the wedding?'

Anjali exchanged glances with Gautam. 'We would have done what was right,' she said, cryptically.

A silence fell over the room, broken only by Ganesha snuffling at a fruit basket he had discovered sitting on a sideboard.

Shaktisinghrao and Prakashrao exchanged glances. 'You have a very intelligent daughter,' said Gautam's father eventually.

'I know,' said Prakashrao. 'And you have a noble son. One I am sure will make her a good husband.'

'So does this mean the wedding can finally go ahead?' asked Poppy.

'About that . . .' said Anjali, looking sideways at Gautam. 'There's a little problem.'

'What problem?' said Big Mother, her eyes squinting with suspicion.

'Um . . . the fact that we're already married.'

A collective gasp of shock rippled around the room.

Anjali sighed. 'Gautam and I knew we wanted to spend our lives together. We were worried that, in spite of our efforts to end the feud – or possibly because of it – the wedding might fall apart. And so we got married a week ago, in a registry office, with no fanfare, and no guests.'

'Oh God, I am ruined!' Gautam's mother swooned into her husband's arms, but his own shock meant that he ignored her and she fell heavily to the floor.

Big Mother grimaced. 'Then why go through with this-this charade?'

'As I said: we needed a reason for our fathers to cooperate. The registry wedding was just a precaution. We still needed a way to bring our families together.'

Big Mother was silent, evaluating her granddaughter's words.

'So what happens now?' said Gautam.

Big Mother wheeled her chair forward. 'I will tell you what happens now. Now, the pair of you will get ready. To be married.'

'But, Big Mother—'

'Don't you "but" me, young lady. You've had your say, and now it's my turn. Regardless of your intentions, you have behaved irresponsibly. You have made fools of your family, and put a great many people to inconvenience. This is not the behaviour of an adult, nor is it befitting a princess of either the Deshmukh or Tejwa clans.' Big Mother paused. 'And so you will make amends. You and Gautam may be married in the eyes of the law, but the royal families of India have their own sense of what is right, a sense honed over thousands of years. And when two great houses are united, there must be a statement, so that *everyone* will know. The light of our kind may be dimming, but we are not gone yet. Until that day comes we will abide by the traditions that we have carried faithfully down the ages.'

Anjali glanced at Gautam. Something wordless passed between them. 'We will do as you wish, Big Mother.'

Poppy clapped. 'So there will be a wedding, after all!' she said, happily.

'No,' said Big Mother, the bones of her face finally stretching into a smile. 'There will not be a wedding. There will be a *royal* wedding. And that is a different matter altogether.'

THE AGE OF SPLENDOUR

'Keep that damned monkey away from me!'

The priest glared at Rocky, the Wonder Langur, as he clutched protectively at his saffron robes. The monkey was perched on Ganesha's back, shelling peanuts with an air of casual menace.

Around them the small crowd gathered in the Bhagat Singh garden for the ceremony talked in hushed voices, apart from Big Mother; she had found a like-minded ally in Poppy's own mother, Poornima Devi, a widow of many years, whose white sari contrasted starkly with the colourful dress of those around her.

The two women were bent in conspiratorial confabulation, loudly berating the modern world and the ungrateful generation that populated it.

The priest, who, by dint of great pleading – and an eye-watering sum of cash – had been prevailed upon to return to the Grand Raj Palace, stepped onto the marriage podium. With one eye warily on the langur, he called the gathering to order.

'May the happy couple please step forward.'

Anjali Tejwa turned to beam a wide-lipped smile at Gautam Deshmukh . . . and then they both turned to watch Poppy and Chopra ascend the podium.

Chopra pulled at the starched collar of his embroidered golden sherwani coat. It had been itching all morning. Well, there was nothing for it but to bite the bullet. After all, the whole thing had been his own idea . . .

Poppy leaned into him. 'This is the best gift you have ever given me,' she whispered. 'Much better than a vacation!'

The words gladdened Chopra's heart. He loved his wife dearly, and there was little doubt that his recent behaviour had upset her. He had racked his brain for a suitable way to make amends. How to make up for neglecting their twenty-fifth wedding anniversary . . .? And then it had come to him. The perfect solution.

Of course, renewing their vows in front of all these people hadn't been part of the plan. Nor prancing around in this silly outfit. He felt like a clown. But that was Poppy all over. Once he had made his suggestion, she had gone to town. He hadn't the heart to tell her that he had only been thinking of a simple affair, just the two of them, with maybe Ganesha and Irfan in attendance.

Still, it was a small price to pay for harmony.

The real ordeal was going to be sitting through the marathon festivities marking the wedding of Anjali Tejwa Patwardhan and Gautam Deshmukh Patwardhan . . .

. . . which began later that evening with an hour-long fireworks display that lit up the southern tip of Mumbai like the coming of the Apocalypse.

Outside the Grand Raj Palace dazed beggars reeled away, leaping over the promenade wall and into the soupy Arabian Sea, thinking that war had been declared and the city was under attack. (It was later said that the fireworks had blown the cobwebs out of the ears of bemused fisherfolk ten miles away on Elephanta Island.)

The fireworks ended with the arrival of a famous American pop star who had been paid an extraordinary sum to parachute in to the festivities. The dramatic entrance was ruined by a high wind funnelling up from the harbour and blowing the star off course, tangling him up in the flag-pole atop the Gateway of India monument and resulting in a strangulated hernia. (The star's voice, however, was not affected. His screams carried far out onto the water, adding to the bemusement of the fisherfolk on Elephanta.)

Once the emergency services had departed the scene, the festivities resumed, with the arrival of a band of eunuchs, their ragged songs of blessing climbing into the night sky. Shaktisinghrao, a man of staunch tradition, rushed out to pay the eunuchs their expected gratuity. They drove a hard bargain, and by the time he had convinced them to leave, he had been all but stripped to his underclothes.

Next came the buglers, and the dhol drummers, the juggling dwarfs and bagpipers, the fire-eaters and sword swallowers, and, finally, the snake-charmers, who caused a minor panic when a basket of cobras toppled over onto the road. As the serpents slithered to freedom, gathered gentry and locals alike fled, some following the beggars by leaping into the harbour.

'Are these people mad?' muttered Chopra, looking on. 'No wonder the royals of India are bankrupt.'

'Well, *I* think it's magnificent,' sighed Poppy, eyes glowing. 'Besides, you only get married once.'

Chopra refrained from muttering that in Mumbai, at least, even that wasn't a given any more. The younger generation appeared to have fewer qualms about divorce and separation. The old taboos were gradually losing their meaning in modern India.

The elephants were on the march.

A line of the beasts swayed down the promenade, bringing traffic to a standstill.

Chopra heard Ganesha trumpeting joyfully. He saw the little elephant skip towards the lumbering beasts, Irfan close behind him. Ganesha's bottom vanished into the crowd of locals, tourists and wedding guests lining the promenade.

Atop the lead elephant, which was caparisoned to within an inch of its life, was Gautam Deshmukh, shimmering in a golden wedding suit complete with golden turban. He swayed vertiginously inside a decorative howdah, a rictus grin on his sweating face.

'Doesn't he look dashing!' said Poppy.

'He looks bloody terrified,' muttered Chopra.

And, after the elephants had passed, came the procession of the nawabs.

Royals from all over India had been invited to this grandest of weddings, the union of two ancient royal houses. A great gathering of the clans, the like of which had not been seen for many years. On they came, thundering along the promenade in their limousines, sports cars, vintage Rolls-Royces, Buicks and Cadillacs and even, for those with a sense of occasion, horse-drawn carriages.

As Chopra watched them process into the Grand Raj, these once-fabulous lords and ladies of the realm, he felt time shifting around him, drawing him back into the mists of history, when men and women like this had ruled the land. For all their faults and vices, they had symbolised something, a certain notion of India, an ideal of hegemony now discredited and folded into the great tapestry of the past. In that moment, he understood how his predecessors might have been seduced into admiration. That this collection of unhappy lunatics, monobrowed misanthropes and brutish vulgarians could be called nobility seemed laughable now, a cosmic jest.

Yet rule they had, since time immemorial.

But now the age of giants was past.

They had lived too loudly and their life force was spent, frittered away like their erstwhile fortunes, a long, lazy decline into moral ruin. Like dinosaurs they had settled into the mud of history, and breathed their last.

The figures before him seemed to shimmer and fade, like ghosts. He was overcome by a sudden, overwhelming sadness. Perhaps, by bringing them together in this final moment of magnificent passion, history was choosing to honour their passing, the passing of an age.

The age of splendour.

Chopra felt a tap on his shoulder and turned to find the artist Shiva Swarup standing before him, a gentle breeze from the harbour ruffling his grey hair.

'May I talk with you a moment?' he said.

They walked to the Gateway of India, where Swarup lit another of his roll-ups and stared momentarily out to sea.

From the harbour came the smell of brine and tar, voices raised in drunken snatches of song, the susurration of water sucking on concrete pylons. 'I wanted to thank you,' he said finally.

'*Thank* me?' Chopra could not keep the astonishment from his voice.

'Yes. I have decided to tell the press about Kunal.'

Chopra took this in silence. He knew that by revealing that he had stolen his dead friend's work to kick-start his career, Swarup would be committing professional suicide. His revelation would not go down well with either the art fraternity or the general public.

Nor would he be the only one facing the wrath of the Indian masses once the full facts of the case came to light.

Even now Rohan Tripathi was preparing a press release that would detail not only Burbank's murder, but the wider aspects of Chopra's investigation. Tripathi had already contacted the commissioner of police and the chief minister. The revelations of the chemical accident that had wiped out the village of Shangarh would send shockwaves around the country.

Chopra knew that the true target of the public's rage would then become the government, the faceless men responsible for the deaths of two hundred individuals. And, inevitably, those who had then covered up the crime. A silent scream that had echoed down the decades would finally find its voice. The media would have a field day, and the ramifications would, no doubt, be felt all the way to New Delhi.

None of this mattered to Shiva Swarup.

'You have set me free,' said the artist. 'I have lived with the guilt of my actions for three decades. It has hollowed me out. You see, it's not just the fact that I stole Kunal's work. It's because I know he would never have begrudged me. He was the sweetest, gentlest soul that I have ever known. Had I asked, he would have given his life for me. In a way, he did.'

Chopra watched the man, his lonely silhouette against the dark horizon. How frail he seemed. And yet, in the relaxed set of his shoulders, the easing of his countenance, he saw that there was, indeed, a weight lifted from him.

Perhaps it was true what they said: redemption, however late it may come, was the only sure road to salvation. Whoever had said that guilt was a town you could never leave was wrong. There was always a way out. Most people simply never looked for it.

'Come on, you're missing all the fun!'

Chopra turned to find Poppy bearing down on him.

She stopped as she reached them, glancing uncertainly from her husband to Shiva Swarup.

Chopra stuck out a hand. 'I wish you all the best. The world is a fickle place. On some days, I can well believe that a man's star rises and falls by the cycle of the moon.'

Swarup gave a wry smile, and took Chopra's hand. 'Perhaps you are right. Perhaps in time I will be forgiven. But if I paint again, it will only be for myself.'

Chopra nodded, then turned and accompanied his wife across the concourse to the blazing lights of the Grand Raj Palace Hotel where the wedding of the century was about to get under way.

AUTHOR'S NOTE

Although the events in this book are wholly fictitious, the idea for one of the major plot points stems from the real-life Bhopal gas tragedy, a gas leak incident in India often cited as the world's worst industrial disaster.

The incident occurred on the night of 3rd December 1984 at the Union Carbide India Limited pesticide plant in Bhopal in the state of Madhya Pradesh. Over 500,000 people were exposed to methyl isocyanate gas. The highly toxic substance made its way into the shanty towns around the plant, killing and injuring thousands. Estimates for the death toll vary from 3700 to 8000. An estimated 40,000 individuals were left permanently disabled, maimed, or suffering from serious illness.

The plant was jointly owned by the American company Union Carbide Corporation (UCC) with Indian Government-controlled banks and the Indian public holding a 49.1 per cent stake.

The cause of the disaster remains under debate. The

Indian government argued that slack management, under-investment, and deferred maintenance were responsible. Union Carbide contends that an act of sabotage by a rogue worker led to the leak.

In 1989, UCC paid $470 million to settle litigation stemming from the disaster. In 2010, seven former Indian employees were convicted of causing death by negligence and sentenced to two years imprisonment and a fine of about $2,000 each, the maximum punishment allowed by Indian law. Union Carbide's CEO and several senior U.S. employees at the time of the disaster refused to answer to homicide charges and remained fugitives from India's courts. The US denied several extradition requests.

The plant site has never been adequately cleaned up.

ACKNOWLEDGEMENTS

Once again I owe a debt of gratitude to my agent Euan Thorneycroft at A.M. Heath, my editor Ruth Tross at Mulholland, and Kerry Hood at Hodder. Between them, this frighteningly talented triumvirate ensure that complacency is given no quarter, and mediocrity is shown no mercy. If the series continues to lurch from strength to strength then it is surely because of their support.

I would also like to thank the rest of the team at Hodder, Rachel Khoo in marketing, Rachel Southey in production, Dom Gribben in audio, Rosie Stephen in publicity, and Ruth's fellow editor Cicely Aspinall. In the US, thanks go to Ellen Wright, Laura Fitzgerald and Nivia Evans, and also Jason Bartholomew at Hodder. Similar thanks go to Euan's assistant Jo Thompson, and the others at A.M. Heath working tirelessly behind the scenes.